C. E. Murphy

This special signed edition
is limited to 1000 numbered copies.

This is copy number 731.

Baba Yaga's Daughter

& Other Tales of the Old Races

Baba Yaga's Daughter

& Other Tales of the Old Races

C. E. Murphy

SUBTERRANEAN PRESS 2012

1/13
40⁰⁰

First Edition

ISBN
978-1-59606-382-2

Subterranean Press
PO Box 190106
Burton, MI 48519

www.subterraneanpress.com

Table of Contents

For Bryant

From Russia, with Love

THEIR MISTAKE WAS IN DESIRING my mother's daughter.

No: let me start at the beginning, when I listened to foolish men make foolish jests that turned, as these things always do, to even more foolish action.

I was a barmaid, not for the money, which was poor, but for the ear to the ground; for the hearing of secrets told and of visitors arriving. My mother likes to know these things, but she is fearsome, and her hut with its chicken legs follows her wherever she goes, so she cannot easily spy. I am a simpler creature, only the daughter of a man my mother later ate, and hardly a witch at all.

They came into our smelly little pub as a pair, the two of them dressed so fine and looking so clean. We lived on the edge of Moscow, my mother and I—at least for now, while her house was content to settle there—and the little bar where I found work was not a place that men such as these came to visit.

The taller was red-haired and jade-eyed, and wore a coat of many colors. He smiled or laughed at everything, but his presence took the laughter of the men around him. He was a weight in the air, heating it, and even when he didn't drag on a thin-rolled cigar, hazy blue smoke seemed to follow him.

The other man was smaller, black-haired and black-eyed, altogether ordinary beside his tall companion. I preferred the red-head's easy, dangerous laughter from the start: perhaps it's because I'm my mother's daughter that I like to play with fire. They say flame will defeat her, but I know the thing which has that power, and it is not the heart of man's red flower.

None of that matters now: that is not the story I am trying to tell. I am telling the story of handsome Janx and small dapper Daisani, who wore somber colors to hide from attention. I would say such a man should choose his friends more carefully, because to be friends with a brightly-plumed bird such as Janx is to draw attention, but I *am* my mother's daughter, and I could see that it was more than friendship that kept these two men together. They needed each other the way the light needs the dark, the way fire needs air: not gladly, but deeply, a bond which only the end of time could break.

They were too finely dressed for our wretched dark pub, but they were free with their coin and made new friends quickly: grubby men eager to tell tales that would keep the beer flowing. So it was no surprise to me to hear stories of my mother, for people like to frighten themselves with whispers of witches when they're sober, and even more when they're drunk.

"She eats men alive," one man said, and that was true, so I said nothing.

"She flies on a giant mortar," said another, and that too was true, so again, I said nothing.

"Her house has chicken legs and goes where it wants," said another, and once more spoke truth, and I held my tongue.

"Her daughter is the most beautiful woman in the world," said the first, and now too many things had been said, and so I said, "But Vasili, you tell me *I* am the most beautiful woman in the world," and he spread his arms and spilled his grog and said, "Why then you are Baba Yaga's daughter, and I bet neither of these fine lords can win your heart."

The red-head turned to me with his eyes alight, and bowed with all the grace of a man born to dancing and fine wines and sword lessons. He drew breath to speak, and the other said, "You have business here, Janx, and if you take time to play at women you will lose," which was how I came to know Janx's name.

"I never lose," Janx said with playful boldness, and what his tone told me was that he never imagined he would lose.

His friend said, "Shall I remind you of London?" and Janx turned from the bar and from me with a flash of emerald in his gaze: a flash of fire, for all that its color was green.

"We both of us lost in London, old friend." There was warning in the last two words, making them entirely other than what they seemed. "We both of us lost, and you're the one who chose to follow me to Moscow, so don't lecture me on business or loss."

"I go where there are promises of riches," Daisani said, and though they'd been speaking my language all along, he suddenly sounded as though he ought to be, deep rich avarice in the rolling words.

"And who better to lead you there than me." Janx came back to me and leaned across the bar to offer a sly wink and a promise that might have fallen from a gypsy's lips: "No woman would choose to love when she knew a bet had been placed on the winning, and so I foreswear all wagers in the matter of your heart. I can't speak to the beauty of every woman in the world, but I'll tell the truth and say you're the loveliest woman I've come upon in Russia. If Baba Yaga is your mother indeed, then her greatest magic is in giving the world a beautiful daughter."

I should not have, but I smiled, and I thought I had better not tell my mother what he had said. Mother is jealous of her magics, and if she thought I was the greatest of them, she'd eat me up like she did my father, to have them back inside her.

"Janx," Daisani said again, with more impatience, and Janx said, "*Eliseo,*" which was the name I first heard for the smaller man, though in time, as his fame grew, I too came to think of him as Daisani.

"Forgive my friend," Janx said to me. "He's long since misplaced a sense of humor." Then, curiously: "Are you Baba Yaga's daughter?"

A fit came upon me, as sometimes happens; a fit that is the price of being my mother's daughter. Instead of a yes or a no, this is what spilled from my lips: "That depends. Are you a son of the serpent at the heart of the world?"

Both mens' gazes snapped to me, and this, I think, was the moment when things went wrong indeed.

The danger was twofold: one, that I had never seen such passion in men's eyes, and two, that I had never felt such heat rise in me in response. Oh, I had known my share of lovers: Russian nights are long and cold and unlike my mother, I do not eat men when I'm done with them, so I have spent some time in the throes of need. But never like this, nothing so raw it tore through me and left me eager to snatch at these men, to taste them and swallow them whole and make them part of me; and that was when I wondered if my mother had begun this way.

I did not think. I only put out a hand, and the coal shovel by the fire—an old thing, blackened with use—leapt to my fingers and I jumped onto it, not astride, but as one might stomp a spade into the earth—and commanded it whisk me away up the chimney.

Later, I knew this to be a mistake. First, I could never return to work at my wretched little pub, for now they knew me to be Baba Yaga's daughter indeed, but second, and more importantly, I ran. For men such as Daisani and Janx, there is nothing more exciting than the chase.

BENEATH THE UPROAR FROM astonished Russians, Janx turned to Daisani with a smile bordering on beatific, the expression of a man proven so thoroughly right that nothing in this world could upset his smug superiority. "I believe I've found my mark."

"Baba Yaga is a story made to frighten children and pass the long winter nights," Daisani said. "You should know better."

"And you, of all people, should know not to dismiss stories of witches in the forest and demons in the dark. Go away, if you want. I intend to make Moscow mine, and so require the most priceless of baubles to draw my rival away."

"'Your rival.' I know his name is Rumi. After all this time, you still won't speak their names to me first."

"No more than you would tell me the names of your brethren," Janx said easily, then paused. "Would you?"

Daisani snorted, and with no more discussion they left the pub and walked into the frozen winter night. Their breath caught in the air, turned to silver glitter, and faded behind them. "Moscow. Russia is cold, Janx. Why here?"

"You follow me to the ends of the earth and only now ask why?" Janx sauntered along in silence a little while, then shrugged. "Because my kind aren't inclined to go where it's cold, and yet Rumi has been here centuries. He must guard a trinket of tremendous value to make him stay, and I simply can't bear the idea of not having it myself."

"So you'll trade away Baba Yaga's daughter?"

Janx blinked in astonishment. "Her daughter? Don't be silly, Eliseo. Give over that jewel of a girl to anyone else? No, old friend, I intend to make a bargain or a bounty of the old witch herself. None of us has such a prize in our hoards, and who knows what might be done with a witch's bones?"

"The same that might be done with a dragon's," Daisani said dryly. "If you can capture her, why give her up?"

Jade sparkled in the taller man's eyes and Daisani dropped his chin to his chest with a sigh. "You're a fool, Janx."

"But an adventuresome one," Janx said happily. "And since you're here, you can help me. You have her scent?"

Daisani looked insulted, but Janx waved it off. "Go on, track her home. You're faster by far than I am, and much more subtle."

Insult faded, then turned to chagrin. Daisani thinned his mouth. "I should know better than to fall for your flattery."

"You do know better." Janx smiled again, the same beatific expression. "But at the end of the day, you can't stand to not be a part of intrigues, and so you're going to go anyway. Besides, if I take wing Rumi will know I'm here, and I'm not willing to give up that advantage just yet. I need you, old friend." He placed a hand over his heart, green eyes wide with pleading. "Without you I have no hope."

"I'm mad," Daisani said, but then there was nothing at Janx's side but a breeze, and snow blurring into the air along a trail cut too fast for the eye to see.

It was Daisani who caught me, and he should not have been able to do that. No: not caught; he did not capture me, but when the magic fled from my coal shovel and I came to rest at the forest's edge—for I have not got my mother's strength, and metal and iron will only defy the world's pull for so long at my command—when I came to rest, small unhandsome Eliseo was at my side as though we'd walked all the way together. He twirled his fingers like a man presenting a flower to his beloved, and though nothing was there, I thought I saw a rose of silver and ice catch the moonlight and scatter shards through the frozen night air. I plucked the imaginary flower from his fingers and tucked it above my ear, seeing it all white and shining against the blackness of my hair. A gift: I should not have taken a gift from a man such as this, but doing so made me smile. "Who are you?" I asked then, "And what does it mean to be a son of the serpent at the heart of the world?"

Daisani tilted his head, giving him the look of a curious sparrow, even to the black glitter of his gaze. "Like for like," he said. "How does Baba Yaga's daughter know to ask, but not know what it means?"

Well. I was not going to answer that, and so could not demand my own answer. We stared at one another, he and I, until a smile curved his mouth. "Janx is here to collect a trinket for his treasure chest."

Anger flared in me, though wit told me not to rise to such bait. Still, I was no trinket, and Eliseo saw my outrage in the set of my jaw. "And you are here because you and he are bound by time and love and loathing," I said before he could banter on. "What's a trinket to him is a triumph to you, if you can steal it before he does. I'm neither to either of you."

"Ah," he said, so lightly, "and yet you already wear my flower in your hair."

I reached to crush the imaginary bloom, but was stopped by Eliseo Daisani's cold kiss. For an instant I was breathless, and then I was alone in the dark.

"You have a stink on you," my mother said as I came into her house. This was the trouble of being her daughter: there were no secrets, even ones I might have liked to keep. "Blood and sex and magic, and none of it made of mortal flesh. Go," she said, without care to the ice drops forming in the air outside. "Wash yourself, or the house will eat you up. Come back when you don't stink, and I will gnaw a bone and tell you of the serpent at the heart of the world."

I stared at her, a bent and ancient crone with sharp teeth and sharper eyes, and thought of the illusory rose and the brief kiss on my lips; of the magic I'd used to run away; and then I went, the obedient daughter, to scrub myself with snow.

There is no good way to wash in a Russian winter: it is all cold and miserable, and best done wearing boots and nothing else. I might have dragged the tub from the house's tiny porch inside and let its packed snow melt in front of the fire, but neither my mother nor the house would bear my stink that long, so I crouched under the house and washed quickly, my face stuck in a grimace against the cold.

"Eliseo's maligned me," Janx murmured, light voice coming from darkness. He should not have followed me, no more than Eliseo, and not with more daring than Eliseo had shown. Eliseo, at least, had only caught me at the city's edge, where Janx slipped into Baba Yaga's territory, and seemed not to worry a whit. I went still, clutching my handful of scrubbing snow, a bit of prey hoping not to attract her predator's attention. But then, I was my mother's daughter, not prey, so made myself bold enough to stand and face him.

He smiled and looked me all over in the moonlight. His gaze weighted me, warmed me, until I thought the frozen air had thawed even though my skin remained puckered and tight with cold. My skin, yes, though heat wakened in other parts of me, and I would have to scrub all over again to rid myself of this new stink. But he was beautiful in the half-light, a scent of cigar smoke rolling through the thin air toward me as he pulled the tub from the porch and let it thump against the ground. "It's true I come seeking trinkets, but you're not one I'd bargain for. I made you that promise at the pub."

"Why are you here?" I had an answer to that, one that made the warmth inside me conquer the frigid air, and every part of me knew that it was not wise to keep speaking with him. That I should call out to my mother, warn the house; that I should let them do as they would with the red-haired man who stood before me. Indeed, a thought trickled into my mind, that Mother and house alike should already know of his presence, that one or the other should have swept down by now to gobble him up. That neither had happened only interested me further, as though I needed something beyond the dark light in his gaze and the slim fine lines of his body to command my attention.

"There are things I need from you, and others I desire." Rue curved his mouth, amusement colored his eyes: we might have been in a ballroom, dancing with words as much as bodies, both knowing we said more than we should and less than we wished. At least, so I imagined: I knew little of ballrooms, and more than I wanted of wishes.

"Tell me what you need," I said unwisely, "and I'll give you what you desire."

Janx smiled his insouciant smile and crouched by the tub packed with snow, putting his fingers in it. Steam hissed from the snow and melting began to spill away from his hand. I came forward, all heavy boots and cold skin, to shovel more snow into the tub with my hands, until I could step out of my boots and into scalding water.

It splashed over the sides of the tub and made ice of the snow around it as Janx joined me, and in a very little while I thought that my mother could tell me nothing, that I had learned all I needed to know of the serpent in the heart of *my* world.

That, then, was when he asked me how to capture a witch.

I LAUGHED, OF COURSE, and perhaps it was the sound of laughter that brought my mother from her house. She is old and crafty, and knows that when love turns to laughing, lovers are easily caught unawares. Not I: I was only surprised she had taken so long to come to us. Janx, though; well, Janx knew nothing of my mother, and was bold besides.

He stood up from behind me, stepped out of the tub, and in the moonlight against the snow he was golden, a liquid metal god with hair blackened by water spilling over his shoulders. Snow melted around his feet, though ice would capture him soon enough if he stopped moving. As for myself, I wished my clothes were nearer, and huddled in the water to hide from cold I hadn't felt while in his arms.

Mother held a bauble in one hand, a thread with a blood-colored pendent dangling from it. She lifted it high and the pendant's thin gold wire caught in the moonlight, making sharp lines across her gnarled knuckles. "Witches," she said to Janx, "are no easier to catch than dragons, but like dragons, we look fondly on gifts. I can count back centuries, and in all that time I can think of no gifts brought to me by the one who calls Moscow his own."

I lifted wet fingers to wet hair, remembering the rose Eliseo hadn't given me, and wondered what my mother would make of that.

"I would give you all his trove save one piece," Janx offered. His head tilted, gaze gone to the crimson pendent, and a quickness came into his voice; an urgency that I hadn't heard as missing when he'd wanted me, but now that I knew its sound, it left me cold and alone with regret. "All but the piece that keeps him here, and that one would be mine."

"Spoils of war are no fit gift," Mother said dismissively. She raked him with a glance and a fit of avarice came into her eyes, a look I knew well enough, for it had been my own not so long ago. I opened my mouth to whisper a warning, but the words stuck in my throat, and that was no doing of my own.

"I know little of witches," Janx said, "and less of how your magics work. But I have three books, taken from three sisters three hundred years ago. Perhaps they'd suit your tastes."

"The grimoires of Birnam Wood," Mother murmured, and bumps stood up on my skin in the cooling water. I knew those books, as anyone who was my mother's daughter might. As any of the old ones might, but there are few of them left now, and their daughters are not what their mothers might have hoped.

"Yes," Mother whispered, "that will do. Come, red lord, let me grant you thanks in exchange." The jeweled wire glittered again, and Janx walked forward, a king to be crowned, and bent his head so she might drop the shining thing around his neck. "A ruby," she said, "bled white in my fist and filled with color again by a virgin's blood."

Janx lifted the stone from against his naked chest and admired it in the moonlight. "I'm no unicorn to be caught by a maiden, old mother."

"Not," my mother said, and the weight of it shivered cold out of the air, "unless the maiden is a witch."

Tension sluiced into Janx's shoulders, and not until it arrived did I realize how little worry he carried in his body. Men were not like that; they moved with strain that belied natural grace, but nothing of concern had marred his form until now. Then something more happened, something unlike any I had ever seen, and that even without it coming to pass properly enough *to* see.

For a violent instant two beings occupied the space he stood in. One was the slim long-legged man whose beauty had caught my eye; the other was a savage thing, impossible in size, struggling to burst through the shape I'd come to know. It was a thing of fire and fury, of burnished color and changeable smoke, blurring, vibrating, unseeable in its struggle to change. Fear should have wakened in me, but instead my breath caught and I knew I had learned nothing of the serpent, after all.

Then the attempt was over and Janx flinched toward me, panting, agape with disbelief and anger. He clawed his fingers at the necklace, and though strain pulled the muscle in his arm, the chain refused to break. "You were no—"

Shame filled my chest. "Not now, but I was once, and my mother does not waste what tools she has at hand." I stood and called my clothes to me with a whisper of power, much less than it took to ride a coal shovel across the edges of a city, and shivered into layers and furs before looking to Janx again. His jade eyes were wide, no longer drinking me up, but searching for answers in my hidden form.

"It was not a trap," I said heavily. "I thought we might steal a while without my mother knowing. But we are beneath her house, and nothing passes here that she doesn't see." Gaze lowered, I stepped past him, but he caught my arm with a fingertip touch. Compulsion brought my eyes to his, and if he had not been chained by my mother's will I might have thought that compulsion to be one he laid on me. But no: it came from within, burgeoned by apology, seeking forgiveness.

Humor and confidence shone in his face: an obvious lie. I was my mother's daughter, and could see fear tight against his bones, could see anger burning emerald in changeable eyes. But there was nothing of falsehood in the words he breathed: "Some things are worth risking all."

His smile left a mark in my mind, a scar that would never fade, and as I climbed the ladder into my mother's house, I heard her whisper, carried on the thin winter air: "And now you know why White Rumi has never left this place. You, though, will go. Change your form and fetch me my grimoires. I command it."

An infuriated roar and an upheaval beneath it sent the house to scrambling, looking for safe ground to stand upon, and when I looked out the window it was to see a blazing fiery arrow climbing into the sky.

A SLASH OF WHITE flew upward, a meteorite falling in reverse. It slammed into the streak of red that was Janx, and Daisani, sitting at the forest's edge hundreds of feet below, sighed and put his palm to his forehead.

The dragons alone fought territory wars. They alone knew when another of their kind took their Old shape nearby, tasting it as a challenge in the air. The youthful among them—when there had been young—transformed often, struggling to steal or win a scrap of land for their own, and then to hold off other comers. It was the way of the young.

Janx, though, had not been young for a long time.

Knowing what he'd see, Daisani dropped his hand and turned his attention to the stars again. They fell, the two dragons in the sky: they fell writhing and spitting and tangling with each other, toward rooftops that housed men sleeping for the night. That was lucky: mankind's population grew too quickly for red Janx, for white Rumi, for any of them to take the kind of risk these two did now, and its only saving grace was that the hour was small and only drunkards would be out in the frozen morning. Daisani wished the moon away and instead watched it catch the brilliance of Rumi's wings as he finally pulled out of the fight to gain altitude again. Janx twisted after him, larger wings driving him higher more rapidly, and even from the distance, Daisani winced as one of Janx's huge clawed feet smashed Rumi in the head and sent the smaller dragon tumbling.

And, against every natural tendency, flew higher still, and cut his way across the night, darkness swallowing him whole. Daisani stared after him, relieved and bewildered. Something had gone wrong with the witch's daughter; that much was clear, but then, that much had been all but promised in the moment she'd called the coal shovel to herself and flew out of the pub. He was no stronger in the face of astonishing events or beautiful women than Janx was: curiosity was a cat to kill them both, though he, at least, he had more sense than to romance the girl at her mother's house.

Fascination bit all the harder with Janx's departure: he couldn't catch a sky-bound dragon, but the other might have answers, and he was still falling toward the earth.

Daisani reached the crash site before Rumi himself did.

Snow smashed upward and caught in the air, fragile glittering bits of light under the moon. Daisani brushed his shoulders clear and climbed a hill of displaced snow, crouching on its crest to examine the fallen dragon.

Blood leaked over the behemoth's eye, a wintery scale torn loose from Janx's kick, and the white whiskers around his mouth looked like silver drool against the snow. He was smaller than Janx, who was of an impossible size, but the same in general form: serpentine, winged, legged, long and slender in all ways. Not even Daisani had often studied a dragon in repose, and he thought the form admirable, if impractical for a world growing more and more populated by man. "Wake up and change back. You idiots may have woken someone, and whatever treasure keeps you here, it won't be worth a dragon hunt."

One of Rumi's eyes peeled open—complex double lids, like a snake—to reveal ice blue before it shuttered closed again. He pushed up on a foreleg with aching care, then rumbled a wordless curse and transformed. Wind rushed by Daisani, knocking his clothes askew, and the echo of transformation left his ears ringing. A white-haired man as tall and slim as Janx sat in the middle of a dragon-shaped depression, and as he stood a ruby pendant on a silver wire slid from beneath his shirt. He tucked it away again, and Daisani watched the impression it made. "I thought the purpose of a hoard was to hide it away unseen."

Rumi scowled, uncertain, then scowled more deeply still. "Vampire."

"And a curious one at that. I've known Janx for more centuries than you've been alive, and in all that time I've never seen him wear decorations. Dragons," Daisani said with easy confidence, "don't. So tell me the story of your silver chain, and I'll be on my way."

Anger worked the dragon's thin mouth, pulling his lips back to show too-long, inhumanly sharp teeth. "I can't," he finally said, and then, more bitterly, "Ask the witch's daughter."

Daisani's eyebrows lifted. "And why would she answer me?"

"She might not." Against all good sense, Rumi slammed back into his dragon form, sound and shockwave powerful enough to send Daisani staggering. "But I *can*not, and so if you want answers, vampire, seek them with her." He flung himself into the air, leaving Daisani still curious and now blanketed in snow.

A WEEK OF WAITING: not so much time, for one such as Eliseo Daisani. He was a patient predator, though many—most—of his kind were not. The witch and her daughter would go nowhere until Janx returned: that was Daisani's bet, even without a taste of blood to tell him which way the wind blew.

He didn't expect the dragon to return with a leather satchel grasped in gold-dipped talons, nor for Janx's wisdom to have left him altogether. The terrible crimson beast that he was came winging out of hard winter sunshine, scattering so rough a landing that Baba Yaga's house leapt aside to keep from being toppled. That was not Janx; in uncountable centuries Daisani had no memory of the dragonlord risking exposure so blatantly. Under cover of night; under cover of smoke and fog and war: those were the times when a dragon might return to his elemental form and trust that mankind's eyes wouldn't see. They were too large, too dangerous, too obvious a threat; Daisani and his kind could take far greater risks, and as for the others, well: the selkies were drowned, the djinn bound to their deserts, and the gargoyles were night-time creatures and cautious besides. That was the price of being birthed of solid steady stone, though by that logic, fiery dragons might well be the most reckless of all the surviving races.

Janx transformed to human shape entirely naked in the snow, dressed in nothing but an expression of rage and a glint of gold at his throat. The daughter came out from the chicken-legged house to take the satchel from Janx's hands, and the human-formed immortal softened, some of his fury bleeding away at the girl's presence. Daisani, hunched in a tree like an over-sized raven, didn't try to hide his grin: this would be fodder for centuries to come.

"Drowned by water," an old woman's voice whispered in his ear, and all around him, snow splashed to meltwater below the sound of chains rattling. Branches, freed of their heavy white burden, sprang upward and snaked toward him, and rushing water bared black dirt between the tree's toes. "Staked by wood, bound by iron, buried in earth."

Janx's wisdom had fled: Daisani's had not. He dove from the tree and sped across the forest, racing a specter whose words followed him: "Forget the serpent's son, Eliseo Daisani, and I shall pursue you no more."

THERE WAS NO JOY in bedding a man bent to my mother's command. Under her whim he was a lap-dog, not a firebrand, his color leached and his eyes dull except when anger moved him. Then he was stirred to beauty, but the red gem at his breast would flare and he would subside again, leaving me aware that I was a fool and red-haired Janx was lost to me. Emboldened by curiosity and loss, I peeked at the pages of my mother's oldest grimoires, the books of magic which lay down the laws of the world. She might have told me herself, had I asked; might have told me of the serpent at the heart of the world, but I disliked the thought of offering her more power over me. My interest was a thing of my own, and I had little enough of that to want to hoard it. That, and I knew now that dragons were real, and so clinging to precious bits of knowledge had a sweeter taste, as though I could make myself closer to the one I'd inadvertently betrayed by collecting and keeping what wisdom I could.

I let myself pretend I was fooling my mother. It's possible I was, but the heart of me, where I was fully her daughter, said I lied to myself as I'd done when I'd stolen an hour with a dragonlord. That time had not been stolen, no more than my dredges of scholarship were: they were granted me by a witch whose foresight ran far beyond mine, and who would find a way to use what little I could eke out and take for my own.

I knew this, and still I didn't care, because what I learned was beautiful.

I had known, of course, that those such as my mother sprang from those places in the earth where confidences were whispered and offerings burnt. They rose up from ashes and secrets, rose up stench-ridden with death and burdened under the promise of silence for sly things shared. They rose up mad things, shaped by their making, greedy for knowledge won at any cost. Frightened peasants told tales that water would not drown a witch but that fire would burn her, and that gave them comfort, false as it was. Only one thing could condemn a witch, and that was exposure of the secret that gave her life. Her first secret: that, and that alone, would undo my mother or any witch. The few old ones who remained had long-since outlived those who'd whispered the first secrets, so long-since that I had thought no one in this world might have been there to watch them birthed.

But now I knew of the Old Races.

If I had been my mother I could have sunk my fingers into the grimoires and drawn the knowledge in through my blood. But we daughters are not what our mothers hoped, and I could only turn page after page, reading hungrily. They were fables, these stories, legends written by the hopeful and the lonely, but they were written in books of magic, and they were written in words of blood.

Dragons. Oh, dragons I knew, in the slim sweet form of the red-haired man my mother held under lock and golden chain. They were born of the hot places in the world, far from my frozen Russia. Like the witch my mother was, they were greedy for precious things, and this is how dear the knowledge of how to hold a dragon was to my mother's heart: it remained unwritten, even in the pages of her own grimoires. In all the world, she may have been the only witch to bind a dragon, and that, *that* was deep magic indeed.

Vampires. Their gift was speed, and answered for me how Eliseo Daisani had come to stand at my side even after my coal-shovel escape. They, too, could be bound; all of the Old Races could be, though none of them easily, and vampires with the most difficulty of all. Unlike the dragon charm, a vampire's confinement was written in the book, proof enough that amongst the ancient crones it was a spell well-known. What lay unmarked in the history of vampires was their genesis: not even my mother knew where they came from, though someone in the writing of this book had hinted that they were not of this world at all.

There were others, though, so many others. Gargoyles, which my people might have called golems, and seal-folk called selkie which were only stories from the ice-bound hunters who lived even further north than my mother's hut chose to go. Mountain-men called yeti, and water-born sea folk whom popular tales called *mer*, but who were written in these pages as *siryn* who swam with sea serpents. Djinn, which were the living wind, and winged angry women named *harpies*. These were creatures of the darkness, all the dreams and fears of humanity given form, and they were dying.

Some had died to fill these pages. Words wrapped around drawings, and more than one of those scrawled pieces of art writhed when my gaze slipped away. Magic pinned them in place, secrets draining their vitality and preserving them forever, though they would remain known only to a few.

There were wonders in the world; that, I had always known. How could I not, when I was my mother's daughter? But they were greater than I had imagined, and I felt the first stirrings of lust in me as I read my mother's grimoires. Not lust for men, or even dragons, but the burning need to learn more. I wanted to tear the living drawings from the book itself and eat them up, to chew them and taste what they were, to learn it and have it in me for all time. That, then, was the witch in me, and wisdom told me to keep my curiosity's flame low. Baba Yaga is jealous of her knowledge, and if my child's interest turned to active desire in her eyes, she would eat me up and make all my thoughts and questions her own.

A week passed while I read, then two. The light began to return, though winter grew more bitter yet. I thought of Janx at times, but more often I thought of the imaginary rose, and wondered that I had been so wrong, that the man called Daisani could so easily leave his partner behind.

When I left the hut it was to discover I could find no jobs that would have me, now that it was known whose daughter I was. I walked muddy frozen streets, listening for what was to be heard, and this is what I heard: Moscow rumbled with discontent, with too many stories of witches and magic. The poor and superstitious spat when they saw a black-haired woman of beauty, while the rich and fanciful cut those same women deep curtseys and bows, just in case they were Baba Yaga's daughter.

Mother had her grimoires and no other cares: she even put the dragon to sleep, that his grumblings should not bother her. Her other pet, the sullen icy Rumi, came calmer at that, and with his calm the city calmed, as though it had become so much a part of him the one could affect the other. Then only I was left with discontent, hungry for a touch that my mother had neutered and searching for the one who might make it whole again.

When he came it was from the wealthy quarter, and there was a determination beneath the artful lightness of his voice. He played at being Janx, I thought, but Eliseo Daisani was that coin's other side, and the act sat badly with him. Still, he spoke with a touch of romance the dragon hadn't pretended to, and my ears were good enough to hear that there was no pretense as he murmured: "You still wear my rose in your hair."

My fingers flew to the nothingness tucked above my ear, the gesture enough to say his words were truth. We were in a square, broad and empty for all that daylight shone down, and he offered me his elbow like a gentleman. "I have been around the joined continents these past two weeks. Would you like to know what I've learned of witches in that time?"

"I would." My mother would not like whatever answer he gave, but at least I would have it to give her.

Eliseo Daisani nodded and we walked a long time in silence, leaving the rich parts of the city and finding its ragged, forest-ridden edge. "Nothing," he said then, as if the trees had shaken loose his tongue. "I have learned nothing at all. Those few witches old enough to carry knowledge carry too much and are a danger, and the young can only tell me that a man bent to a witch's will is caught beneath a binding spell. I ought to have heeded Rumi, and asked Baba Yaga's daughter first. How do I free my friend?"

"Why would I tell you?"

Daisani smiled. "Because I'll kill you if you don't."

"That's little incentive," I said, and heard myself from a distance; heard myself make a choice that had to do with the fire gone from Janx's jade eyes and the secrets revealed in my mother's grimoires; a choice that spoke to the aching loss in my breast at those secrets caged by a witch's spell. "That's little enough incentive," I said again, and then oh so softly, finished, "for you'll kill me if I do."

My walking partner stopped, a terrible stillness that swept out from him and made him all the things his slight dapper form gave lie to: made him alien and dangerous, made him a killer and a drinker of blood. Then he turned to me, black eyes gone bright, and whispered, "Ah," so that I knew he understood me.

He took my wrist and turned it up, exposing skin to the winter air before tracing a fingertip over blue veins. "Bloodlines," he breathed. "Blood is ever-important."

"It is," I whispered back, "and you will want to run far and fast, Eliseo Daisani. Cross a river and an ocean if you can. Then my mother cannot follow you, for she's a witch bred and born, and running water has its power." By then we were far from the city, lost in a frozen forest, so there was no one who might hear me scream if

I chose to. I did not: first, because I thought the heat reborn in Janx's gaze was worth the chill of mine, and second, because—to my surprise—there was no pain. There might even have been seduction, had we willed it, but no: this was a thing done of a duty running deep as mountains reached high, and lust, should it ever come, would come at another time.

It never would come, for me, and as the blood emptied from my body, I felt my heart drawing back what it had once given, calling all parts of me to it so it might keep beating, and in so doing, drained the rubies of their color.

A DRAGON BURST FROM the chicken-legged hut, scattering its pieces across a snowy landscape. Rage shrieked from the dragon's throat, fire bursting over bits of shattered wood, and below that an ancient crone shrieked too. Agitated chicken legs ran about, their animation comical and terrifying all at once, but no more than the old woman or the pieces of broken house did they burn. Janx hung in the air, spitting fire again and again, until the forest itself was alight, but Baba Yaga refused to burn. Only when her screams cut through his own bellows of insult and fury did Janx take wing to the sky, chased by a witch on her mortar as she shouted, "My daughter! My daughter! My daughter is dead! You will pay, you will burn, you will die!"

A flash of black on the snow below: Janx dove and captured Daisani in gold-tipped talons, and together they fled Russia and the rage of a witch, followed by promises of their doom should they ever return.

I AM, YOU SEE, my mother's daughter, and it is not only blood that flows in my veins and gives me life. There is magic, too, and it is lucky for me that Daisani slipped me into a cold deep snowbank to bury me when I died, for my mother would have eaten up my body to take the magic back into herself. Then I would be dead indeed, and there would be no one to tell this story the way I could.

But not even Baba Yaga can sniff out a corpse in an ice field in a frozen Russian winter, and her re-made hut had moved on before spring came to Moscow. The earth thawed and a dream came to me: a dream of the serpent at the heart of the world, and the world's heart was a tree, growing up toward me, around me, waking life in an icy body. A tiny woman came from the tree to bend and kiss my brow, and a bond snapped inside me.

Power took its place, the kind that could call a mortar for me to ride as long as I might want; the kind that could bind a man or eat him up; the kind that could steal magic back from others infused with it; the kind that made me my mother's daughter in more ways than blood. I thought of her, and of her house, and of all the stories of fear and warning that rode with her, and I thought of Eliseo Daisani and the one called Janx. They are in the world, shackled like thirst and drink: the one no good without the other, but those are chains they've chosen, and not ones forced upon them.

For myself, I rose up out of the snow no longer my mother's daughter, and that, I think, is enough.

Five Card Draw

HER EARS AND NAPE ARE cold. Neither the diamonds on her lobes nor the mink at her throat do much to warm her; there's something in the difference between upswept hair and locks cropped short that lets the chill creep down her spine and leave her fingers bloodless. Women have worn their hair long her entire life. Embracing the daringly short new style is, to be honest, unlike her, which may be part of why she's done it. That, and the blunt cut suits her angular face: she looks a little like a film star now, and glamour has never been something she's aspired to. She finds it appealing, in a transient way. Time will bring her back to a more customary look; that much, at least, she's already learned.

There's a thin blue smoke in the room, enough of it to suggest a fire to take away her chill. But the heat here is electric, stolen from the city above, and the smoke is an affectation of the man who designed this room.

Everything about it is sumptuous: thick carpets, expensively upholstered chairs, rosewood and mahogany tables. The colors are red and gold, colors of warmth themselves, and the lights set into curving walls offer a cheery ambience. She could seat herself at one of the tables near a heater, entertain herself with the chess set, its pieces carved of ivory and ebony, whose game has been left to wither. Instead she stays where she is, a little too cold, examining one stained glass window and then another.

The speakeasy is an unnatural place for such art. Tens of feet beneath the surface, there's no sunlight to spill through them and cast their colors on the carpeted flagstone floor. The architect has made allowances for this, has built electric lights behind the windows to illuminate them so they become more than dull colors bent inside the walls of an abandoned subway station. She wonders what will happen when the lights burn out, if there's a way to reach them, or if they will be allowed to remain nothing more than blackened memories of what was once a brilliant pastiche.

The very mortal part of her, the dour aspect which accepts death as an inevitable part of life, whispers that such an end might be ironically fitting, reflecting in glass what is almost certain to be the fate of the Old Races.

"Vanessa, join us?"

For a moment she doesn't answer, though her heartbeat jumps the same way it always does when she hears her name unexpectedly from that smooth voice. For a moment she pretends he won't have heard it, and keeps her gaze on the stained glass.

She is the only human being who has ever seen the windows as they are meant to be, a layered tapestry depicting five immortal, inhuman peoples. A sinuous dragon winding its way around the outer border; the long-extinct selkies built into the ocean's blue. Temperamental djinn at the sea's shore, rising in dune-colored dervishes, and a gargoyle's hunched grey form where beach turned to mountainous earth. Behind them all, hardly more than a murmur of black lines, was a man in a segmented cloak who was no man, but a vampire, whose true form no one lived to report.

The vampires, it was said, did not come from this world at all, and Vanessa Grey turns now to acknowledge the one who told her that, and who has invited her to their game.

"Winner takes all," Eliseo says gamely, and Janx, the jade-eyed dragonlord, snakes out a long leg to snag the crosspiece of a nearby chair and drag it to their table. He even pats the seat, and offers a wink meant two parts in jest and one part in calculation: she has spent nearly forty years at Eliseo Daisani's side, and if Janx can woo her away even now, then he will win another mark in their endless battle of wits, finances and lust.

"I'm very bad at card games, Eliseo. You know that." Vanessa comes to sit with them regardless, taking her place as one of five at the small round table. Lazy, insouciant Janx is to her right; small dapper Eliseo, less handsome but equally compelling, is to her left. There's no subtlety in placing herself there; it says she is his right hand, but no one in this room would doubt that anyway, not even the men across the table.

Vanessa has only come to know them recently. One is a djinn, a master of wind and glassworking genius; the other is a gargoyle with a heavily scarred face and the strength and stoneworking capability to have made the subway speakeasy a place of sealed-off, remote beauty.

They are all, Vanessa assumes, terrible cheats at cards. Eliseo's impossible speed could allow him to look at every card on the table without anyone being the wiser, while the blue smoke sailing from Janx's nostrils (whether his cigarette is lit or not) is distraction enough should he wish to work a bit of sleight-of-hand. The djinn can become incorporeal and drift unseen around the room; there is no guarantee, certainly to her dull human senses, that there is not a second such creature in the room, observing the hands that have been dealt and whispering them on a breath of wind to his compatriot.

The gargoyle, she admits after a moment's consideration, may not be well-suited to cheating. His people are supposed to be honorable—honorable to the point of irritation, to hear Janx tell it—and though she understands that their stony race can use a kind of mental sharing between one and another, a second gargoyle in the room could not go unnoticed. It's possible that of the five players, Vanessa and the scarred man called Biali are the only two who will not be cheating.

It is likely, in fact, because of the five players, she suspects only she and Biali are uninterested in the outcome.

"I've nothing in the pot," she says even so. "Are you sure you want to play it winner takes all?"

"I've seen you play cards," Janx says drolly. "I think it's a safe risk."

Her heartbeat jumps again. After forty years, it shouldn't, not anymore, but even after all this time, it seems the slightest reminder of her mortality, her presumed inferiority, her humanity—even in teasing, even as a joke—still stings. She was fifteen and in pinafores when she met Eliseo Daisani; twenty-three when she learned his secrets and the world he belonged to, and became his life-long companion. In all those years she has never imagined herself to want to be like him, but only to share the life he knows. And yet the needle pricks sharp and deep when she's obliged to face any comment that she isn't one of the Old Races, and never will be.

Someday, she realizes in a rare moment of clarity, someday this truth will make her bitter.

"Your deal," Janx says, and offers her the deck of cards.

Her fingers are clumsy and thick as she shuffles, then deals out the deck. It's partly that her hands are cold, partly that she can't help remembering the slick swift sounds of Janx's own dealing; in comparison, even the most skilled of human dealers are slow and numb-fingered. Janx, imagining he is doing her a favor, glances away as if to avoid pointing out her awkward deal.

Across the table, the djinn's lip curls as he regards his cards. Vanessa might think it a tell, except she's rarely seen another expression on Tariq's face. His is the quintessential lemon pucker even at the best of times, as though such expressions had been invented to accommodate him and him alone.

The gargoyle, of course, is impassive. A poker face worthy of the phrase, which almost brings a smile to Vanessa's lips. She has no idea if he wants the thing they play for; he has certainly put as much time and work into the speakeasy as any of them, but gargoyles are creatures of mountaintops and the sky. Had she wings, Vanessa would not want to live under the earth.

Janx and Eliseo are uninterested in the other two; the game is between them, as far as they're concerned. It always has been and always will be, long after the vitality supped from Daisani's blood has left Vanessa dead and ashes. She lifts her cards with that thought in mind, wondering, as she sometimes does, how many years two sips of a vampire's blood allows a mortal woman.

More than a century: that much is clear. She was born before the War Between the States, though it broke out only a few weeks after her first birthday. She is over sixty now, and looks hardly older than she did the day she drank of Eliseo's gift. One sip for healing, he told her; two sips for life.

Three for death.

The cards are a blur of hearts and diamonds, red as blood as she places them face-down and deals new cards to the men who have, as it were, discarded theirs. Tariq is an impatient player, demanding four new cards; Janx, whose very personality bubbles over with acquisitive eagerness, only asks for one. If Eliseo is cheating, there should be a breeze from his motion, a ruffling of the cards or a stirring in the air. Perhaps he's decided not to in light of her own incapability. Even her heartbeat, so mercurial and alive, could give away the strength of her hand. In that light, the fact that it betrays her so often may be a gift; perhaps there's no telling a thump of excitement from a crash of desire.

The gargoyle asks for two cards; Vanessa passes them over with the unguarded idea that he, the other party who seems uninterested, holds a handful of dark suits to complement her bright ones. Eliseo declines new cards altogether: either he is confident or he is cheating after all. Vanessa discards and collects two for herself, and coughs lightly on Janx's exhalation of smoke. He puts a hand over his heart and offers a mocking seated bow, a pretense at apology that amuses her, though she doesn't let a smile curve her lips.

"Fold," Biali says in disgust. Vanessa is caught unawares, blinking wide-eyed at the scarred gargoyle as he throws his cards down. She had decided this game was between him and her, in the same way Janx and Eliseo played no one but each other. She wonders, briefly, where Tariq fits into these unlikely alliances; it seems no one has partnered him.

This, she thinks, is why the Old Races are dying, but it's not a thing she would say to any of the men she shares a table with. They're right not to trust humanity, and they deny their natural alliances with one another.

She believes she has many decades to live, maybe even centuries, but if the vampire blood that runs through her veins is kind, Vanessa will die before the last of the Old Races does. She would not wish solitude on anyone, least of all the dark-haired vampire who has been the center of her life for forty years, but even less would she wish it on herself. It is small and petty, but it's easier to think of Eliseo Daisani going on without her, than of herself going on without him.

"Fold," Tariq says after a much longer silence, and the look he gives Vanessa is poison, as though he suspects her of deliberately giving him poor cards. She tries to imagine, briefly, how she might have succeeded in doing that without his superhuman senses catching it, and then puts the worry away.

Eliseo and Janx are watching each other like predators, neither willing to lay his hand down prematurely.

She has seen this time and again over the decades, whether in cards or at the horses or in building empires and watching as they crumble down.

And yet, even after so many years of observing them, she can't see the moment of exchange, the instant of unspoken agreement that lets them move in tandem and spread their cards on the table. They do not give way to one another, these two not-men, and their ability to dance around the point of concession is a thing of legend, at least to Vanessa's mind.

She looks to Eliseo's cards first, naturally; he is, after all, her lover and her friend, and his hand is a very good one. Good enough that she understands why he risked taking no cards. In a game with five players, a full house is more than a safe bet: even Vanessa, who professes to know little of card games, knows that. Eliseo displays nines and sevens, three of the higher cards and two of the lower.

Janx, though, has lain down a straight flush.

For an astonished moment they all stare at his cards, a glittering row of red diamonds numbering five through nine. Triumph flashes through the dragonlord's jade eyes, his charmer's smile laced with avarice. "It's only fair," he says in a tone Vanessa recognizes as meaning to be magnanimous, "that we should all make use of this place we've created together. You are all welcome here any time, of course." Welcome, but at Janx's leisure: it is a draught he enjoys drinking of.

"Forgive me," Vanessa murmurs, and watches both her lover and his rival turn surprised gazes on her. They've forgotten she's playing, just as she dismissed Tariq only moments ago.

With a heart-pounding glee she barely remembers from childhood, she places her cards on the table in a fine, carefully spaced arc.

The ace of hearts, and its king. That card is Eliseo Daisani, in Vanessa's world, and when she dares she imagines herself the queen lying alongside it. The jack that sandwiches them is the son they'll never have, and the ten which completes the royal flush is a number, nothing more, like the ageless years she'll have with her immortal lover. "Forgive me," she murmurs again, "but I believe the speakeasy is mine."

MONTHS LATER, VISITING HER subway sanctuary, her hands are once again cold. She sits at the card table and makes a mess of shuffling the deck, thick clumsy fingers full of awkward motions. She remembers the uncomfortable air that surrounded her as she dealt cards to the men who'd built the speakeasy, and feels a warm blush come to her cheeks at the recollection.

She remembers, too, the grandfather who played at cards and magic tricks when she was a child, a man whose livelihood came from the skill to distract as much as to shuffle a deck. She turns her cuff up to consider how an astonished dragonlord and a delighted vampire never thought to check her sleeves after she'd taken their prize away from them, and smiles.

After all, she is only human, and could never manage to cheat the Old Races.

Hot Time in the Old Town Tonight

SHE WAS TOO YOUNG, EVEN for a man with no age, but she caught his eye. Slim, dark-haired, with long fingers caught in the skirt of a shapeless dress, she was clearly not a child of wealth. She no doubt belonged to the riverboat upon which she stood, a shabby thing that had seen better days. Even so, in the fire's light they both bent toward beauty.

It was her gaze, fixed on the sky, which arrested him. Others watched the fire, drawn in by its glow and movement, but she looked upward as though she could see what soared above the smoke. That was quite impossible: even knowing who danced there, Daisani could barely see them himself, but the girl watched as if she knew. Such seeing eyes were enough that he might have gone to her then, despite her youth, but tonight; tonight Chicago was burning.

New York, 1923

FLAME TREMBLED, DANCED, THEN fell into darkness. Vanessa murmured a sound of impatience and rose to find matches. Her lush speakeasy refuge had electric lighting, but she preferred the warmth of fire. She had since childhood, though there'd been no electricity then to weigh it against. Then, she had loved its power, even when it destroyed, even when it haunted her dreams; now, she loved its gentleness on her eyes, on the lines of her face, though she, of all women, had little cause to worry in that regard. Still, she read and played chess and cards by candle-light, and the flame that had died left the room just that much too dim.

A spark; a scent of sulfur; and an idle thought that the guttering candle would have been better served with the living flame from another rather than the recalcitrant matches. A second strike woke a second spark, but no blaze caught. "For pity's sake."

"Allow me." A man's voice where there'd been no one a moment before, first startling and then waking a whole new level of impatience. He stood behind her, close enough to be a lover, and folded long cool fingers over hers, as though he'd strike a new match himself. He didn't: a scrape of his thumbnail against his fingerpad brought flame to life, and the candle's glow warmed the cup of her palm as he guided her hand to light it. "There," he said with evident satisfaction. "Much better, isn't it?"

"It might have been, if your arrival hadn't blown it out in the first place." Vanessa turned in his arms and put her fingertips against his chest, pushing him away. He fell back one step, expression all jade-eyed injury, and was obliged to step backward again as Vanessa returned to her chair.

Well: not obliged, perhaps. She had known the red-haired man more than thirty years, and if obligation had ever sat on his shoulders at all, it had done so lightly indeed. Book in hand, seat re-taken, she turned a deliberately piqued gaze on him. "What on earth do you want, Janx? Eliseo isn't here."

"My dear Miss Grey." Janx cut a more extravagant bow than usual, then fell into the chaise lounge across from her and cocked a knee up, fingers spread wide in supplication. "It's not Eliseo I want at all. Surely you know that by now."

It wouldn't do to laugh; it would *never* do to laugh at Janx's theatrics. He had everything Eliseo Daisani lacked: fire, vitality, humor; a face which would see him beloved in the moving pictures, if he were fool enough to take vanity that far. He was not, though, a fool. A fop, yes; a showman, without question. But never a fool, and Vanessa dragged her gaze from him to the surrounding walls, the better to remind herself of who and what else he was.

No one else—no one else human, at least—had ever seen the tapestries from whence the speakeasy's abstract glass windows came. Curved to fit into subway walls, as they stood they were beautiful rushes of color, lit from behind because this room was buried, a secret meeting place for a handful of men who were not human at all.

Men who had, as it happened, lost its ownership to Vanessa herself, and who now came and went from it only at her whim. Largely, at least; Janx was ever disinclined to follow someone else's strictures. Truthfully, she was surprised any of them obliged her winnings and her privacy as much as they did. She was only human, and a clever bit of card-play could hardly stop them if they chose to make this place their own again. But Eliseo and Janx admired cleverness, and what they deigned to accept, the others tended to follow.

Unless the chosen object was a thing *one* of them had chosen to accept, and by doing so left the other to want it. "You don't want me, Janx. You only want what Eliseo has."

"And are the two not one and the same?"

"Not," Vanessa said with a faint smile, "from where I'm sitting. I doubt you came down here alone to try to seduce me. Half your entertainment comes from doing that in front of Eliseo. So what do you want?"

"I want to know how you won this place." Janx spread his arms, encompassing the room's curved walls, the rich carpets and heavy, warm furnishings. "I want to know how you managed to cheat us. Oh, I don't care, I'm not going to eat you." Fluttering hands made light of the way her heart lurched. "It's simply curiosity, my dear, and I'm so much like a cat. My curiosity shall kill me."

"My concern is that it shan't kill *me*."

He gave her a smile, candle-light never dim enough to hide the too-long curvature of his canines, or their too-sharp points. "Of course not. Not if it finds an answer."

She doubted he would do it. Not for any love he had for her, but because of the delicate dance between himself and Eliseo. If she were to die here, in the speakeasy she'd won as her own, Eliseo would have no doubt as to her murderer. It would lack subtlety, and Janx was too much a master of their game for that.

And yet it wasn't a bluff to call. Not so obviously, at least, as by refusing him. Vanessa set her book aside, studying the lanky red-head across from her. The firelight was good to him, making his skin gold, bringing life to his reposed form. Living shadow danced where light would not fall and brought with it memories so long occluded she could only half believe they were real. No: more than half, now, and for a long time since, but there were questions she had never dared lay at the feet of the men she'd come to know.

Questions which now, unexpectedly, had an opportunity to be asked. "A curiosity for a curiosity, Janx. I'll tell you for a price."

He sat up in an explosion of movement, interest brightening his jade eyes. "You surprise me, my dear. Name your price, and we shall see if I'll play your game."

"No." She knew better. Neither Janx nor Daisani, nor any of the others she'd met, were men with whom to settle the details of a bet after the fact. "This is the game. One of your curiosities satisfied in exchange for one of mine, or we both go away unsatisfied."

The impulse for low-brow humor scampered across his face, but she'd been right, before: it was only in Eliseo's presence that Janx truly enjoyed flirting with her. His humor was replaced by petulance and he waved a hand sullenly. "Oh, very well. What do you want to know?"

Triumph spattered through her. "Tell me what happened in Chicago."

Janx's silence was so complete, so still, that it seemed the candle-light had died. That Vanessa was alone in the dark, with no companion but her heartbeat, and then he said, oh so softly, "Her name was Susannah, and like the best of you, she was only human."

Chicago, September 1871

HER FEAR GAVE HER away.

That was to be expected; that was, indeed, part of the plan. But knowing a man could count the rapid beat of her heart or breathe in the scent of her terror was one thing. It was a different thing entirely to see flat hunger in his eyes as he disengaged from conversation, searching the room for a tantalizing prize.

She had every right to be afraid: gamblers' halls and saloons were men's territory, the only women to walk among them prostitutes and actresses. Susannah was neither, nor even pretending to be one of them. Her dress was of extraordinary quality, better than anything she'd ever owned, and her hair was done by the expertise of an upper class ladies' maid. The scenting man was not the only one whose attention she'd gained, though of all of them, he was the most dangerous. He was also, of course, the target.

She'd been warned. She'd even watched, from a distance, as he and his kind moved through the city. She'd been taught to recognize their slightly-too-smooth movements, and to notice how even the most elegant of humans seemed a little thick and clumsy in their wake. She saw it again now as he made his way through rough and gentle men alike. The gambling hall equalized them, sinners to a need.

"Madame," her quarry said with utmost courtesy when he reached her, "you cannot possibly belong here."

"No." Her voice was far too frail. She swallowed, trying to strengthen it, and felt the pulse in her throat. Saw his gaze go to it, and felt it leap again. She would be no use at all, if her fear stayed this real. She swallowed a second time, then pulled a nervous, determined smile into place. It suited both her barely-contained panic and the role she was meant to play.

It had seemed easier, this part, before she walked on stage.

"My brother," she managed, then tightened her hands in their gloves. Soft kidskin gloves, as fine as the dress; finer than a secretary could ever own. But tonight she wasn't a secretary, nor would she be for many nights to come, if this first encounter was successful.

If it wasn't, well. She would be dead, and so not a secretary then, either.

"Your brother," he prompted. "A ne'er-do-well?"

Offense welled up in her, genuine enough to be funny if she didn't need it so badly. "I should think you're not one to talk, sirrah, given that you've come from a gambling table to greet me."

A smile cut across his face, making him compelling, if not handsome. That surprised her: she had expected beauty, but he was merely tall and rangy and graceful. Combined with the sharp smile, it could be mistaken for attractiveness, but it was by no means the seductive masculinity she'd imagined.

Then again, she knew what he was, and that, perhaps, colored her perceptions. "Would it help my case," he wondered, "if I swore I never gamble? That these premises are mine to run, but not to indulge in?"

"No," she said as acerbically as before. "A man who profits from a den of iniquity is no better than those who lose their money to them."

"Such as your brother," he said smoothly, and Susannah winced even as she admired the circle she'd been run in.

"He looks like me," she said more quietly. "His hair is sandier, perhaps, but his eyes are the same, green and wide-set in his face. His jaw is stronger, and...please, has he been here? He's only seventeen, and I was meant to care for him after our parents died. I've done all I can, but he's drawn to the cards and the horses, and I'm at my wits' end."

His gaze darkened, another sharp smile sliding across his lips. "Alone in the world. How tragic for both of you. I've seen no youths of such rare beauty, miss. Oh, but he must be," he said as she blushed. "If he looks like you, he must be. Perhaps you would accept my escort to some of the less reputable establishments on Hairtrigger Block, that you might search for him in safety."

"Please." It took no effort at all to put a quaver of relief in the word, nor any thought to slip her hand into the crook of his elbow when he offered it. Her heartbeat was dizzyingly high, and she wondered what he made of it. If he thought it heightened from gladness that she needn't face the gamblers' row alone, or if he imagined, as many men here would, that she had come to sell herself for the first time, and that terror had the best of her. There were other explanations, but those were the two most likely, and neither had any bearing on the truth.

It was unseasonably warm beyond the gambling hall walls. Within them it had been muggy and smelled of sweat; desperate men made a stench difficult to wash from the skin. But outside was almost no better, though a breeze took the smell away. Torches threw scattered light on the street, alley-way openings gaping between them like dark maws. Susannah glanced down them nervously, and her escort offered a reassuring squeeze. "The heat is making everyone temperamental, but you're safe enough with me."

"It's just I fear I'll look down one of these and see him," Susannah whispered. "That all the years of watching over him will come to naught. See—!" Her breath caught on the word and she pulled away from her escort, taking quick steps toward a shadowed alley. "I saw, I saw—!"

"You saw nothing." Impatience colored by deliberate tolerance filled her escort's voice. "I would have seen, or heard—"

"No, I'm sure of it!" Susannah gathered her skirts and dashed down the alley, heartbeat pounding in her ears. The gambler behind her cursed, then followed after; in someone else, it might have been a gentlemanly gesture.

Even running blind, she knew how many steps to take. She had practiced so many times, wearing this very dress, these very shoes. Running over rough cobbled streets, over smooth paved stones, over mud and dry dirt, over mucked-out straw; over every kind of earth she could think of, until she was confident in every step, certain of every possible fumble. Fourteen strides, so far back into the alley that no hint of torchlight danced there, before she flung herself to the ground, sprawling crosswise across the filthy alley floor.

Her escort's boot caught her ribs, tripping him, and he fell forward into a black iron cage, invisible in the alley's darkness.

She rolled to her knees, no pretense of getting to her feet, and dragged a wooden stake from within her right sleeve: from the arm he had been unlikely to take, when he offered her his. This was the part she'd never done before, never driven wood through a living man's body, though she'd practiced hundreds of times on pig cadavers, and twice on the bodies of dead men whose presence she had not questioned. Surprise was on her side. Surprise and so many rehearsals that it was easier than she expected, plunging oak into his back.

Neither the pigs nor the dead men had screamed the way the vampire did.

It tore at her skin, a sound of knives and pain in a register no human voice could reach. On and on, his body arching back against the stake, fingers gone to black claws as they tried to reach her. *The heart is best,* she had been told. *Best, but not necessary: it's the wood impaling them that binds their form.* Even as she repeated the promise to herself in words whispered aloud, his changing fingers shriveled and became human again. She dropped her weight down on the stake, shoving it through until it moved more easily. Until his screams lost air, for she'd struck a lung, she thought, not the heart.

Only then did she dare seize one of his hands and manacle it within the cage, and then the other. He fought, even without air, but that was two. Two of the four elements of a spell to bind a vampire. It wouldn't hold forever, but it would hold long enough.

When the cage was closed, a vast darkness came out of the sky and beat wing above the alley. Taloned feet reached for the cage, seized it, carried it high. Vampires, it was said, could not die. But they could be bound, and once bound, there was another thing never yet tried. *Drowned by water. Staked by wood. Bound by iron. Buried in earth.*

Burned by fire.

Susannah, shaking, exhausted, fell back in the mud to stare skyward at the black shape a dragon made against the stars.

It had not started this way, but then, she never could have imagined where it would lead, when it began.

August 1871

THE DOORBELL'S QUIET CHIMES were flat in air bitter with heat. Susannah glanced toward the door, but whomever had entered had already stepped away, beyond her line of vision. All that was left to see were the etched glass words, arching backward on this side of the door: THE PINKERTON AGENCY. It was the agency's files she had in hand, tucking them away into neatly labeled drawers. "One moment, please. I'll be right with you."

"Miss Stacey?"

A woman's voice, rare on this side of the door; even when a woman was in need, she usually came with a male proxy. More often, she simply trusted a man to plead her case. Crossing beyond the threshold of a Pinkerton office suggested desperation, and a lady was never desperate.

Susannah Stacey, at twenty-eight and unwed, with a temperament poorly suited for nursing or teaching, had long since passed over desperation and taken up a banner of independence. She called it independence, at least: there were men who would be grateful to rent a room in their uncle's home and accept employment at their uncle's business. By that standard, she could be as satisfied with her lot as any man.

"Miss Stacey," the woman said again, more urgently. "I must speak to you."

That was the sole reason her uncle had agreed to employ her. Once in a while, a great while, a woman did pass through the agency doors. Almost inevitably, those women were more comfortable speaking with another woman in the room, pouring out their stories to what they saw as a kindred spirit. Very few of them, Susannah imagined, ever thought through what it meant that she was there at all. They would hardly consider her of their class, worthy to share anything with, if they realized she worked as the agency's secretary. She expected they saw her as more of a prop, a convenience brought out in order to sooth their worried souls.

It was, she reminded herself daily, a better fate than preparing meals and exchanging wifely gossip. Her uncle wanted to believe education had put her above herself, but was stymied by the bare fact that she'd had none beyond the necessary accounts and letters to run a household. His wife thought her unnatural, which made Susannah smile each time she recalled it. She was still smiling as she put the files aside and stepped around the wall separating the foyer from the stacks.

The woman waiting for her was not, though she put on a brief grimace approximating pleasantry when she saw Susannah's expression. It hardly mattered: she didn't need a smile to take the air from the room. Susannah's uncle would call her *full-blown,* though the phrase did no justice to the woman's lush figure or rich coloring. Red highlights in black hair and coppery skin tones hinted at Indian heritage, common enough in Chicago, and her strong features had enough of the exotic in them to lend credence to the thought. A deep red cloak hid her dress, but even so it was clear she'd foregone wide skirts and bustles. Susannah thought she'd only be half-surprised if the cloak disguised trousers and suspenders, rather than something befitting an appropriately modest woman.

She made Susannah feel pale, wan, and slightly amused at her own despair. "I'm afraid Mr. Stacey is out at the moment. Would you care to wait?"

"Mr—" Incomprehension slid across the woman's features, then faded into dismissal. "You mean the Pinkerton? No, I've no use for him. It's your help I need. You are Miss Stacey, are you not?"

"I am, but—"

"And you know something of the Pinkerton methods? Of searching out missing persons, of apprehending dangerous men?"

"I suppose I do, but—"

"Then I wish to hire you."

Susannah folded her hands in front of her stomach, a poor show of holding astonishment inside. "Madame, you must misunderstand. I'm only the secretary here, hired help to keep the paperwork in order. I'm not a detective. I don't investigate. I—I'm a *woman*."

"Yes." This time a genuine smile flashed across the other woman's face, and the brittle dry air in the room warmed as though she'd brought a small fire back from the embers. "As am I," she said as if in confidence. Then, less slyly, she added, "And I assure you, this is not a job that can be done by a man. It may not be one you people can do at all."

A flare of injured family pride stiffened Susannah's spine. "I'm quite certain the Pinkerton Agency is capable of—"

"No, my dear." The woman's smile gentled and she patted Susannah's cheek with cool fingers. "Not the Pinkertons. I mean you charming, fragile, foolish human beings."

SHE OUGHT TO HAVE something witty to say. That was her only clear thought, repeating itself like the wash of lake waters on the shore. There must be something clever to say, in the face of preposterous statements. She could think of nothing else, only that she *should* be able to meet absurdity with drollery, and became faintly aware that the desire to do so was a cocoon, keeping her safe from trying to comprehend impossibilities.

"My child is missing," the woman said into Susannah's silence. "I know who, or rather what, has taken him, but I can't hunt them myself. It's against the covenants of my people. I believe in this case I might be offered some leniency, but I prefer a subtler hand if it can be found. I cannot trust a man, Miss Stacey. They're too easily challenged, too determined to prove themselves master of what they face. And a woman is less likely to be seen as a threat, which is of some importance to your survival."

A trill of frightened laughter burst from Susannah's throat as she was given something to hold on to. "My survival? Are you mad? What are you talking about? I'm a *clerk*, madame, not a, a—"

Words failed her, but the woman took up where she left off. "You're a clerk, perhaps, and unquestionably a woman, but a woman of some rare boldness, my dear. You might have taught, you might have governed, you might have sewn; those are the legitimate occupations offered a woman in this city. Instead you bullied your sole remaining family member into hiring you as secretary for a business which deals in dark and dangerous acts. I know who you are, Miss Stacey. The question is whether you're willing to find out."

"How do you know?" Susannah wet her lips. "How do you know any of that? Who are you?"

Sympathy slid over the woman's face. "I think your uncle would keep you sufficiently protected that my name would mean nothing, but if it's of any assurance, he knows it. You may call me Fina."

Susannah echoed, "Fina," obediently, then took a sharp breath. "Fina. Serafina Durke! Chicago's dark lady. You run brothels," she said accusingly. "You seduce girls from good homes, you—"

"Not just girls," Fina said in mild offense. "So you do know who I am. And I pay so well to keep my name out of the papers."

Susannah glowered. "That's what my uncle says. But you can't keep your name out of his files. Your bruisers take tithes from shopkeepers in the city, you have your hands in the fur trade, in the railroad, in politics, in—I thought you were dead. Everyone thought you were dead. It's been more than two years since we've had a case that involved you."

"I've been indisposed. The child," Fina murmured. "Given who I am, given what you know about me, do you think I would come here if I had any other choice? I don't believe you've yearned for adventure, Miss Stacey, because I don't believe its possibility was ever tangible enough to make it a worthwhile dream. I could change that. I could give you excitement beyond your imagination."

The air was unseasonably warm, but not warm enough to account for the flush of heat that rose in Susannah's cheeks. Her heartbeat soared, giving the lie to any hint of sensibility she might have clung to. Men struck out on their own, chasing adventure through hazardous territory; women faced too many greater challenges—their more frail bodies, their desirability, their feminine weaknesses—to follow suit. If she had ever had such dreams, they'd died a-borning.

But the desire for them, it seemed, had not. It had only slept, able to be awakened by rash promises in an office lobby. Susannah raised her hands to her cheeks, fingers cold against their warmth, and Fina smiled.

"We have very little time, and all I can tell you before you choose is that it is as dangerous for me to make it as it will be for you to accept. To explain myself I'll have to break the commandments of my people. To ask what I must of you will mean the sacrifice of my own life if we're caught. Adventure," she concluded with a brief smile, "is not for the faint-hearted. Choose now, Miss Stacey."

Curious alarm made a difficult knot to breathe around. She felt buffeted by wind, by heat, as though Fina's presence took away the need for thought and consideration. Susannah flattened her palms against her skirts, chin lifted in determination. She'd spent all the years since her parents' death refusing to be bullied by family, refusing to set herself on the path they most desired. She would not permit a domineering stranger to change her ways now. "Why so little time?"

Exasperation rolled across the woman's face. "Because I'm impatient, my enemies are quick, and my child in danger. Choose."

You fragile, foolish human beings. As if Fina herself was something else. As if she *could* be something else, and if she was, what a host of wonderful, terrible things that would mean. A modicum of sense prompted one question: "Will I regret this?"

Fina laughed, warm rich sound, and ducked her head before looking up through her lashes. "Almost certainly. The real question is, will you regret not accepting even more?"

Nervous excitement fluttered in Susannah's belly and she pressed a hand over it, trying to calm herself before whispering, "I suppose there's only one way to know."

Fina's astonishing smile blossomed and she offered Susannah her elbow, taking her out of the hot dry office and into the streets. "This is a violent city, Miss Stacey, you know that, yes?"

A chill of anger buoyed by fear spilled through Susannah. "Frontier towns are violent. I'm not afraid of Chicago, Miss Durke."

"Fina," the other woman said. "Those tongue-tangling longer names are for your people, not mine. How violent?

How many homicides would you say are perpetrated annually, my dear?"

Susannah frowned. "I don't know. Dozens."

"Hundreds. And those are the ones which are reported and investigated to some degree. There are so many more disappearances."

"Something you know more than a little about."

Fina gave her a sharp look. "I rarely have cause to make people disappear, Miss Stacey. There are enough gamblers and whores already, without thieving more off steamboats and trains. Come, step along lively." Amusement dashed the sharpness off her features. "Or are you wary of Hairtrigger Block?" The streets were still broad, but pervaded with the scent of alcohol now, and the men and women who lingered there looked hard up. Susannah's conservative dress of wintery brown wool looked exceedingly well-made and well-fitted amongst the other women, and Fina's brilliant deep red cloak made her a fox among wolves. "I'll bring you worse places than this before we're through, dear heart, and you'll bring yourself to worse places yet. This way." She snapped her fingers and a disreputable-looking man stepped forward, dragging a card house door open.

Susannah balked, color in her cheeks high all over again. "I can't go in there. I shouldn't be here at all!"

"Ah." Fina pursed her lips, examining her, then shrugged. "Then there's less to you than I thought there was. Nevermind, my dear, though I'll not trouble myself to walk you home. I may be able to find some other woman with a real Pinkerton heart." She breezed through the open door, and her erstwhile doorman looked Susannah up and down with a leer.

Outraged frustration forced her through the door to hiss, "You're manipulating me!" at Fina's cloaked back.

The dark-haired woman smiled over her shoulder without a hint of repentance. "Of course I am, dear heart, but look how well you're responding to it. And in just a few minutes it won't be a matter of manipulation anymore, that I promise. You'll be eager to help."

Susannah, warily, said, "...or?"

Fina opened a second door on wooden steps leading into darkness. "Or you'll be dead."

A DRAGON FILLED THE room.

It was unlike any dragon Susannah had ever seen renditions of: the classic paintings were all of squat creatures with bulky bodies and long necks, but she had no other word for what she saw, and no doubt that *dragon* fully applied. The beast was long and lithe and slender, with spiny wings and long narrow claws, and it twisted on itself to stare down at her with fathomless black eyes. There was nothing of Fina the woman in that gaze, and yet Susannah had stood and watched, agape, as the one became the other.

She wasn't fully certain how she'd traversed the distance between the cellar door and the enormous sewer room she now shared with a dragon. Fina's words—her threat—had been so calm, so matter-of-fact, that it was as if Susannah hadn't fully heard them. Hadn't fully comprehended their meaning, and so had tripped lightly down the stairs aware but uncaring of her encroaching doom. Fina had said nothing until they reached the cavernous room beneath the city, and then had said, "The rest will be easier to believe once you see what I have to show you."

Then a blast of air had knocked Susannah against one of the curved walls, hard enough she fastened on the idea that she'd hit her head and was imagining things. But she hadn't: there was no throb of pain in her skull, no stars dancing in her vision. There was only a dragon, vast and black with hints of red gleaming in its scales' depths.

It would take two bites, she judged. It would take two bites to eat her, and made the manner of her likely death clear. She hoped the corsets would stick in Fina's gullet and choke her, though from the size of her teeth it seemed unlikely. Whalebone and human bone alike would no doubt be pulverized with ease. It was a curiously neutral observation for a woman studying a dragon, and she recognized it as the same protective, cocoon-like thought that had wrapped her earlier. Someone said, "I can see why this is easier to show than explain," in a cool voice, and only belatedly realized it must be herself: it seemed impossible that the writhing monster before her might speak.

The explosion of air as Fina transformed back into human shape was as rattling as the first. Susannah put her palms against the sewer wall, pressing herself there as she waited. Long seconds passed, long enough to count, and then long enough to worry, before Fina spoke. "Chicago is dangerous, my dear, because the oldest of the Old Races have come here in their numbers. Vampires hunt this city."

A woman had just become a dragon, and changed back again, as Susannah had watched. She only nodded, accepting the impossible as fact.

Approval flickered in Fina's gaze. "One has taken my child. My egg. I had only turned my back." A snarl came into her voice and distorted her face, leaving a mark of the dragon there, to Susannah's eyes. "They are *fast*, the vampires. They have no especial strength, no deadly wit, but they have speed, and by the time its scent reached me, it was already gone, and my child with it. I cannot fight it, Susannah. Even if I could catch it, the strictures of our people, of the Old Races, forbid battle between one race and another."

"The Old Races." Susannah's voice echoed in the chamber in a way Fina's did not. "Dragons and vampires?"

"There are others." Fina made a throw-away gesture, disdain curling her lip again. "A few children of an era far older than humanity's, who still survive. They do not matter, Susannah Stacey. It is the vampires who are my enemy. The vampires, whom I would train you to fight."

New York, 1923

"THIS," DAISANI SAID FROM the shadows, "is not a story I would expect you to tell, Janx. Ah, here you are, Vanessa. I wondered where you'd gone."

Never, not if she should live ten centuries, would she become accustomed to the silence with which he and the others could enter a room. Nor would she ever be able to control the leap of her heart when he arrived and announced his presence in such a way. A rush of breath left her, but it was Janx who spoke first.

"I delight in doing things you don't expect, Eliseo. What are you doing here? Vanessa and I were having such a fine time together without your interference." Janx folded his hands behind his head, feet kicked up as he leaned back in the chaise lounge.

For show, Vanessa thought: all for show. He'd been more intense, more intimate, before Eliseo's appearance. She wondered which was the facade: the easy relaxed man he was now, or the one offering confidences in the protected light of candles. Watching him—as she rarely did; it was simply easier not to, given his relationship with her lover—it seemed that both were the dragonlord in equal parts, and probably more besides.

She moved her belongings—the book she was reading, the deck of cards she whiled away hours with—to the chess table beside her, offering Eliseo space to sit. He smiled as he passed by, but shook his head and took another seat. Playing a part just as much as Janx did, perhaps; playing that they weren't close, so that she might be less a temptation or target to his ancient adversary. None of them was fooled, but in five decades she'd learned the rules, and was content with them.

"It seems I've come to make certain all of the tale is told," Eliseo answered. For a moment Vanessa thought he spoke to her own thoughts, then remembered Janx's question, for all that it hadn't really wanted an answer. "How much have you left out, Janx? Susannah's story is barely yours to tell."

Janx made a dismissive sound, flicking away the scolding with his fingertips. "It's frightfully dull, Eliseo, you being proper all the time. Besides, who better to tell it than myself? After all, 'dragonlord' has its place as titles go, but don't you think 'Father of the Dragons' sounds better yet?"

"I think you never earned it, at the end of the day." Daisani lowered his lashes, almost coquettish, then looked up again so sharply as to emphasize how deliberate the shy glance had been. "Or am I not to remind you of that, old friend?"

September 1871

"DID HE BURN?" THE question came unwillingly, and yet couldn't go unasked. Susannah's hands were a Gordian knot in front of her stomach, and like that knot, seemed they would require the sword to loosen them. Whether it was anxiety or excitement that drove their wringing, though, she was unsure. Both, perhaps: there was no reason they couldn't be coupled. Hours after the vampire's capture she still suffered moments of shaking limbs and weakness in her body that were thrown at odds with a terrible, breathless pride. "Is he dead? Did he...know anything of your child?"

Fina paced, sinuous exploration of the room which seemed to be not so much movement as a transference of her attention from one place to another. It was impossible to see her dragon form when she'd taken the human shape, but that vastness lent weight and heat to her presence. It had dried the air the day Susannah had first met her; now, at least, she understood why. That day, though Susannah hadn't known enough to recognize it, desperation had driven the dragon female. Now it was success, though the questions brought her up short. "He burned. Whether he's dead..." She shrugged. "His ashes lie scattered around a stake of oak, bound and drowned in an iron casket, and all of it is buried far beneath the earth. If he isn't dead, he certainly isn't *well*. You must hunt again tonight."

She swung toward Susannah, gaze gone black in the torch-lit underground room. "Tonight, before they notice one of their own is gone. He knew nothing, this one, not even bragging tales told from one idiot to another. Someone will know, in time, but time is so *short*. The egg will hatch, Susannah. The egg will hatch, and unmothered the dragon will die. It has been eight hundred years and more since one of my kind was born. I cannot let it die."

"So you've said." Susannah sank against the wall, grateful that Fina had insisted on new corsets. It had been weeks since the dragon discarded Susannah's fashionable steel-lined stays and offered her new ones which had boning of corded twill cotton. Nor would the dragon have them tight-laced beyond what was necessary for support; the point, Fina insisted, was flexibility and the ability to breathe freely in battle. Susannah argued that she wasn't of a class to train her shape to a wasp-waist, that her corsets were comfortable and permitted free movement, but the new ones were astonishing in the range of motion they allowed. She would not have wanted to run from the vampire in her old stays. She *could* not have sunk against the wall as she did now. "I don't see a difference between you playing bait for them and me doing it, Fina. You're the one who took him away and burned him. Isn't that breaking your covenants?"

"They would see me coming. You're human. I can never be." A familiar argument there, too, and having seen the vampire's grace up close, Susannah could read its echo in the way Fina moved. They were *not* human, neither of the self-proclaimed Old Races, though she would never have noticed their unusual fluidity without Fina there to train her eye to it. "Humans," Fina muttered, "are dealt with, when they hunt the Old Races, but there's admiration for your daring. I would not be admired."

"So they must imagine I've hunted, bound, and burned them. Me. An ordinary human woman. Does this admiration reach so far as to include clemency for murdering your people?"

"You will not be caught." Fina shook off her own moodiness and came to Susannah, crouching to catch her hands. The dragon's fingers were unexpectedly cool, serpent-like, though Susannah had no doubt of the flame that burned within. "I've told you, my dear. We will take them one at a time, every night, until we've found the one we need. They hunt alone, so there's no risk that your scent will grow familiar to them, and they haven't the imagination to fear a woman. Those who have hunted us have ever been men. Stay bold, dear heart. One success begets more."

"And wisely or not, I'm long since committed anyway." Susannah tipped her head back against the wall, eyes closed. Without vision, Fina's presence was a comforting warmth, though her hands remained cool. That grasp steadied Susannah, reminding her that Fina was extraordinary even without the secret Susannah held. Everything about her, most especially her heated gaze, was alluring and dangerous. The former was more compelling, which was no doubt how she had earned her name and place as Chicago's dark lady. But that was among men: Susannah would have thought herself immune to Fina's beauty and wit.

But not her strength. *That,* the utter certainty in self, the confidence with which she'd offered adventure which women were rarely permitted; *that* was as irresistible now as it had been weeks earlier when Fina had demanded her help at the Pinkerton offices.

She had learned, in the past weeks, to use a gun. To kick and strike out, and to trust in physical strength she hadn't known she possessed. Women were smaller than men, yes, but not as much the weaker sex as she'd always been told. She was surprised at how strong her legs were, and more surprised at the changes in her body that had come over six weeks of hard training at Fina's hands. The independence she'd sought as an employed woman faded in comparison to the trust she'd developed in herself. Her uncle, she thought, wouldn't be able to defeat a vampire.

Or accept a dragon's existence. Susannah opened her eyes, studying the dark-eyed woman crouched before her. She was a gift, an answer to impossible dreams. If she could be, then nothing Susannah wanted lay outside the bounds of possibility. "Would you still eat me, if I walked away?"

Fina arched an eyebrow. "Is there any danger you would?"

Humor blossomed deep in Susannah's chest. "That's not what I asked." She squeezed Fina's hands, and the other woman stood, drawing Susannah to her feet.

"I would not," Fina murmured. "But neither, I think, would you."

Susannah ducked her head close enough to breathe in Fina's scent. Earthy flame, not the rich sharpness of wood smoke, but something deeper and more subtle. It was nearly a flavor, something to be supped on and filled by, and it, as much as her own growing strength, bolstered her surety. "Not with another vampire to hunt tonight."

October 1871

NOT UNTIL THE TENTH night did anything go wrong.

He was one of them, so unquestionably one of them, now that Susannah knew what to look for. Taller than most, with a slim build and dark red hair, he moved with a gentleman's grace. More than a gentleman's grace, but in strictly mortal terms, there was no better way to describe him. He was better dressed than most, too, his fine-cut suit and waistcoat's splendor only rivaled by the first vampire she'd trapped. Even so, that unfortunate looked something of a country cousin compared to the red-haired man.

Unlike the others, she found him at the theatre. Not to watch the women on stage as though they were delectable, but to fold a knuckle over his mouth as he smiled or frowned, entirely taken with the story unfolding before him. When he applauded after the show, his enthusiasm seemed genuine; the others had been poorer actors, too intent on the hunt to become so nearly disguised by humanity.

She lingered after the performance, making much of a pebble lodged in her shoe. Making much of being alone, and insisting to those few men who stopped to offer assistance that her escort would be at her side in moments.

And he was, heralding his arrival with a murmured, "But you arrived alone," and a smile when she looked up in half-real surprise. "Don't look so startled, my dear. Of course I noticed a beautiful woman attending the theatre alone. Especially when her attention is less for the stage than my own august person. But then, I am splendid, am I not?" He made an act of showing the cut of his coat, of his trousers, then offered an extravagant bow that made his hair, unfashionably unslicked, fall into astonishing jade eyes.

A trill of laughter escaped her, surprising her further: none of the others had made her laugh. "You are, sir. Very splendid."

"For pity's sake, no, my dear. You mustn't call me sir. I shall think myself positively antediluvian if you do. My name is Janx." He caught her fingers to kiss them, then held her hand quite captive as he murmured, "And you are Susannah Stacey, and you must stop what you are doing."

THERE WAS NO ESCAPE: he held her hand too firmly for that. Terror made her heart leap and she cast a single panicked glance toward the sky: Fina was up there somewhere, her only hope of rescue from a deadly creature who knew who Susannah was and what she was doing.

Janx's gaze followed hers to the sky, then came back with the weight of ages in it. "No, Fina won't come, not until she hears the clang of your iron cage. Even if you should scream, I'm afraid she has the sense to keep away. You, discovered alone hunting vampires, would be—forgiven," he decided archly. "She would not be."

"She said I would die." Susannah's whisper was an edged accusation, meant to direct her fear elsewhere. It almost worked. It was something, at least, a show of bravado that might do a man proud. Her uncle had told her where boldness was pretended, it often followed, and she would need every inch of bravery she could eke out of herself in order to survive. The cage wasn't so far away, and the wooden stake was safe in her sleeve. She'd never yet fought a vampire who knew her purpose, but she had trained with Fina night after night, and the dragon had never pretended to be caught unawares.

Interest, perhaps admiration, quirked Janx's eyebrow upward. "How unusually forthright of her. She is, of course, correct. You would be forgiven in that it might be expected for a human who learned of our existence to hunt us, but that forgiveness would come in the form of execution." He smiled, the same long-canined smile that Fina often showed, then unexpectedly offered her his elbow. "Fina, however, would not be forgiven, and so this must stop now."

"She would rather die." The words sounded childish with defiance the moment they were spoken, but curiosity twitched Janx's eyebrow again.

"You're only mortal, my dear Miss Stacey, so I'm afraid you can't appreciate what Fina would lose if she were to be discovered in this madness. We do not hunt one another." His voice dropped, turning silky but overlaying steel. "We cannot afford it. There are too few of us as it is, and far too many of you. Nothing at all is worth such insanity, and I know better than you what she now has to protect, and therefore stands to lose."

"You know nothing." Susannah's fear receded into sharpness. "And why should you care? Why not kill me and try to kill her instead of trying to dissuade either of us? It's your kind we're hunting, after all."

Janx slowed, then chuckled. "Ah. No, my dear, it's my kind I'm protecting. Fina's of my people, rather than me being one of Daisani's."

"Daisani?"

"A vampire, and not one of any relevance right now, though Heaven forbid he should hear me say that. Miss Stacey, I can't imagine what's set Fina on this vendetta, beyond Chicago being her claimed territory and the vampires running amok through it, but believe me when I say she has too much to lose to continue this game. I'll stop her myself, if necessary, but I would prefer she ended it herself."

"You know nothing of what she's lost." Ice, as pure as the silken warmth of Janx's voice, edged Susannah's. "If you're one of her kind, why aren't you talking to her instead of me?"

A hint of impatience flickered in Janx's eyes. "Because we dragons do not share territory gladly, Miss Stacey. I'm here without Fina's express permission, and would prefer not to exacerbate that. Intervening with you not only alerts her of my presence, but if I'm fortunate and you've any sense, also means I'll be on the next train out of town. It's ideal for everyone." He paused, looking down at her, then sighed theatrically. "Well, not for me, perhaps, as I'll be unable to pursue this courtship beyond the end of this lane, if I must go so quickly."

Aggravating humor bubbled up again, though Susannah took care not to let it through. He was relentlessly charming, this dragon, though perhaps not quite as irresistible as he imagined himself. "There is no courtship here, sir, and I can assure you you're wasting your time. Fina won't stop."

"Well, why ever *not*?" Janx demanded petulantly. "She knows this is insanity. She knows the cost. And she's involved you in it, which is unkind. Why did you agree?"

Susannah, thoughtlessly, said, "Because she's beautiful," and frowned at Janx's answering laugh.

"That she is, but there must be more, my dear, because no one in their right mind accepts a commission from a dragon unless they have nothing else to lose." Silence broke, loud and considerate, before he said, "Ah. You're unmarried, then. No children. I suppose I knew that, else you'd not be a Pinkerton, but what a delightful surprise for me. Married women are often easier to seduce, but spinsters are much more interesting."

"I'm not—" *Not a Pinkerton* was the protest on her lips; the other, the matter of spinsterhood, was an unassailable argument. At twenty-eight, it was unlikely she would ever marry, even if it had been her inclination. And she could not, by law and by virtue of her sex, be a Pinkerton.

Yet if not a Pinkerton, what? A hunter, but of such extraordinary creatures she could never define herself as such to another mortal. To be a Pinkerton was strictly impossible, but outrageous as the idea was, it was a name she could take for herself. Something people would understand, even as they disapproved.

Disapproval, Susannah had found, became easier to bear with each year that passed beneath its burden.

Janx was waiting on her, interest dancing in his too-green gaze. She could leave him dangling for whole minutes, she thought: he was too taken with what she might say to prompt her and possibly change the words she decided on. The city around them was remarkably quiet, as if it, too, waited on her, or as if Janx had commanded it lie still and not disturb her while she considered her thoughts.

Though if that was a talent the Old Races commanded, she was happier not knowing it. "I'm not here to entertain you, sirrah. I have no interest in your games of seduction. I'll tell Fina you're here. I'll even pass on your warning, though it will do no good. But don't imagine your handsome face and smooth tongue will win me to your side."

"My dear Miss Stacey." Janx caught her hand and bowed over it, eyes bright. "You've had no experience at all with the smoothness of my tongue as yet. I assure you it would be my delight, as well as yours, to share its talents with you."

Incomprehension left her hand in his a moment too long, before a furious blush belittled her attempt to withdraw coldly. Janx's smile broadened and he let her go merrily. "Here we are at the end of the lane, Miss Stacey, but if you're so certain of Fina's refusal, then it's my pleasure to believe this isn't yet the end of our relationship." His voice softened as his humor faded. "I'm staying at the Hotel Sherman, my dear, under my own name. Fina will be able to find me, and find me she must. This cannot be allowed to continue."

Embarrassment fled before impatience. "So you've said."

A twitch of interest wrinkled Janx's forehead. "You're not afraid of me at all, are you?"

Susannah lifted her chin, defiance startling her with its inherent conviction. "Vampires can die. I'm sure dragons can, too, Master Janx."

"Of course." Janx touched a fingertip to his lips, shaping a smile around it. "Ask Fina how, when you give her my greetings."

"WITH ALMOST AS MUCH difficulty as a vampire."

It was the answer Susannah had expected. It still made her smile, though she kept the expression hidden as Fina stalked around her parlor. They were no longer hidden beneath the city, not when there'd been no successful hunt, no potential pursuit to lead astray. Instead they had retreated to Fina's enormous home, near in distance but far in society terms to the self-same streets where Fina ran whores and gambling dens.

It had been easy enough to call Fina to her; it had only taken the clang of the iron cage's door to send the dragon swooping into the alley. Fina had been surprised enough at the cage's lack of contents that she'd transformed then and there, human features better suited to expressing astonishment than her serpentine form. Astonishment only, though, no anger: that was good, as anger might well have spelled Susannah's own doom. Fina had even waited on explanations until they'd reached the privacy of her home, though the way her countenance had darkened at Janx's name suggested she'd have been happier in the sewers, where she might have vented her anger.

"He's old," Fina had said, when pressed. "Very old, and flaunts the same laws he would have me abide by. Not hunting," she added reluctantly, at Susannah's startled sound. "But he walks with humans as though he's one of them, and I know he's given our secrets away in the past. He's also the child's father."

Shock seized Susannah's heart, turning her breath cold. "Then all you have to do is explain—!"

"Dragons," Fina had said, almost wryly, "don't listen well."

Susannah dropped her face into her hands, then asked the question Janx had told her to. Had gotten the answer she expected, and when she glanced up again, watched Fina storm about the room in agitation. She wore the crimson-shot black she favored, the color reminiscent of her dragon form, and within the confines of her parlor looked like a caged thing eager to be set free.

"We're too big," she said abruptly. "We're simply too large to kill easily. Of all the Old Races, the gargoyles are most dangerous to us for their strength alone. The vampires and their speed are nothing, and the others less than that. It's only you humans who manage to murder my people, and even that rarely enough. The first dragon your George slew was in human form when he died. We revert," she explained bitterly. "When we die, we transform to our true selves, or he never would have known we existed so he might hunt more of us down."

Astonishment made Susannah's voice small. "But people must have seen that, then. We should all know you do exist."

"You do know it." Fina turned to her with a smile, but not a gentle one. "In dark tales, in stories of the night, in legends and fables, we are there. And you dismiss us as just that: stories. But you keep telling them, Susannah. You keep sharing them, and you always look carefully when there's a sound in the darkness. We're there, buried in your hearts and minds, and none of you wants to admit we still survive."

Susannah shivered. The warmth in Fina's voice was dangerous, like water coming to the boil around her. "But there must be proof. If Saint George killed a dragon "

"We know when one of our own dies. We come for the body, and bury it in the volcanoes. Return it to the fire from whence we're born. There's nothing for your people to find except whispers and fear."

"...do you hate us?"

Fina said, "Yes," without remorse, then sighed. "And no. You in specific, no, Susannah." She came to join Susannah on the couch, tucking up against her as though she were much smaller and younger than she really was. "You're so foolishly bold, as a species. So eager to explore. So curious. It's impossible to hate that, even as you encroach on our lands, take away our territory, hunt and hound us to sewers and caves. The only way we can survive in your world is to pretend to be you, and it chafes, my dear. Oh, how it chafes. And yet I find the alternative unthinkable," she murmured. "To hide away beneath the mountains in the world's fires until I rot. To sleep until your people are grown enough to accept us, or until the plague of humanity runs itself out and the world is left to us again. No. I would rather play at being you, and grasp all the risk it entails, than wait an eternity for something that may never come."

"Do some of you?"

"Wait?" Fina lifted her head to catch Susannah's expression, then nestled down again, pressing her cheek against Susannah's shoulder, cat-like. Her hands, her skin, were always cool, snake-like, but curled against Susannah's side, she was a source of heat and comfort. Like coals were banked within her, Susannah thought, waiting until they were uncovered and her true self revealed. "Yes. More of us than not sleep now, waiting for a tomorrow that's little more than a dream. We don't share territory willingly, and there are so few places we can hide. A few dozen of us, perhaps, still walk the world in waking hours."

"And Janx has come here regardless of territory protocol. He must be very certain he's right," Susannah said cautiously, then held her breath on a hesitation before suggesting, "Or afraid for you, Fina."

The dragon's laughter broke, rich and deep and unexpected. "We attach very little sentimentality to breeding, my darling. He wouldn't have a care for me. Being the mother of his child is meaningless."

Determination steeled Susannah's spine. "Normally, maybe. But you said yourself this child is special. The first one born in centuries. That makes you special as well, a female who can still have children. If I were Janx, I would be concerned for your well-being. I'm not Janx, and I *am* concerned for it, Fina," she added rashly, and the other woman sat up again with a smile.

"Are you? I've put your life in danger, Susannah. I've introduced you to a world likely to kill you, and you're still concerned for me?"

"I could have refused you." Could, but never would, have. Not with the memory of Fina's presence in the

Pinkerton offices burned in her mind like a brand; not with the challenge the woman had thrown down. It had awakened in Susannah a longing for something more than the life she'd known, a life she'd been satisfied with until Fina's arrival in it. Few women of her class had the wherewithal to be as independent as she'd become, and yet what she'd achieved had paled by comparison to what lay beyond the limits of her imagination.

An imagination which, now aroused, would never fail her again. "Let me talk to Janx, Fina. Let me play intermediary. He seemed to like me."

Amusement curved Fina's mouth. "Janx likes beautiful things, Susannah. I mean no insult, but he has no interest in you yourself."

"I'm not beautiful, despite what you all keep insisting." It wasn't false modestly: she had spent enough time at the mirror to be certain of herself. She was pretty, but not remarkably so, with her square face and thick hair. She could make herself lovely through carriage and dress, but beauty lay beyond her. In her girlhood she despaired of that, but as an adult she had come to appreciate ordinary attractiveness. Had she been beautiful, she would have found herself married whether she liked it or not, beauty's advantage greater than an unfashionable name or thin pocketbook.

"All of us?" Fina asked, curious.

Susannah shook her head. "You. Janx. The first vampire." She hadn't asked his name, nor any of the others: it was job enough to hunt. Giving them names would only make it harder. "Your standards are too low."

"Or we see in humanity a fire you cannot see in yourselves." Fina touched her cheek, smiled, then sighed and flung herself against the sofa's far end in a fit of childish dramatics. "What will you say to him, dear heart?"

"Her child has been stolen."

Janx went still, preternaturally still, and in that moment became less human than Fina had ever seemed. There wasn't so much as a pulse in his throat, a detail Susannah, mere weeks ago, never would have thought to notice.

They had met in a restaurant so far beyond Susannah's means she hadn't known it existed. Private booths allowed only glimpses of those coming and going, but glimpses were enough to know that she would never belong to the class of men and women who were patrons here. Even the best gowns Fina had arranged for her weren't bustled or crinolined, and her new corsets provided only support, not stricture. The other women had waists even Susannah could have spanned with two hands. Although half-hidden from their view, she felt thick and ungainly.

Janx, though, looked the part, and if the staff had disapproved of her they'd shown none of it as they fawned over her escort. They had been served appetizers so delicate they had almost no presence, and then had been brought a Napoleonic wine. Janx, to Susannah's private amusement and the staff's horror, had sniffed disdainfully, and when the stricken waiter retreated the dragon had turned a blinding smile on Susannah. "That should ensure either utter privacy for the evening or an interruption every time we say two words. Susannah my dear, I'm quite certain your agreeing to an evening alone with me means Fina has chosen to be unreasonable, and yet I can't quite bring myself to regret that fact. I'm sure she's told you I'm an untrustworthy reprobate, and I'm afraid it's probably true. But if you've drawn Fina's attention, if she's trusted you, you must be profoundly remarkable, and I have a great weakness for remarkable women."

Most women, Susannah imagined, very likely had an equal weakness for him. She thought he tried too hard, though: his rushing charm and affectations of enthusiastic interest were amusing, but Fina's direct challenge held more appeal. And she was there to argue her dragon partner's case, not be swept away by Janx's easy banter and quick compliments. He would, if she permitted him, be at this engagement all night, wooing and flirting in hopes of—

To tell the truth, she wasn't sure. He'd plainly claimed seduction, but for all his outrageous advances, she wasn't certain she believed that. Not that he *wouldn't*, she was certain, but what he *wanted* was Fina's good behavior. Susannah's own virtue would merely be a delightful secondary prize.

Irritated at the idea, she cut across his breezy patter, words cold and precise: *Her child has been stolen*, and he took on the aspect of a sculpture, frozen through and through.

No, not through and through after all: fire built from within him, shading his eyes to a dangerous color. Nothing external changed, but the booth, then the room, gained heat as Janx's fingers lay still and quiet on the tabletop. "A vampire," he finally whispered, and if Susannah had thought Fina's anger was compelling, Janx's might have laid down bridges for men to walk across as they sought immolation in his presence. "She hunts for the child. *You*.

Hunt for her child. Oh, Eliseo, my friend, how badly you have lost control, that it should come to this."

"Eliseo," Susannah whispered back. "The vampire you said was inconsequential."

The rage in Janx's presence was suddenly tamped, his gaze bright and normal again, even cheery. "Even more inconsequential than I'd thought, it seems, but at the same time distressingly vital. What a shame," he added softly, and with an unexpected air of regret. "I'd hoped I mightn't have to share you, my dear."

"You labor under the misapprehension that I'm yours to share."

Mercurial emotion swept him again, this time ending in satisfaction. "So I do, and your boldness in pointing out the error of my ways only makes me that much more determined to convince you of the error of yours. Susannah." He leaned forward, uncouth elbows on the table, and offered her his hand. "She'll have explained to you the importance of this child," he murmured. "And you will have believed her, as you should. And I see now, yes, why she will not stop. The situation is untenable." The buried anger flashed forward again, making his gaze crackle. "You people have a most evocative phrase, Susannah. One might as well be hanged for a sheep as a lamb. You're familiar with it?"

"Of course." Cool dread spilled through Susannah, and she refused the hand Janx offered her, instead edging forks into a flawless line on the tablecloth before speaking again. "So if I've taken the lamb, what is the sheep you would have me hanged for?"

"*Continue*." The word came out cold and sharp, entirely at odds with the casual line of Janx's body and the softness of his smile. "I'll mitigate this as I can, but until then, forget everything else I've said. Let it continue, Susannah Stacey. Hunt, and hunt well."

New York, 1923

"SOMEHOW," DAISANI MURMURED, "THIS is an aspect to Susannah's tale you never shared with me, old friend."

"Of course not. That would have been indiscreet." Janx flashed a disarming smile at the vampire, but it came to rest on Vanessa and lingered there even when she glanced away. She had no secrets at all worthy of the story he told, much less the small one which had won her the speakeasy. Janx, as if following her thoughts, put another smile in his voice. "But your Vanessa asked, and I do hate to refuse a lady anything, Eliseo."

"You might have paid dearly for your decision then."

"I might have, but I didn't, and who will scold me now? You? The truth is, I was right, and you wouldn't condemn me to our brethren even if I was wrong. The years would be too long and lonely without me."

A rush of air left Vanessa's lungs, so soft it would never have betrayed her to mortal men. These men, though, were anything but, and both of them looked to her as she tried to steady her breathing.

"Forgive me." Something in Janx's inflection made her look up to find a trace of genuine sympathy in the dragonlord's eyes. "I meant you and your companionship no insult, my dear."

"But even two sips of a vampire's blood won't grant immortality," Vanessa said calmly. "There's nothing to forgive, Janx. You've hardly surprised or insulted me."

"Perhaps not, but it's never easy to be reminded there are those who are in your lover's life longer than you have, or shall, live."

A smile creased Vanessa's lips. "You think like an immortal, Janx. Maybe I find it comforting to know that regardless of how long I live, there will always be someone upon whom Eliseo can rely. It's against your laws, isn't it?" she asked more swiftly, setting aside the uncomfortable question of her own limited years. "Even if Fina were discovered, or you were in condoning her actions, the Old Races only exile one another from the greater community. You don't have a death penalty."

"For the usual transgressions, no." It was Eliseo who spoke that time. "For betraying our presence to humans, for breeding with humans, for killing one of our own, no, and those are our three greatest strictures. On the other hand, through Susannah, Fina was responsible for the destruction of a dozen vampires, and Janx allowed it. The circumstances became extenuating."

"A dozen?" Vanessa's voice rose and she clapped a hand to her throat as if she could lower her pitch by doing so. "She must have been the greatest hunter the world's ever known."

Janx and Daisani exchanged glances. "Very nearly," Eliseo finally said. "Only Abraham Van Helsing bested her."

"They made a hero of him," Vanessa said into a silence that was suddenly too loud. "Why not of Susannah?"

"Go on," Eliseo murmured to Janx. "It's your story."

Chicago, October 1871

JANX NO LONGER RECALLED when they had begun their games. With the rise of human civilization, perhaps, though that seemed unlikely even given his fondness for dramatic flair. Humans wouldn't have struck them as particularly dangerous, that far back. They wouldn't have yet realized how quickly and thoroughly humanity would encroach upon the world. So early on there would have been no impetus to manipulate and investigate human lives, no need to hide amongst them and pretend to be one of them whilst working to gain advantages over the other.

On the other hand, there had been Sumeria, so perhaps their rivalry stretched back so far after all.

Never in all that time could he remember summoning, or being summoned by, Elisco Daisani.

It was clear, when the vampire arrived, that neither could he remember such audacity, and that he resented it with every fibre of his being.

Resented it, yes, but still he came. Black-clad and somber, Janx's very opposite, he entered the Hotel Sherman like a streak of outraged night. Everything surrounding them spoke of gentility, from the rich wood panel walls to the parquet floors, from subtle welcoming music played by an even-more subtly hidden quartet to furnishings some of the city's wealthiest would admire. Eliseo Daisani came through it all radiating insult that made even the most arrogant and confident-seeming of men back away.

A less cocksure man than Janx would have made their meeting private for that very reason. But there was no appeal in that, no fun to be had. Confrontation was best performed with an audience, and better still if not one pure and absolute truth could be spoken in front of that audience. The hotel lobby, inviting and comforting to men of means, was an excellent stage, and Janx didn't try to hide his grin as Daisani stopped before him in a glower of cloak and leather.

"Nothing," Daisani hissed, "can be so important as to call me across half a continent, and so rudely. This isn't your territory, Janx. Remember what happened last time we were here."

"Vividly," Janx murmured in response, and gestured to the seat across from him. "That's precisely why I've called you, in fact. And you came, Eliseo. Rude summoning or not, you're here, and unless I miss my mark, in better time than even the fastest trains could take you." He put a hand against his heart, eyes sparkling. "You ran. I asked for you, and you dropped everything and ran to me. I'm overcome, old friend. I weep with emotion." He touched a fingertip to the corner of his eye and mimed flicking away a tear.

Daisani made a sibilant sound of exasperation and threw himself into the chair opposite Janx with an excessiveness more suited to Janx himself. "What have you done wrong now? The lady of this city cannot possibly be as great a fool as you are, and ready to fight over your presence here."

"It is not my people who are the problem here." Janx spoke with a precision unusual to him, words crystal in the air between them. Daisani noted it, holding momentarily still before his chin lifted a scant inch and comprehension slid through his gaze.

"It's not their fault, Janx. The hunting grounds are so rich here, and they are..."

"Impulsive," Janx said through his teeth. "And yet you, who names yourself master of your kind, are not."

"How do you think I got to be master?" Daisani shrugged one shoulder and let the gesture fall away again. "A hundred thousand men and women here, Janx. Crossroads of a nation. The canals, the rivers, the railroads, they all lead here. Itinerants move through constantly. It's difficult to resist. And I'm surprised you care."

"I care because they're careless, and can be discovered and hunted themselves. We can't afford that, and you know it. But I care all the more, old friend, because their impulses have led them to steal Fina's child."

Rage, cunning, curiosity, humor; those were expressions familiar to Daisani's features, and to Janx's knowledge of the vampire. Shock, though: it was nearly impossible to shock a creature of great age, much less to send horror flickering across his face in equal, brief part before he regained mastery over what emotion he showed. "I see."

"You will control them," Janx whispered. "You will find the egg, and return it, or in this, Eliseo, I will defy every law we have ever imagined, and I will make war on your kind. It has been eight hundred years since a child was born to my people, and I will have vengeance if that life is lost."

Daisani lifted a palm, the action as graceless as he could be. "Stop being melodramatic, Janx. None of them, no matter how impulsive, should be so stupid as well. Thieving one another's children is too close to an act of war itself. I'll find the child and punish the fool who dared this, and if I fail..."

"Then you'll look the other way while I seek retribution."

"Yes," Daisani murmured after a moment. "Yes, I suppose I will. Give me a week, Janx. Even I can't corral them with a word, and if whomever's stolen it isn't a complete fool, he'll have hidden it far enough away that canvassing the city, even as quickly as I can, won't find it. Besides, your mate will have searched already. Did she call you here for help?"

Janx shifted his gaze away, then returned it to the vampire. "'Mate' implies such permanence, Eliseo. Fina won't even see me. This thing must be settled."

"Or you'll never know her tenderness again," Daisani said half-mockingly. "Give me a week."

"You have three days."

SHE DIDN'T SEE HIM coming until it was too late. Focused on the hunt as she was, it never occurred to her there might be a second vampire partnered with the first. And the first had been easy, this time: she had proven Fina's prediction true, and taken herself to places more dangerous than even Fina would send her. It was easier to play the part of a riverside doxy than she'd expected, making a pretense of selling wares no man had actually known. The vampire had come to her from well down the banks, slower and smugger than his kind usually were. It was only when newsboy criers told stories the next morning, stories of a woman found dead and drained of blood on the riverbank, that Susannah understood why he was as slow and uninterested as he'd been.

Not so uninterested, though, that she couldn't lead him into the trap she and Fina had set. Not so slow that there wasn't satisfaction in rushing away, playing her role as victim until it was time to turn the tables. He had screamed; they all did, and she was becoming inured to it. The door had slammed shut and Fina was there, taking him away and leaving Susannah triumphant and prepared to return home.

Home: that was Fina's mansion, now. Had been more and more so each day as Susannah had grown away from her position as a Pinkerton clerk and had become more comfortable as a hunter. Her uncle thought she was being courted; his wife was scandalized that she spent nights away from their safe walls. Susannah knew the woman would have her ousted if her uncle's heart was just a little harder.

Never in her life had she been so unafraid of the idea. She would go west if she had to, would proclaim herself a widow if necessary, would make herself a Pinkerton—an investigator, at least—in fact, even if the agency itself might never be convinced to license her. There would be a few people, perhaps women, ready to hire a woman for jobs they believed men couldn't succeed at. Where Susannah had once doubted her ability to survive outside her uncle's generosity, she now knew she could, if she must.

Given a choice, though, she would simply remain with Fina. Help to save the child, and then to watch it grow however quickly a dragon might, and hunt or fight to keep it safe. To keep them both safe from a world which loathed the prospect of offering women adventure and autonomy, nevermind facing the profound truth that humanity was not the only wily race to walk the earth.

The thought lent her strength and quickness, and she was nearly out of the docks when the second vampire struck.

Fina had warned her of their speed, but none of the eight or nine she'd trapped had shown signs of it. Too late, Susannah knew she'd been complacent. More, that she'd been a fool to believe she ever had the upper hand with the creatures she'd fought. She'd had trickery, that was all: the thing that came at her now moved so quickly that in the darkness she couldn't lay eyes on it, not truly. Still, she knew how to fight, and miraculously threw up a wrist to block a blow whose speed jarred her to the bone.

Pain ruptured through her arm, fingers going numb as fire spilled toward her elbow. Fina had never hit so hard, and through bright sparks in her vision Susannah realized the dragon had held no illusions about Susannah's ability to survive if their traps should turn to a fight. There'd been no need to introduce her to real agony: if it had gone that far, she was already as good as dead.

Still, the vampire's second blow missed. Not because of her newly-honed fighting skills, but because she'd simply fallen, clutching her arm and gasping for breath. A little of the pain receded as she hit earth, and she scrambled forward on hand and knees, searching the dry dark dirt for anything that might be a weapon. The vampire pounced after her, weight bearing her to the ground, and she screamed as he caught a hand in her hair and drew her head back.

The nerve in her elbow shrieked dismay as she slammed her arm back, catching the vampire in the ribs. He let go of her hair, more surprised than injured, and she surged forward again, hands still spread in search of a weapon.

Her fingers jammed against a slab of something cold. Wood, stone, something laid down to mitigate the filth dredged up from the river during wetter days: she didn't know. But it came free in her hands and she swung around, throwing her weight with it, and caught the vampire in the temple.

He collapsed as obligingly as a man might, blood leaking from his skull. His form trembled, then shriveled and changed, darkness too complete for her to fully grasp what she saw before a man's quiet voice said, "No one sees a vampire's true form and lives to speak of it," almost conversationally.

Susannah shrieked again and scampered backward again, stepping on her skirts and collapsing the few inches to the ground. Three: three was unfair. Three was, without question, more than she could survive. But the third vampire stepped from one shadow to another, crouching above the one she'd knocked unconscious, and from there gave her a mild and interested glance. "Susannah Stacey, I presume."

Hysterical laughter burst from her lungs. "Why do you all know my name?"

"Janx thrives on gossip. What were you going to do with him now that he's down?" The third vampire nodded at the prone one, then lifted an eyebrow at Susannah.

"Stake him and manacle him and throw him in the river," she snapped, taking refuge in asperity so fear wouldn't control her. "I don't think I'd have time to dig a grave, not with the ground hard with drought."

"You've been well taught." He straightened, caught in a bit of torchlight from somewhere down the river. Like the other vampires, he lacked the outrageous attractiveness shared by Janx and Fina. Instead, his slicked-back dark hair and expensive black coat lent him an air of fastidiousness. "By Fina, I suppose. I applaud her ingenuity. How many have you taken?"

Susannah swallowed. "He's the ninth. Who are you?"

He stepped forward to offer her a hand up without answering. Helpless, she took it: she would be dead already if he wanted her that way. His hands were warm, almost hot, unlike Janx or Fina's, and she wondered at the differences in their creation that made one Old Race run so warm and another so cold. Especially when those with cold hands seemed to have, as the adage went, warm hearts, whereas the vampire before her seemed the personification of cool regard.

He was only barely taller than she, a diffident height for a man at best. But his gaze was absolute, making her feel as if she were the unchallenged center of his regard. Everything else faded away: the ache in her arm, the danger presented by the unconscious vampire, even her intention to escape back to Fina's home. He smiled, brief expression with none of Janx's charm, then inclined his head slightly and took a small step back from her. "I'm Eliseo Daisani."

"Oh," she said, unwisely. "The insignificant one."

Daisani's eyebrows shot upward. "*Excuse* me?"

Horrified heat rushed Susannah's cheeks. "I'm sorry. That was unforgivably rude."

"Without doubt, but what on earth would possess you to say it?"

Susannah mumbled, "Janx. He said you weren't important right now."

A *hnf* of offense slipped through Daisani's teeth. "I trust that was before he determined the need for my presence here to keep my people in rein."

Susannah said, "I'm sure it was," in a tiny voice, and for a moment wished she dared hide her face in her hands, embarrassment nearly stronger than the desire to survive. "Can you?"

"Keep them in rein?" Beyond Daisani, the fallen vampire stirred, then came to his feet in a blur of outraged speed. Susannah made a choked sound, fear suddenly bright and strong, outweighing shame. Daisani snapped his head toward the second vampire, jaw extending too far as he let out a dangerous hiss, and to Susannah's astonishment the second creature froze, snarling angrily. "You," Daisani murmured to him, "are most certainly indebted to me, as this young woman has means and willpower beyond nearly any I've met, and your pathetic life would have been hers to end had I been a single moment later."

Susannah thought she'd never experienced so many heady emotions so quickly. Pride made her chest tight, and she wondered briefly if it was misplaced given the source of the compliment, or whether the unlikely source made it that much more powerful an endorsement.

"Go," Daisani said, still softly, still speaking to the other vampire. "Leave Chicago, and do so now, never to return. Your scent is known to me; in ten minutes I will follow your trail, and if it doesn't lead miles beyond this city's streets I'll return for the woman, and allow her to finish what she began. *Go,*" he said again, and the vampire was gone.

Susannah fell back a step, heartbeat so quick she feared it might seize, as her father's had. Daisani turned his gaze back to her, casually slow and disconcerting when she knew the speed he could command. “Well,” he said after a while. “I see why they like you.”

“Faint praise from an executioner,” Susannah whispered, and complex emotion slid over Daisani’s features.

“It was meant as sincere praise, and what makes you think I’m an executioner?” Daisani turned a palm out, modifying his words: “*Your* executioner?”

“Fina said I’d be killed if I was discovered.” Susannah was surprised and pleased at the steadiness of her voice. Repeated exposure to the likelihood of death, it seemed, had calming, rather than distressing, effect. She could face its reality with equanimity, in due time.

“Does one condemn the bullet or the man who holds the gun? You’re a tool, Miss Stacey. A deadly weapon set loose by another. Fina’s right, of course. Almost any of us would see you dead.” The corner of Daisani’s mouth turned up, pretense of a proper smile. “But in this instance, I understand her rage, and admire her choice of weaponry. Janx and I are both…intrigued,” he decided. “By extraordinary women. He might never have come here, but I would have, eventually. Word of a hunter would have reached me. I would have come to kill him, and found you instead. And, in so finding, would likely have found clemency to grant as well.”

A ghost of humor rippled through Susannah. “So I may go about my business?”

His eyebrows shot up again, expressively. “The business of binding vampires? I’m not sure I can condone that, Miss Stacey. Isn’t it enough I let you live?”

“No,” she said, surprising herself. “Not until Fina’s child is found. I promised her.”

"As I now promise you. I intend to bend my considerable talents to finding it. Anything else begets war, and that's a game we can't afford. Your people would notice. Imagine. If you, a solitary woman, can trap and bind eight vampires, then armies of men with great intent could hunt us to extinction. I will not permit that to happen." He glanced toward the riverside, then back again. "Surely we can find somewhere more pleasant to discuss these matters."

Susannah gestured at her doxy's dress. "With me in this? We couldn't. I'm the only one who knows how to trap your kind, Master Daisani. Why let me go?"

He gave her a look that suggested he wore pince-nez, and was peering over their top edge in disbelief. "Would you prefer I killed you now?"

A spike of alarm went through her, making faint mockery of her belief that she'd gone beyond fearing death. "Not at all, but I—" She stepped forward suddenly, hands extended but knotted together. "I want to understand. You have so many rules, so many laws, and none of you are paying heed to any of them. I know the circumstances are unusual, that the child makes everything different, but…you're creatures of magic," she whispered. "I'm only mortal, and on the edge of your world. I want to know it better."

"Laws," Daisani said after a moment's pause, "are for the law-abiding. Which even I must be, most of the time, the better to set an example for my brethren. But some one among them has gone beyond the law in spirit if not in letter, by taking the dragon's child. If Janx and I choose to go beyond it in pursuit, there's no one to tell us no. So you, Miss Stacey, may live, and Fina will in time be convinced to release the vampires you and she have bound. I may even allow her to keep the one responsible, as a warning to other fools."

Susannah clenched her fists in her skirts, head lowered in hopes that her gaze wouldn't give her away. Fina's captured vampires had burned, all of them, and Susannah couldn't imagine that they might rise again from that. Daisani clearly didn't know, and her own life might be the price for the dragon's thoroughness.

But not tonight. Skirts gathered, she dipped a curtsey, then looked up again. "Will you walk me home, Master Daisani? A woman could have a worse escort than you, I think."

"Far worse," he agreed, and offered an elbow. "We understand each other, then?"

"We do." Understanding wouldn't prevent Susannah from hunting, but between Janx and Daisani, she doubted she would be the first to happen on the vampire mad enough to kidnap a dragon's egg.

They spoke of inconsequentialities on the journey home: the unseasonably dry weather and the scent of smoke in the air from a fire across town; common gossip about society; the threat of the city's darker side. They might, Susannah thought, have been any ordinary couple out for a walk.

Might have been, at least, until Daisani took his leave of her, and in so doing sped away so quickly there was only dust left behind him, and not the shadow of a man. Susannah stared after him, then sank down onto the steps of Fina's grand home, and put her face in her hands.

Long minutes passed before the door opened behind her, and Fina, without speaking, came down the stairs to sit beside her. Cool fingers touched her shoulder, then tugged her sideways, and Susannah leaned into the embrace, gaze still downcast. Fina's heartbeat was slow, solid, reassuring: not the flighty thing Susannah's had been all evening.

"Are you afraid?" the dragon eventually asked.

Susannah lifted her head, finding Fina's warm smile and fiery gaze close enough for reassurance. There was strength there, unimaginable, inhuman strength. Some part of it had become Susannah's own, wending its way inside her to take up residence in her soul. "I met Eliseo Daisani tonight," she said instead of answering directly. "He's...less comfortable than Janx."

Laughter creased Fina's eyes. "I think they would both be pleased to hear that. And what am I, if Janx is comforting and Daisani is not?"

Susannah said, "Beautiful," as thoughtlessly as she'd said it to Janx, then blushed in surprise at the confidence of her answer.

Fina's smile deepened. "I could ask for nothing more. Come, dear heart. A glass of brandy, and I'll warm a brick for your bed."

"It's much too hot for bricks." Susannah let Fina draw her to her feet, both women smiling, though Fina's expression turned wicked as she led Susannah up the stairs.

"Then I'll have to find something else to warm, won't I, my dear?"

"The brandy," Susannah suggested, and blinked with puzzlement as Fina's laughter preceded them into the house.

"WAKE UP. WAKE UP, dear heart." The words were breathed by Susannah's ear, so quiet they barely had the strength to carry warning. For a moment they made no sense, neither the words themselves nor the import they had, but then Susannah's eyes flew open to thin dust-laden strains of golden morning sunlight, and to Fina's cautiously tense expression.

Her bedchamber was stifling. It had been weeks since Susannah had awakened early enough to see morning sunshine, a detail which would scandalize her uncle's wife. In that time, she'd become accustomed to Fina's housemaid slipping in and opening windows so that by the time she woke, what movement of fresh air could be had, had taken some of the unbearable late-season heat from the room. Waking to it was almost as alarming as Fina's presence, and her air of worry.

That concern was almost washed away beneath a warm smile, but lines of tension remained around the dragon female's eyes. "Good morning, my dear. I'm afraid you must go. Now."

Susannah came fully awake, pushing up on her elbows. "What? Why? What's happened? Did they find—?"

"No." Fina put a fingertip to Susannah's lips, stopping the rush of questions. "The child hasn't been found. But I've made a miscalculation, Susannah. An error that will very likely cost your life, if you don't leave Chicago now."

"Leave *Chicago*? Are you mad?" The thought that she might have to had crossed Susannah's mind, but to be ordered to do so ran deeper than anger and into pure astonishment. "Why?"

"Because it seems Eliseo Daisani's precipitous arrival here hasn't gone unnoticed. Nor, I'm afraid, has the disappearance of so many vampires. They know there's a hunter now, Susannah. I will not have you exposed to them."

"I've been exposed all along." Susannah sat up, tugging the shoulder of her night-dress into place. "No one has found me yet."

Fina whispered, "Susannah," and took her hand, leading her from the bed. Leading her to the curtained window, where she flicked back the drapes a few inches to expose the street below.

At a glance, it was full of the pleasantry of a Sunday morning, well-dressed families and individuals pausing to speak with one another on their way to and from church. Coaches drew by, or riders on horse-back passed through, though neither with the business to be expected on a weekday. The startlement of a sudden waking still ran through Susannah's blood, but she shook her head, seeing nothing out of place.

Fina said nothing, only waited as Susannah glanced at her. Susannah frowned, then breathed deeply to steady her heartbeat, and turned her attention back to the street below.

It took another full minute to understand. Not all: oh, not all, not by any stretch, but far too many of the men and women below moved with unnatural grace. With astonishing fluidity, as they paced from one end of the street to the other, exploring the block but always returning to mark a path in front of Fina's home. A dozen, perhaps even one or two more, all watching and waiting.

Vampires.

Susannah fell back from the window, arms clutched around herself. "I thought they were night creatures. I thought that's why we hunted them at night."

"Not at all." Sorrow and surprise mingled in Fina's voice. "If they were bound to the night I would have sent you hunting in the day with iron manacles and wooden stakes. We hunt at night because *I* can't take to the skies during daylight hours. I would be seen."

Heat rushed along Susannah's jaw. "Of course. Why are they *here*? Not in Chicago, I understand that. But at your home?"

"I have two suppositions for that." Fina glanced out the window again, then retreated to Susannah's bed, smoothing the duvet as she sat on it. She was no more prepared for the day than Susannah, wearing a silken dressing gown over her nightdress. "I'm the mistress of this city, which is no secret. If there's a hunter in my streets, I should know about it. So perhaps they're watching to see how I react to being watched. There are one or two others whom I imagine might also be under their observation."

"Dragons?" Susannah came to sit across from her on the bed, knees drawn up to wrap her arms around them. She should be getting dressed, preparing to make an escape, but a core of calm certainty rose in her at the realization she would not, despite Fina's demand, flee.

"No." Fina smiled, but shook her head. "Not unless they're haranguing Janx, which isn't an unpleasant thought in itself. No, there are a few others who interfere with or belong to our world. A bookseller downtown, and a gargoyle guardian or two. Though they're dull to observe in daylight, frozen in stone as they are. Nevermind," she added more gently, as Susannah felt confusion spill over her face. "They're waiting, perhaps, to see if any of us acts out of character. Which means I shall have to challenge their presence, and means you, dear heart, must escape the city while you can. We've been careful, but if one of them should have your scent…."

"One escaped last night." Susannah got up again, moving to her wardrobe, though she had no intention of acquiescing to Fina's wishes. It was something to do, though, action to steady herself with as she spoke. "Eliseo Daisani let him go and banished him from Chicago. If he met with others, told them about me, they could have come from far and wide, could they not? Given how fast they are? And perhaps they would have my scent, but if they did, I would think they wouldn't wait on your move. They'd have come after me already, whether I was in your home or not."

She found a dress, not one of the finer ones Fina'd had made for her, but lightweight enough for both the late-season heat and for running or fighting. And it was pale green, a flattering shade for her skin tone, though the idea that vanity should rear its head just then amused her. "I don't want to leave you, Fina. My life is so much more, with you. I don't want to give that up. I don't want to give you up."

"You've changed, Susannah." Fina's voice was soft, and when Susannah turned back, dress gathered in her arms, the dragon woman was smiling. "I always knew you had the capacity for boldness, or I'd have never come to you at all. But I thought adventure might prove too much for you. Instead it's whittled courage from curiosity. I don't want you to go, either. But I want to risk your life even less, my dear."

"Well." Laughter splashed through Susannah's response. "You should have thought of that earlier. Now go find your maid, Fina. We both need to be dressed, no matter what happens. It would be undignified to die in our nightgowns."

"Really, if we're dressing to die, you have much more magnificent dresses than that, Susannah." Fina stood, though, still smiling. "But perhaps dying isn't really your plan."

"Not when I'm only just beginning to live." Susannah returned to embrace Fina, inhaling her warm spicy scent, then released her and nodded toward the door. Fina dipped a maid's curtsey and scurried off in a pretense of obedience, and Susannah laughed, glad the sound would follow Fina out the door.

Only when the dragon was gone did she allow herself to sink down at the foot of her bed, and bury her face in the fabric of her dress. Her heartbeat, briefly so controlled, felt like a bird beating wing inside her chest, taking up all the room she might have had to breathe. Fina wouldn't, she was sure, think less of her for her fear, but it had seemed important for her own sake to hide it.

One vampire at a time they could fight, at least under night's cover. A dozen was suicide, maybe even for the dragon, and Fina clearly believed there were more still in the streets beyond hers.

Their only advantage was Eliseo Daisani. Daisani and perhaps Janx, who had as much stake in the child as Fina did. Susannah pressed to her feet and dressed herself, grateful once again for the less-binding corsets Fina had insisted on, and quietly left the dragon female's home in search of those who could help them survive.

IT DIDN'T SURPRISE HER that she was followed, but after a moment's consideration she chose not to try and hide her path. First, given their speed, it would be nearly impossible; second, the more who followed her, the fewer would be on hand to harass Fina once it was realized to whom Susannah was going.

False comfort, that: with their speed, word could spread before Susannah had so much as spoken with her quarry, much less laid out battle plans. She laughed at the idea, small rough sound: she'd never dreamt her small show of independence, her determination to hold a job at her uncle's investigative agency, would lead to such thoughts as *battle plans*, much less ones she herself expected to instigate.

The doorman at the Hotel Sherman recognized her, and cut a bow before he opened the door. Susannah smiled her thanks, and was unsurprised when Janx appeared in the lobby to greet her. "But it's not a social call, is it," he asked with only half-mocking dismay. "You and Fina have seen who's come to town."

"We can't possibly hope to survive without you," Susannah murmured. "I'm fair game for them to hunt, but do you really think they'll stop if they realize Fina taught me? Your laws nonwithstanding, do you really think they'll stop?"

"Of course not." It wasn't Janx who spoke, but rather Daisani, adjusting his cufflinks as he stepped from the hotel's elevator. "Even if I commanded them directly, they wouldn't stop. Not with so many of them. I've been about the city," he said to Janx. "There are the eight or so remaining whom Miss Stacey here hasn't encountered, and some three dozen new arrivals besides. I don't recall the last time I saw so many of my own people in one place."

"Rome," Janx said without hesitation. "Although they were as good-natured and controlled then as I've ever seen them."

"You would be too," Daisani said sourly, "with such a feast as was presented then."

"Speaking of which, how long before their attention strays and we begin to find bodies?"

Susannah covered her mouth with both hands, the idea one beyond her preconceptions. Daisani shot her a look of faint sympathy. "It's a matter of when we begin finding them, not when their attention strays. There will be dozens dead already. Something will have to be done about that, as well."

"I can burn them, if necessary." Everything the two men said was spoken so softly it barely carried to Susannah's ears, much less beyond. Yet the horrors of which they spoke seemed so great that she thought the words must echo like a tower bell ringing out across the city. She was mildly astonished that no policeman came to take them all away.

"It would be wisest," Daisani said to her, "for you to leave now."

Susannah's heart knocked in her chest again, but she lifted her chin and managed a smile. "Fina said something similar."

The two men exchanged glances, Janx shrugging an eyebrow in expressive dismissal. "Fina wouldn't have asked a wallflower for help."

"Nor would you have found a wallflower so enticing."

"Oh," Janx said with a sniff, "as if you're immune to bold beauty and wit. My dear Miss Stacey, if you lack the sense God gave a goose, and refuse to retreat, then perhaps I might suggest a position for which you are uniquely suited."

Wary, Susannah asked, "What's that?"

"*Bait.*"

IN THE END SHE agreed, because the thought had been at the back of her mind anyway. She had always been bait, right from the moment Fina had taken her from an ordinary life and thrust her into the world of the Old Races. Armed bait, yes. Knowledgeable bait, even, but ultimately, her frail humanity was what drew the vampires to her, and therefore was the best hand she had to offer.

She was much less afraid than she should have been, walking down the most dangerous streets in the city. Her clothing marked her out as a target for human and inhuman hunters alike: the soft green dress spoke of at least moderate wealth, and the appearance the others insisted on calling beautiful drew many eyes.

The first to approach her was a man one swallow shy of stumbling drunk. Everything about him was genteel: well-bred features, soft-looking hands, expensively-cut coat. But his gaze was hard and greedy, and he made a proposition no gentleman ever would.

Susannah, to her own astonishment, laughed in his face.

He surged forward, flushed with anger, and she stopped him with her fingertips. There were too many extraordinary dangers facing her for a mortal man, no matter how ill-mannered, to make her afraid.

"You're a boor," she murmured. "An embarrassment to your family and a blight on this city. Have some pride in yourself, sirrah. Go home. Bathe. Put away the bottle and the gambling cards, and make some effort to rejoin the human race."

She pushed, and he staggered back, too shocked to protest.

Actual applause rose up around her from scattered passers-by. One or two men fell in step with her, a kind of honor guard of ne'er-do-wells trying to get an equal rise from her. They faded away when she ignored them, and the next man to intercept her path wasn't a man at all.

He was paler than the others, or perhaps it was just that she'd never seen any of them in sunlight. No: Daisani was swarthy, and this one as white-skinned as a baby. "A fighting spirit," he said. "I like that. May I offer you an escort, lady?"

Susannah withdrew into herself, gaze as fierce as she could make it. "You may not. I need no escort, sir."

"Oh, but I insist."

She still wasn't prepared for his speed. Fina had sworn vampires had no particular strength, but the unutterable quickness with which he moved made up for that. She was between steps when he snatched her, so fast she thought watchers would barely realize anything had happened. One moment she was in the street, and the next in an alley, slammed against the wall hard enough to knock her breath away.

This kind of hunting, she thought, would have seen her dead inside a day.

She didn't see her attacker enter the alley. Nor did she see Daisani, so quick on his heels that the only sign of their entrance was a veritable dust devil of air rushing around. Then the vampire was against the wall, pinned there by Daisani's arm across his throat, until Janx wandered in to take the master vampire's place. He was beautifully dressed, red hair slicked back and a monocle hanging from his lapel, but he carried with him the same weight Fina could, a dangerous heaviness to his dapper presence.

"My dear, please do tell me you're all right?" he asked with such flawless solicitation that Susannah's shaking breaths turned into giggles. She nodded, and he turned a long-toothed smile on the captive vampire.

Whose gaze was for Daisani alone, now. The smaller vampire had fallen back a step and was adjusting his suit as though nothing particularly untoward had happened. Only when he was quite satisfied with his own appearance did he glance up, looking almost surprised to see the vampire still pinned in place. "Is there anything you'd care to tell me about a dragon's egg, Mikal?"

The vampire paled even further. "How do you know who I am?"

Great patience came into Daisani's expression. "Because I'm Eliseo Daisani, you fool. I know each and every one of you, and you cannot possibly hope to outrun or outwit me. This young woman you were about to do violence to has a remarkable skill for binding our kind, and so I would like to suggest you answer immediately, else I'm afraid I'll let her have her way with you. I've no use for idiots, after all."

Mikal shot Susannah a look of venom, then spat, "I know nothing of dragon eggs," at Daisani.

"Mm," Daisani said with mild but clear disappointment. "Very well. You'll leave this city for good when you're released, or you'll regret it for your few remaining days."

Mikal snarled, stared from Daisani to Janx and Susannah and back again, and when the red-haired dragon released him, he was gone.

BY TWO HOURS AFTER sundown, Susannah had only been required to bind three of the fifteen they'd interrogated.

The sixteenth was smarter, or had been warned: he ran, when he saw Susannah, though by that time she was bruised and her dress dirtied from violent encounters throughout the day. She felt, rather than saw, the rush of Daisani's pursuit: wind skipped up in his wake, blowing hair into her eyes and briefly, blessedly, cooling her.

Janx joined her a few moments later, far more out of place on the city docks they'd been exploring than she was. He, somehow, hadn't gotten dust on his shining shoes or lost the sharp creases in his suit pant legs, whereas the hem of her dress was an indescribable color now, and her feet ached in her own dirty shoes. Nor did he seem to sweat, and she wondered if dragons burned off their excess heat some other way. "I hate it when they do that," he said mildly. "I'm always afraid I'll miss something."

Susannah coughed laughter. "You could run after them."

"In these shoes?" Janx sniffed disdainfully, then smiled. "I couldn't catch them even in my natural form. But he ran, my dear Miss Stacey. I wonder if he ran because of you, or us."

"He wasn't supposed to see you," Susannah reminded him, but Janx shrugged.

"We, like you, have been hunting—no, I'm sorry, what did you call it earlier? *Investigating.* All day. We too are tired, and it's not entirely impossible we've made mistakes. In fact, since they may be off chasing one another across the countryside for some time, might I entice you with a meal? A cool drink, perhaps? I'm sure Eliseo will tell us the story when he's caught his wayward youth."

"Nowhere in the city would let me in, looking like this." Susannah gestured at her filthy, worn dress. "Maybe just home for a little while. Fina will be worried. I left without telling her, this morning."

"I'm surprised she didn't come after you." Janx offered his arm, and Susannah, weary, slipped hers through it, glad to lean a little as they began their way back into the city.

"I don't know if she could. There were so many vampires outside the house. Some of them followed me. I think we chased those ones off, so maybe the others weren't warned who I was seeing, but if they were..." She shook her head. "I'd have stayed inside, if I were she. At least until nightfall, when she could change."

"Hard to change inside a house," Janx murmured, then frowned at the distance. "She hasn't changed. I'd have felt it. By that same token I can say with assurance she's alive, because we know when one of our own has died."

Relief surprised her with the strength it sapped from her limbs. "She mentioned that. I'd forgotten. And I've been worried all day."

"What is it you people say? Worries shared are worries halved? And who else could you share that particular trouble with, I ask you? I'm wounded, my dear. Wounded that you didn't unburden yourself to me." Janx put a hand over his heart, looking injured. "Here I've been trying so very hard to win your lust, and—"

Susannah laughed even as a blush climbed her cheeks. "Don't you mean love, Master Janx?"

"Well, perhaps, but lust is so much quicker. I could then take the time necessary to woo you into love. Really," he added with a touch of credible dismay, "don't you find me at all devastating?"

Susannah patted his arm. "Of course I do. I'm sure you'd be irresistible, if I hadn't met a different dragon first."

"Inured you to our ways, did she?" Janx sighed dramatically. "And here I'd been certain that any mortal we exposed ourselves to would certainly find undying love in their hearts for us."

Susannah, still smiling, slipped her hand to Janx's and tugged him forward. "Come on. I want to get home to Fina."

SHE STEPPED IN A puddle as they crossed through the city center, and then another one. There was an ugly scent in the air, tangier than the smoke that had filtered through the city since the fire the night before. It was only with the third or fourth puddle that wrongness settled clearly into her mind. It had hardly rained all summer, much less enough in the past few days to leave puddles.

Janx stopped her as she tried to turn back and see. "Don't," he said quietly. "Don't, Susannah. The vampires have hunted here, and you don't want to know what you're walking through."

"Oh, God." She fixed her gaze straight ahead, suddenly sure he was right. "How many people? How many, to leave that much…" *Blood,* her thoughts whispered, but she couldn't force the word aloud.

Janx shook his head. "All of them, Susannah. All of them in this part of the city. Enough to call it a plague, if an answer needs to be given as to how it happened. *This,*" he snarled, his calm suddenly gone. "This is why they should never gather. They're dangerous and foolish enough alone, but together they run rampant, and leave behind stories almost impossible to decry. They'll kill us all and your world will be the lesser for it, and you'll never even know it."

"I'll know," Susannah whispered ferociously, and Janx looked at her as though he'd forgotten who he was talking to.

"I dare say you will, and that you'll weep for us, Susannah Stacey. Here, we're almost home, not that Fina would thank me for describing her domain in such a way. Careful, my dear, there may be—"

"Vampires," Susannah breathed. More than she'd left behind that morning. The street teemed with them, and in equal parts lay deadly still, empty lumps of flesh fallen by the wayside. A single window was lit in Fina's home, and her silhouette was visible there, a challenge to the dozens of graceful creatures in the street below her. "Why don't they go in? Why haven't they gone after her?"

"Because no dragon would hunt vampires." Janx caught Susannah's shoulder, pulling her back a few steps into the safety of a shadowed alley. "Our laws forbid it, and they can't quite believe she'd break the covenant. They're waiting for her to move, so they have an excuse to attack. Susannah, we have to find another way in. My presence here might be the trigger they're searching for."

"If it's not," Daisani murmured, "they'll find some other excuse." He had a hand over Susannah's mouth as he spoke, stifling her shriek, sending her heartbeat soaring. A few long seconds passed before she exhaled against his fingers and nodded, telling him she was calm enough to be released. He said, "My apologies," as he came to her side. "My brethren are enough focused on Fina's home they might not have noticed you yet, but a scream would have sent them running."

Susannah nodded, fingers clenched in front of her stomach as she tried to regain equilibrium. Daisani's smile was only half-visible in the faint alley light, but there was sympathy in it, more than she might have expected to see.

It changed, though, as he looked to Janx. Became deeper, more regretful, as did the tenor of his voice: "I'm sorry, old friend."

Tension slid into Janx's easy posture, making him taller and narrower. "Sorry?"

"He ran because he was the thief. By the time I caught him…"

"Say it." Janx's voice dropped octaves, a harsh rumble that had nothing to do with his usual pleasant tone. Horror knocked through Susannah's chest, taking her breath with it and leaving her heartbeat so loud she barely heard Daisani's confession.

"He must have known his own existence was already forfeit," Daisani whispered. "I was no more than seconds behind, but by the time I reached him, the egg was lost. I'm sorry, Janx. I'm so sorry."

There were no words to Janx's answer, only a roar too large to come from a mortal chest. Concussive force smashed Susannah to the side, crumpling her against collapsing walls. Bricks glanced off her, numbing her arms where she raised them to protect her head, then weighting her skirts when their tumbling stopped. She lay half stunned, gazing upward as the dragonlord took wing above Chicago. He was the color of flames, red and orange, vast talons tipped in gold, and he hung against the city night screaming his fury at the vampires below.

An answering scream came from Fina's home before it too erupted, fire and fury birthing the black dragon who had been her friend. She was delicate beside Janx, perhaps a half of his size, but no less enraged.

This was the gift Susannah had been given: the luck, the damnation, of being the only mortal alive in a city block to see the Old Races go to war.

The vampires were so hard to see. Unconstrained by mortal limitations, they flung themselves skyward and snapped out insectoid wings to carry them closer to the howling dragons. Janx bit and snapped and burned at them, and they darted away on wingtips, then circled back to attack with pincers that did no damage to his enormous gleaming scales.

Fina threw herself at the earth, skewering their changing black forms and pinning them to the ground so she could breathe huge gouts of flame. The vampires screamed and writhed, and when she left them to burn, crept away into the shadows. More than one took a human body with it, and too many of them then returned, stronger and eager for the fight again.

Thoughtlessly, almost aimlessly, Susannah began removing the bricks that held her captured. Daisani had disappeared, leaving her to get up on her own, and she did with a distant gladness that she still could. Cold went deep inside her, making a place of calmness. Her heartbeat was solid, not fast, but loud enough in her own ears that she was surprised the vampires hadn't heard it yet; that they hadn't been drawn to her as a source of sustenance during their battle with the dragons.

There was a moment, surprisingly clear, when Janx looked down from the sky and saw her, and saw what she intended.

She was quicker than he, at the end of the day. Quicker because she had the element of surprise, as she'd had while fighting the vampires all along. Quicker because no human who knew what she faced would be foolish enough to fling herself into battle against dozens of demons.

It would be easier, so much easier, if they would simply *die* when wood was driven through their hearts. She was good at it now, striking with surety. But even with stakes hidden in both sleeves, she couldn't have had enough to take down so many, even if they'd been decent enough to die like normal creatures.

Janx fell from the sky to flank her, air erupting as he shifted back to his mortal form and in it, showed a physical strength he hadn't in their pursuits earlier. Breaking necks and bones, though that wouldn't hold the shape-changing vampires for long. Nothing would, not unless the earth itself flung up iron manacles and the dry skies opened to pour binding water over the throng of monsters. But if she could make it to Fina's home, burning though it was, she might get the tools they all needed to capture the vampires. The wood and the iron, so water and earth could come later.

"You should be running." Janx's warning came through the roar of fighting, and it came filled with a chagrined admiration. Susannah ducked a vampire so intent on the form-changed dragonlord it didn't see her at all, and turned to drive her stake into its back as it leapt for Janx. It went down with an aborted squall of astonishment, and Janx, with casual strength, ripped its head from its shoulders.

"I am." Susannah gave him a grin, emotion tightly lashed down despite the expression. Her fear was gone, perhaps, but horror would cripple her just as certainly, if she let herself consider too closely what was being done. "I'm running that way." She nodded toward Fina's home, then struck forward again through flame and heat.

The second dragon had taken to the air again, spitting fire on the houses below. Wood frames were already failing, wind whipping smoke into a blur that half-hid Fina as she took vengeance on the vampires. Hell couldn't be any less violent, any less hot, Susannah thought, nor any less peopled with creatures out of demonic imagination.

Janx grunted, a sound of agreement if not approval, and they fought shoulder to shoulder, striving for Fina's house. There were cool cellars below it, perhaps a safe haven from the flames. If not that, though, Susannah could at least find the weapons she needed there. A pinprick of clarity came through the smoke, a single thought of things that needed doing: the vampires had to be vanquished, or the dragons sated, before Chicago's fire brigade arrived. The war between them couldn't be allowed to spill into her world any more visibly than it already had, or even the most skeptical of observers would begin to believe there were Hell-born beings populating the city. Urgency set her running, and she ignored the shout that came after her.

She barely felt the daggered fingers in her back, cutting through the sturdy denim cords of her corset like they were butter. Steel or bone, she thought as she fell. Steel or bone might have fared better, though then again perhaps not. Something was terribly wrong with her legs: they refused to respond, and there was no pain at all. Wetness slid down her spine, but she only felt its sticky river for a few inches, as if someone was cleaning it away before it ran further.

The vampire into whose arms she fell was a ruin, itself. Blackened with flame, its skin bubbled over shredded muscle. Its jaw extended horrendously, bone gleaming through burned-away flesh. She was life to it, and she felt almost no regret at that.

She felt even less when Janx tore this one in half, too. Her smile bubbled up, tasting of blood. "Janx. You saved me."

The dragonlord fell to his knees beside her, his expression stricken. "Not so well as I might have hoped, I fear. Susannah, don't speak. We only need Eliseo. Daisani! *Daisani!*" The shout was too large, again, to come from a human chest, but it did, shaking the foundering walls around them. "He'll be here soon," Janx promised. "Just wait, Susannah. Only wait a moment longer."

"Fina…" She reached for Janx's hand, catching it in hers. His fingers, like Fina's, were cool, but her own were colder still. "Tell Fina…"

The jade-eyed dragonlord bowed his head over hers, the battle around them forgotten as he brought her knuckles to his lips. "Anything, my dear."

"Tell her…I would have regretted…not accepting… more. Tell her…" She smiled, relaxing in his arms, and after a long time Janx brushed his fingers over her eyes, closing away fire reflected in their glassy surface.

New York, 1923

"WHERE WERE YOU?" VANESSA'S voice broke the hush after only the longest time, all three caught up in their own silences and what the story made of them.

Eliseo sighed, forehead pressed against steepled fingertips. "I was in Catherine O'Leary's barn, knocking over an oil lamp so the winds would carry fire into the city center. I was never going to stop the battle, and there needed to be some excuse for the fires they were setting. By the time I made it back it was too late. Susannah and the city were lost." He inhaled, long slow breath, then lifted his gaze to Vanessa's. "And so I went to the river, and watched Chicago burn."

"So did I," Vanessa whispered. "I was eleven that year. I remember watching…I remember that I thought I saw…" She glanced at Janx, then back at Daisani, who smiled.

"I saw you. A girl looking to the skies. Looking at the dragons. A girl with no eyes for the earth-bound, that night. Nor did many of us, but I couldn't, in the end, forget her. Not even after years abroad. Not when she saw so clearly what she wasn't meant to see at all. It took a long time to find you again, Vanessa."

A shiver wrapped around her heart and held there in an aching mix of regret and relief. To think Eliseo had been so close, and had gone unseen, cut in its own way. It whispered that her life had never been her own, not since childhood; that the Old Races were her inescapable fate.

"I'm surprised," Janx said petulantly, "that it wasn't me you wanted, Miss Grey. How could you resist, having watched us burn the city?" He leaned forward, petulance evaporating, and caught a candle stub in his palm, cupping the flame. "I know you're drawn to fire."

"Perhaps I owed you too much." Vanessa's gaze remained on Eliseo, though she saw comic surprise shift over Janx's features. "My grandfather berthed our boat in Chicago the night it burned. When the fire was over, we took his winnings to the bank and invested in rebuilding. By the time I was twenty, we were merchant princes. I had wealth and status when Eliseo began courting me. I hadn't known," she added softly. "I hadn't known I might have drawn your eye without those things."

Daisani inclined his head, gaze gentler than he usually allowed it in Janx's presence. "Not might have. Did. Always, Vanessa. Always."

"Winnings," Janx said across their murmured words, with such disgust that Vanessa laughed.

"Is it this uncharacteristic show of tenderness you object to, Janx, or is there something more?"

He repeated, "Winnings," in the same tone as before, and gave her a look full of daggers.

"Grandfather was a cardsharp. Really, you didn't think I would entertain the notion of playing poker against four of you without an ace in the hole, did you?" Vanessa took up her deck of cards and shuffled them with grace earned through decades of experience, then spread them in a fan and offered them to Janx. "Pick a card. The speakeasy's yours if I name the wrong one."

His gaze darted to Daisani, who only spread his hands and smiled and in so doing sent Janx's attention back to Vanessa. She lifted one eyebrow, then smoothed the cards on her lounge chair. "There. Now I can't even feel which one you take. One card for a speakeasy, Janx. Isn't that worth playing the game?"

He stood and in one fluid movement stepped over to her and selected a card, then tucked it into his breast pocket without so much as looking at it. "The speakeasy's yours, Vanessa. I would never try to steal something fairly cheated for. And I have my answer now, as you have yours. I shall name myself satisfied, and bid you goodnight." He bowed, then exited just slowly enough to not be called a retreat.

"And?" Curiosity lit Eliseo's voice. "Which is it?"

"There's only one card that matters to him, Eliseo. There's only one that matters to you." Vanessa turned the end card up, flipping all its brethren over in a quick ruffle. "Who else could it be, but her?"

Eliseo's, "Ah," came after long moments of silence. "It is not...*always*...about a woman, Vanessa."

"Yes." Vanessa touched a fingertip to three queens, sliding them loose from the others. The fourth was missing. "It is. One doesn't come to understand and live with what you are without understanding that. It doesn't bother me." She glanced up to offer a faint smile. "Perhaps he won last time, but this time, my love, he only has the card."

Daisani got to his feet, extending a hand toward her and smiling in return. "Then I've won more than he knows."

Chicago, 1871

THE RIVERBOAT WAS NOT the one the girl had belonged to. He had considered, then discarded the temptation: she was young. Too young, even for a man with no age, and he was wise enough not to put her in temptation's way. But it was the memory of her slim form, gaze alight with fire as she watched the skies, which drove him to the river and its steamboats at all. He booked passage with thoughts of the muggy Southern summers in mind, and ordered his trunks carried to his berth, all save one.

That one he carried himself, even knowing it would cause comment. Knowing the deckhands and other passengers would notice that a man of his evident wealth considered only one of many parcels to be precious. They watched him bring it to the small room that was his for the journey, and none of them saw him carry it out again in the small hours of the night.

A different man might have thrown it to the river: that, he knew. It represented danger in myriad ways, but most of all as a rebirthing of the Old Races in a time which would not bear them. But there was no game in that, and there was little else that mattered in his life but the game. The bundle fitted under the steamboat's roaring coal furnaces, silk coverings shrinking away, almost alight in the heat.

Daisani lifted a finger to his lips, sly hushing gesture, and with a wink, returned to his berth, certain that his dragon egg lay safe.

When in Rome

"YOU WERE *DEAD*."

These are not words a woman wishes to hear from a lover; from a man who was closer even than that. From a man who has brought her to the edge of death and beyond, indeed. No, they are not words a man should speak in greeting.

Not even when they are true. Most especially, perhaps, not when they are true.

But this is a secret I will share with you, because my birth was not like those of other witches, and secrets hold no power over me: it was worth it. Worth half a century's wanderings, half a world's exploration, worth leaving the long winter nights that were my birthright to be here, now, in a city mortal men think of as ancient, to see blank shock on Eliseo Daisani's face. To see that there is something which can surprise such a man as this.

Vampires, after all, do not expect their victims to live.

But I am—or I was—Baba Yaga's daughter, and of all men, Eliseo Daisani should know that a witch holds untold power in her claw-like hands. And so I smiled, and touched a half-remembered rose that was never tucked into my hair. At that gesture, the angry confusion in Eliseo's eyes faded, replaced by astonished delight.

"You were dead," he said again, and this time offered his hand. "How pleased I am to see it didn't take. Does your mother know?"

His skin was warm, unlike that of the man he was partnered with: jade-eyed Janx, called dragonlord, without whom Eliseo Daisani is incomplete. They were yin to the other's yang, a concept I learned in the first years of my freedom, when I still dared not cross a river and so traveled the breadth of Russia until it became Mongolia and finally China. I walked the wall there, and when I came to its end, I had learned so much about the world that I had never known. Oh, I had studied Mother's grimores, but those were lessons of magic, and it was man I knew so little about.

Not that Eliseo, or Janx, or any of the others who called themselves Old, were men. Not that I had not, at the start, understood their inhumanity or their bond well enough. Mother, though, had understood them far better, and both had nearly paid the ultimate price for her understanding. "Of course she doesn't know," I said, though the answer was self-evident in my survival. "If she knew she would have hunted me and eaten me, to take my magics for herself."

"If she knew," Daisani said thoughtfully, "she might forgive her vendetta against me, and I might once more travel Russian roads."

I snorted, not a very elegant sound. Not a sound that should come from a woman who looked like me, fine-boned and dark-haired and lovely. Half a century had not changed that, nor did I think the same again, or three times it, would. Mother was a crone, yes, but Mother was as old as secrets, and time had caught her up. Then again, the man who walked at my side, amused at my inelegance, was perhaps that old as well, and none of that could be seen in the lines of his face. In his eyes, perhaps, for those who knew how to look, but not in his unhandsome and compelling countenance. Janx: Janx was the beautiful one, of the two, and Daisani more than content to let him be. One was flash and the other fastidious, and I was searching the side streets for the flash, waiting for him to put in his appearance.

"Mother rarely forgives," I said then, "though if she was to eat me up and gain my magics, she might. More likely she would take my magics and then take you, and so I would not test it, if I were you. Where is he?"

"Am I not enough?" Unless I mistook it, there was a note of genuine grievance in Daisani's voice; a whisper of injury which I had not meant to cause.

I did not like that. A thing I had learned from Mother was to hurt with intention, and while I claimed no longer to be Baba Yaga's daughter, it was true that she had shaped me, and that I defined myself even still by the things she was and I was not.

Careless was a thing neither of us, nor any witch, should ever be. So I touched the faded rose that was never in my hair, and said, truthfully, "You are. But you are also rarely without him."

"You've met us once," Daisani said, this time more lightly, as though he pretended to be Janx. "Do you know us so well?"

"Do I not?" I did not mean to be coy, and Eliseo knew it, shrugging the shoulder closest to me in a motion so minute I would not have felt it were we not holding hands. "You belong together."

"I am out of his favor." Daisani's smile was thin and quick, revealing teeth that no vampire of legend would lay claim to: flat, human, ordinary. It was dragons whose eyeteeth curved too long. Mankind knew there were monsters in the dark, but the details had been so badly maligned it was no surprise that the deadly could walk amongst them unknown.

And when the dangerous wore beauty as a cloak the way I did, foolish men saw no threat at all. I asked, "What have you done," as lightly as *I* could, but my heartbeat had quickened with interest, and Daisani marked that with a miniscule turn of his head.

"I have not controlled my kind," he said with slow precision, as if selecting those words took unusual time and thought. "And he has lost something precious as a result."

Russian winter came to life in my blood, turning it cold. Daisani felt that too, and this time turned his head more fully, the better to see me and let me read the curiosity in his eyes. "What," I breathed again, "what have you done, Eliseo? What have you taken from the dragonlord?"

"Who said I'd taken anything?"

The ice in my blood crystallized. I had been born in the snow, had died in the snow, had thawed from the snow in spring. My magics were cold, frost touching my hair even in the warmth of a Roman autumn, and they made a clear warning of power manifested against the vampire's hot skin. *Things*, ***things***, witches hoarded knowledge as *things*, grimoires and secrets and unreadable writings, but I was a witch's daughter, and not what my mother might have dreamed. "You will share it with me," I whispered, and the truth of that spilled through my power as heated gold down a sluice. "You will give it to me, because you have such need of me, master of the vampires. I will take from you what you have rightfully stolen, and I will have it now, before it is birthed into this world."

Daisani—plain, dark-eyed, sallow-skinned Eliseo Daisani—was not a soul to be surprised once in a century, much less twice in an hour. He went still, no longer my walking partner, no longer a man at all, for nothing in this world that I have seen can call stillness upon itself as can one of the Old Races. He might have become a sculpture, for all the life within him: no breath stirred his lungs, no flicker of motion in his eyes, and so when he finally spoke it grated all the more, voice clawed from a thing with no soul. "What is my need, that is so great you lay claim to my possessions with such certainty?"

"The keeping of your kind." The answer sang through me, shivered ice to ice water, made my blood run clear and black the way it does in the depth of a Russian stream choked by winter. "Oh, the keeping of your kind, Eliseo. The bait to draw a vampire in. For tell me, tell me, tell me true. Tell me that there is another drink like that which you tasted from my veins. Tell me true, that there is something so sweet as a witch's blood, and I will cross running water and burn myself with silver to hear you lie."

Silence, silence, silence, and then in a full and furious voice, Eliseo Daisani said, "*Damn.*"

DRAGONS HOARD. THIS I knew from my mother's books, and from the avarice in Janx's green eyes when he had looked upon me. But neither the books nor I had understood why: *why* it is that they are compelled to surround themselves with beauty, to make heaps and piles and hills of precious things. Everyone who tells stories of the beasts simply knows it to be true, in the way that it is known that a starless sky is black and the wind cannot be seen.

But I know now, because I have seen a dragon's egg.

Knowledge: that is what witches wish for, all the knowledge and secrets in the world, to be kept close to their wicked hearts so they might live forever. It was a desire for knowledge of the Old Races which awakened in me the witchery to survive a vampire's kiss, or so I believe. That lust was the hungriest I have ever known, stronger even than my longing for the dragonlord, and that had been great enough to trap us both.

My want for the egg beggared it all.

A depth of pearlescence made it seem I could sink my hands into the shell, so much so that touching it, feeling the curve so far above where my eyes thought I should reach, shocked me. Gold and silver flexed beneath my hands, pressure making rivers of molten metal swirl deep beneath the surface. My breath glittered over it, the promise of diamond mines and more, and I understood. Oh, I understood.

Dragons hoard so they might have somewhere to hide their eggs.

I turned to Eliseo and found him smiling. Not a happy smile, but one of sick comprehension. He was no less taken with the egg than I, and he knew already that against his own every wish, he would give it up to me. "When will it hatch?"

His shoulder lifted and fell. "Soon. The colors are richer every day."

My own smile felt like my mother's, sharp and pointed and full of cruel teeth. "Then we had best hurry. Give me a bowl to bleed in, vampire."

Aggrieved injury changed the shade of his eyes, dark to darkest, and I cursed myself for a fool a second time. Too much of Baba Yaga remained within me, or not enough. I turned my head to show him the pulse in my throat, and closed my eyes to bring a wicked tongue back under control. "Eliseo," I said then, and he said "Witch," in return.

I looked at him again, and saw reservation in his gaze. Reservation and deeper understanding, now, and so I nodded. "We are what we are, all of us who walk the immortal paths of this world. I am not good, Eliseo Daisani."

"But neither are you bad," he said softly. "Not yet. I wonder which road you will travel, Baba Yaga's daughter."

I said, "I have so, so long to make that decision," but Daisani shook his head.

"These things come on us while we think we are choosing. There is less time than you imagine, and the choice may already be made. We will need a third," he added, voice so different there could be no return to the conversation just past. "A third, because I cannot be the one to bind them myself."

I let those words linger in the air, not ignoring them, but hearing only the ones he'd spoken before. I did not like the thought of decisions being taken from me; that had been the shape of my youth. I had done my mother's bidding and dipped my toes in the cold waters of her magics, and had not minded until the cost of both was a red beast's freedom. Janx and Daisani had opened the world to me. I would not have it closed off again in any manner save my own choosing.

"A man," I said, to drown the noise of my own thoughts. "One who will not betray the Old Races even as he destroys the vampires."

"A man," Daisani said, drolly, "because a woman is less likely to succumb to your charms and conviction."

As his had before, my shoulder lifted and fell. "At least I will not eat him up when I am done with him. A wise man, Eliseo."

He lifted two fingers, tapping them together to make a rhythm as he chanted, "Wise man, jester, cowboy, thief. Doctor, lawyer, Indian chief?" Then laughter came on him, bright and brief, to see me scowl in confusion. "It's a children's rhyme older than you are, though it changes with the years. Most things mortal do."

Hairs stood up on my nape, ice sweeping my skin as magics danced with insult. I did not like to be laughed at, perhaps because I had so little experience with it. My mother rarely laughed, and never at me except when I was foolish. I felt foolish now, and ice faded with heat in my cheeks. "Doctor," I said, and the word came out sharp and hurt. "A lawyer would not understand the rules of the world you have made for yourselves, and would betray us all to humanity."

"First we hang all the lawyers," he said agreeably, and between one blink and the next he was gone, leaving me in a silent room with a dragon's egg to warm.

I DID NOT KNOW how long I sat, my hands on the always-changing shell. It might have been hours; it might have been weeks. Though I ate of bread and soup like anyone, it was in truth magic which sustained me, and had been since the last drops of my mortal blood had gone to feed a vampire. The egg itself could have fed me forever, had I chosen to leech life from its glorious colors. But that was something my mother would do, and I had not risen from the snow only to be her daughter again.

I knew long before Daisani returned that the being within the shell was female. I knew that like any child—perhaps like any dragon, grown or not—that she was a curious creature, and bold. And I knew that even from within the shell, this dragon child knew that something was *wrong*: that her mother's fires had left some time ago, and that whatever had caused that was the enemy. I did not know if human children had such clear perceptions of who did and did not belong, but this unborn babe radiated an anger that defined her even before she broke shell.

I, who knew a thing or two of anger, bowed my forehead to her encasement and whispered charms of ice. I could never be a creature of heat, not as dragons were; I had been rebirthed in cold, and the best I might do was to temper the fire burning within the infant's breast. I was not the enemy: this I told her time and again. I was the one who would take her from that enemy, and together we would grow old and strong and see the world. These things and so many more I promised her, and one thing I did not.

I did not promise her vengeance. That, I would not do. Daisani claimed a vampire could be bound but never die, but it was not a game I would play with his life. Not as a promise to an angry child, for promises must be kept, and I still wore his rose in my hair.

By the time he returned, her rage was less than it had been, and I no longer feared that should the shell crack while Daisani lingered, that my daughter's first moments might be her last, fearsome fighting instinct meeting age and speed in a deadly battle.

He returned with a man of excellent aspect, if not the wicked sly beauty that had drawn me to Janx or the reserve which made Eliseo appealing. Unlike almost any man I had ever known, he gave me a mere glance and nod, and gave the shell little more. Neither it nor I were dismissed, only observed, taken for what we were in a moment's assessment, and set aside as specimens worthy of further study. Men did not react to me so: I was a witch, and Baba Yaga's daughter, and beautiful, and so I stood for a moment in childish insult before gathering my wits to say, "You are a doctor?"

"And you a witch, and that a dragon's egg, and this a vampire," he said in a voice deeper and richer than I had thought to imagine. "None of which I would choose to believe, had this creature offered me a choice."

"There is always a choice," I said, and because I was my mother's daughter in some ways still, new thoughts and words came to me even as I spoke them. "You might have chosen the darker door you knew would be the price of disbelief. You might have walked through that door, and found your son again, and a wife whose sensibilities are not lost."

I took pleasure that he stiffened; that the whole of his body changed pace, and that the cast of his features said he would whisper *witch!* if he did not already know that word to be no more than base truth. Then my pique faded: he had paid the price of not acknowledging beauty or wonder, and it was now behind us, safe in history where only a gargoyle might bring it to life. And because my anger was fleeting, I finished more kindly, a soft song to my speech as I sounded out the truth that flowed before me. "You are not a man to hunt vampires in hopes of finding death, then. No, you seek the other: you seek immortality in deed if not in life, and this I will promise you, Doctor. Choose your name and choose it wisely, for you will be remembered in all ways as the greatest vampire hunter who ever lived."

"Then I choose my own name," he said almost so softly in return, "for my son is dead and my wife is mad so there will be no other get from my loins. Let the name Van Helsing be remembered, witch. Let them know Abraham Van Helsing, so that my family, my boy, my life, will not be forgotten."

My fingers splayed, sharp motion of their own, and from their tips sprang wisps of cold so strong they steamed in the warm Roman night. Forward, forward, hissing through Daisani, through Van Helsing, and becoming inextricably twined as they rushed into future history to make their mark in times and places yet to be.

"So it will be," I said, and Daisani, forgetting all romance in the name of practicality, said, "If you survive."

"THE BLOOD MUST BE fresh."

"The blood must be *sweet.*" We had made this argument a dozen times, Daisani on one side and my own self on the other, a wrist lifted to slash as I had offered with each reiteration of the disagreement.

"The blood must be *warm,*" Abraham said in clear disgust, and we two supernatural creatures looked at him in raw astonishment. "If it is hers, it is sweet, yes? Sweet or not, cold blood has a stench to it, and no vampire will be drawn to that, not at the heart of a trap. You do not intend on feeding them at all, do you?"

Guilt filtered through Daisani's eyes, so exquisite it made me laugh. "It seems not," I said for him. "He only wishes my blood for himself. What happens, Eliseo, to a vampire who drinks too often of witch blood?"

He said, "No one knows," in a way that made me know he wished to discover it. "I doubt, though, that it's a question of too much or too little, but rather how many times."

The words welled up from nowhere: "Once for health."

Daisani's gaze sharpened and he looked from the witch's daughter to the human doctor and back again before deliberately loosening his expression, Janx-like. "I assure you there's no question as to my well-being."

Abraham Van Helsing was mortal, not a fool, and looked between us as though he sipped at bitter dregs. He muttered, "There is too much here I do not know," but pressed it no further: a wise man indeed. "How do we keep it warm, to draw them in?"

I was born of ice, but I had learned a thing or two of heat in my years, and so I said, "I can do that," which brought both men's attention to me.

"I did not imagine," Eliseo said after a moment, and carefully, "that you might intend to hunt with us."

"I would be a poor witch indeed if I could not be warmed by, and warm in turn, my own blood, no matter how far from my veins it might travel. I will not hunt with you, Eliseo Daisani. I am not my mother. But if my blood is to run hot for you, well then, I know of only one way to best do that."

Soft, soft, and so soft: "I thought you preferred dragons."

"I was young then, and Russian nights are cold."

Eliseo smiled. "Dragons are cold too. They like hot places so they can sun themselves like lizards."

"And vampires are hot, like Rome. Like tonight. Perhaps like calls to like, within me." We moved as we spoke, small steps like dancing, until with the last words we swayed in each other's spaces, little between us but a promise. "You cannot drink me, if my blood is to be bait."

"A taste," Daisani whispered, and I lifted my chin so my throat might take the teeth of a vampire a second time. No pain, and this time all the seduction promised in the first. It is a heady thing, a lightening thing, to be loved as blood slips away, and for a long time I knew nothing but Eliseo and the near-silent splash of red liquid into a narrow-necked urn.

When I opened languid eyes, Van Helsing had very sensibly gone.

WHETHER IT WAS TIME or whether passion offered a subtle heat to wake a sleeping dragon, a crack had appeared in the shell. I took a breath to murmur Eliseo's name, then held it captured behind my lips and instead rose, silent and careful, to cross to my egg and kneel beside it. Its curve rose above my eyes, from that position, and I placed my hands on the ever-changing surface to feel the heartbeat within.

The shell bulged under my touch, a living response unlike any that had come before. Then stillness, such utter stillness that my heart, too, went still, in unimagined concern for the infant I had claimed as my own.

All babies are born hungry. I had not thought what that might mean, when the babe in question was a dragon.

Glorious shards erupted under my hands, scattering across the room, digging into my palms. I fell back, and that was a mistake, too, for it showed weakness. My daughter sprang from her shell with jaws gaping, and teeth as long as my finger slashing for my flesh.

A lamb, half-grown and bleating, appeared between the child dragon and myself, and fed the hunger that I had nearly sated. Blood and sinew splashed, turning dangerous teeth red; turning my naked skin red, and making me that much more a meal.

A second lamb, and a third, appeared and were devoured as swiftly, and by the fourth, my daughter slowed her haste, and I, still gasping with astonishment and rabbit-hearted fear, began to understand what had happened. I said, "You were sleeping," not in accusation but relief, and Daisani's chuckle rolled across me.

"Resting. Vampires rarely sleep, and even if I had been, I would not have slept through *that*." He came into my line of sight and nodded—nodded, did not gesture, because his arms were full of still another lamb, this one dumbstruck with horror at the carnage around it—nodded to indicate the broken bits of shell that had heralded my daughter's birth. "Lucky for you I'm quick."

"Lucky indeed," I whispered. "Why so many lambs, and not a sheep?"

"I'm quick, not strong," he said drolly. "A dozen lambs are easier than a sheep or two. She's nearly done with that one now. You might give her this last, so she sees you as a provider of food, not a source of it."

Bloody, reverent, and as bold as I could make myself, I did this thing, to the infant dragon's purr of delight. She was lovely, as long as I stood tall, and crimson-scaled, though the edges of those scales were stained with black. "You know me, child," I said as she fed, and she tipped her head to examine me with one emerald eye. A sinuous shrug rippled the length of her: acknowledgment or dismissal, I did not know. Her gaze fastened on Daisani, and two things happened then. First was the hiss, a sound longer than she was, from behind shreds of flesh and dripping ichor. Second, though, was the flare of fine nostrils as she looked to the lamb she devoured, and though I could not say for certain these were her thoughts, so they seemed to me to be: *Enemy, but the female thing, the mother thing, accepts it and bids me to as well. Enemy, but it has brought me food. Enemy, but I shall not eat it. Yet.* Yes, she seemed that much a thinking being, even in those first minutes of life, and nothing in the years to come told me otherwise.

"Holy Mother of God," Van Helsing said from the cavern's mouth, and I could not help but laugh to see us as he did: savage infant and naked witch kneeling amongst fragments of lamb bones, well-dressed somber vampire—because of course Eliseo had dressed, though whether he'd done it before or after fetching the lambs I did not know—somber vampire standing over us as a grim father. The second phrase whispered by the doctor was one I could not understand, but the tone was reverent in a way his first words had not been. He entered, strong features alight with wonder, and crouched some safe distance from my daughter, who lifted her head, studied him, and to my mind determined his height and breadth to be too great to consider him as lunch. That too made me laugh, for of the two men, Van Helsing was the easier mark for one such as she, but to a newborn predator's mind, Daisani's smaller frame made him the likelier meal. "Would you have me hunt them as well?" A note of regret echoed through Van Helsing's deep voice, and relief made crags around his eyes when Eliseo shook his head.

"Dragons have difficulty resisting beauty only. I fear my own kind are more impulsive and easily distracted than that, and they are always hungry. They have become a danger to themselves."

"And to you." Van Helsing looked to Daisani, who inclined his head.

"I intend to preserve my people, but it's true I have even more vested in preserving myself. I have the blood, Master Van Helsing. Are you prepared to hunt?"

"Is the blood ready?"

"It is." I rose from my red-toothed infant and lifted the urn, staining its china surface when it had drunk of my blood unblemished. It was cool now, but that was of no import: I only called the chill to me, sister to my icy start, and in moments it forgot all it had ever known of snow and cold. I folded that trace of bitterness close to my heart: close, but not touching, for bitterness born of something so uncaring as cold was not a thing I wished to embrace. So we make our choices, I said to myself alone, and offered the urn to Daisani. "I would join you on this first hunt."

His eyebrows lifted, swift and questioning as he glanced toward my daughter. "And leave her alone?"

I too looked at her, gnawing slowly on lamb's guts, her eyes half-lidded with sated pleasure, her long tail twitching and curling like an infant at the breast. "A newborn babe sleeps and eats and expels," I said. "She will sleep soon, and has no need of a keeper to change soiled clothes. And I will return before she awakens again, for how long can it take to catch a vampire?"

Daisani dipped his head over the urn, inhaling. A delicate shudder ran through him, and my answer was given like a prayer: "Not so long at all."

BEYOND THE ENTRANCES OF caves the temperatures are steady, comforting, unnoticeable, and there is no difference between night and day. I was surprised, then, to exit our hideaway into full-blown daylight, Roman sun beating down and heating the very drops of water in the air. I could scoop it, gather it, weave it, if I so chose, but this was Eliseo's hunt, and not my own at all. A city on seven hills lay before us, streets worn down with the passage of many feet over many years, marking a lust and love for life. Perhaps it was natural that vampires should gather in such a city; perhaps especially because at its heart lay the church which perpetuated so very many wrong legends of that kind. Crosses, silver, sunlight: these were not things to slay a vampire with, any more than they might kill a man when brandished at him.

And so the man who walked beside me did not rattle with the sounds of swords or announce his presence with the stench of garlic. He carried wooden weapons only, perhaps some choice of timber sacred in his native land, and the iron chains he bore were slight and muffled well. *Drowned by water,* my mother's voice whispered in my ear. *Staked by wood, bound by iron, buried in earth.* She had the ingredients, but not the order of it: no unbound, unstaked vampire would submit to being drowned or buried, and their quickness made up much for their lack of strength. Van Helsing came as prepared as any man might, and had trained with the master of them all, but even so, I walked with them at least as much to see him fail as to wonder at his success.

I had not thought that failure—or success—would be within the Vatican itself.

Even I, who knew little and cared less of human religion, hesitated at crossing that threshold. They burned women they thought were witches, these fools, never knowing that the number of true witches was so scarce it barely rose above twenty and four across all the world; never knowing that there was not a witch who walked the earth who could be undone by fire. And yet I hesitated, until Daisani looked amused, and then my pride was greater than my caution, and I walked with them into a heart of mortal power.

"Tell me," Van Helsing muttered, "that we are not here for the Pope."

Daisani's amusement turned to a laugh. "Not the Pope. Only a cardinal. The next Pope, perhaps, if we are unsuccessful."

Van Helsing blanched, a hand moving to the iron chains he carried, and Eliseo smiled again. It was I, though, who spoke: "A Pope such as that one might free you from your mad wife, Abraham. Think twice on whether you wish to pursue this hunt."

The look he gave me was venom, and Daisani's, curious. I lowered my gaze in a pretense of contriteness, but his answer was what I had hoped for. He was a good man, determined to do right, and that was the path of his choosing. I did not know if he had chosen it time and again, or if once set upon it, it became inviolate, nor how I might know such a thing for myself. It had been easier to be only my mother's daughter, but that had been so long ago.

Occupied with these thoughts, I hardly saw the marble floors we crossed, the elegant arches we passed beneath. I did not know how we came to the inner chamber where a man of medium build and slow eyes languished in robes far too warm for the summer heat, but I knew when we entered the room that this was our quarry.

And he knew us as well, or at least our leader: his stillness when he saw Daisani told me that. Then his gaze came to me, and thin anticipation slid across his features. "A gift to the church, Master Daisani?"

"Never. But to you, perhaps." He uncorked the urn as he spoke, and even I caught the sweet scent of blood rising.

The vampire cardinal came to us like a man, slow careful steps: wise enough, for a vampire. Disguising what he was, in the expectation that neither Van Helsing or I knew him to be other than a man. Expecting, too, that we had no knowledge of the liquid within the urn, or wisdom would have him choose not to bend his head over it for a deep inhalation.

Van Helsing moved more quickly than I thought a man his size could do. The iron chain about the vampire's neck; the wooden stake slammed through its ribs to beget a scream. But the neck was not enough, and though the creature shuddered and shifted, oily black skin breaking through the countenance of humanity, he also turned and dug long and deadly claws into Van Helsing's gut.

Foolishness grasped me and I stepped forward, prepared to help. Daisani lifted a hand, arresting my action, and we both stood mute to watch the blood drain from Van Helsing's face and leave desperate determination behind. He ought not have had the strength to wrap iron around the vampire's elongated hands, binding its wrists, and yet he found that strength within him, then savagely pulled until the creature's hands were at its own throat, rendering it nearly helpless. Bleeding, white-faced, grim, the hunter bound the vampire further, ankle to wrist, its spasms and screams increasing even as its ability to shift from one fluid shape to another faded.

Van Helsing silenced its screams with a second shaft of wood driven through its skull, and only then collapsed on the slick and bloody floor.

Eliseo Daisani, with due and graceful deliberation, gave to me the urn of my own blood, and knelt by Van Helsing's side to say a curious thing: "You are not as good as Susannah was, Van Helsing. She took nine of my kind without an injury of her own, and now I see why Fina chose a woman for the job instead of a man." He pulled Van Helsing's clothes apart, revealing murderous holes in his ribs. The man cried out, low and hoarse, and for a long moment Daisani remained beside him, letting his life blood mix with the vampire's.

As for me, I waited to see what things Eliseo Daisani chose to be, and was neither surprised nor unsurprised when he muttered a curse and opened his wrist to give a dying man a taste of a vampire's blood. "One," he snarled. "One sip alone, for health, Van Helsing, and with that sip you are mine. Do not fail me again."

Grievous blue eyes stared at the vampire, but the desire to survive was stronger than fear of failure. Van Helsing drank, and as I watched the injury sealed itself, healed itself, until all that remained was a scarlet ridge, the color fading even from that. "Now," Daisani said, low and harsh, "go to find some young brother, some impressionable child, and have him gather his kin and take this beast below. Bury him, soak the earth with water, and command them never to speak of the monsters you bring to cage beneath holy places. Make it clear their duty is jailer, not hunter."

"Is that wise?" Van Helsing and I spoke as one, but Daisani spat a dismissive sound.

"Holy men are better than any at keeping secrets, and only some very few of them are truly bold. Most will not want to hunt, and those who do will die of it, and their secrets with them. I will bring you across the globe," he said to Van Helsing. "When Rome is cleared of my brethren, then I will take you elsewhere, and you will hunt and bind and bury, and the holy men will watch over my people for eternity. We have very little time to accomplish this, now that it's begun, so waste no more of it. Go."

Van Helsing came to his feet slowly, fingertips exploring the wound that should have taken his life. He nodded once, then stalked away, only pausing at the door to glance back at me, a certain recognition in his eyes. "I think we will not meet again, lady. Watch the child. It is precious."

"Is it? Is it not a monster?"

"All children," Van Helsing said softly. "All children are precious. Remember that, lady. Remember it well." Then he walked away, and it is true that we were never to see one another again. His words, though, stayed with me, and I forgot Eliseo Daisani as I left the Vatican to return to the birthing cave, there to consider my daughter.

Daisani, though, did not forget me, and though he waited some time before entering, I knew when he joined us that he had walked in step with me all the way back. "Will you bind her," he asked from the cavern mouth, and I looked at the child who was born as tall as I was.

She slept now, crimson scales flexing in small ways as she breathed and shifted. In a week or a month, I might seem as a meal to her: small, delicate, fragile. It would be in all ways wisest to bind her; to make a gift of a glittering thing as no dragon could resist, and hold her to me thus.

My answer, though, came without my bidding: "I have no blood of a virgin—"

Daisani made a disbelieving sound, and I finished with the briefest of smiles. "Witch, Eliseo. A virgin witch. You did not think it was a human virgin's blood which could hold a dragon, did you?"

Either he had not thought on it at all, or had not thought it through fully, for chagrin momentarily colored his eyes before he shrugged and passed it off with a wave of his hand. "Vampires can be bound by mortal tools. A dragon might have been, too."

"By a great many mortal tools working together. A magical binding might require only one component." I was not questing for an answer. I was *not,* but Daisani pinched his mouth closed and sent a dour glance my way. I could not help but smile then, and look back to my young dragon. "I have no blood of a virgin witch," I said again, and then more softly, a revelation even to myself: "No. No, Eliseo, I will not bind her."

"And so we are as we choose," Eliseo Daisani murmured, but I thought I heard approval in the quiet words. "What will you call her?"

"Jana," I said, as unbidden as before.

Fresh approval darted across Daisani's face. "A proper dragon's name." Then approval faded before curiosity, and he tipped his head, examining me. "And what shall I call you?"

I had not thought he'd noticed, that my only name was a title. But I shook my head, and instead of the answer he wished for, said only, "It is best, I think, if you continue to think of me as Baba Yaga's daughter."

He lowered his gaze, pretty gesture better suited to Janx, but when he lifted his eyes again, there was an honesty in them that Janx could perhaps never achieve. "So long as Baba Yaga's daughter wears my rose in her hair, I am content with that."

I touched the imaginary bloom and smiled. "Always, Eliseo Daisani. Always."

Satisfaction slid across his face and he nodded once. Then in a darker voice, a warning voice, he said, "And none of this will ever be spoken of."

"Who would believe it," I said lightly, and wondered how long past his hunting days Van Helsing would survive. "Go, Eliseo. You have the blood to tempt them and the man to hunt them, but you have little time before word spreads that their master moves to bind them."

"You're trying to get rid of me," Daisani said in amusement. "To raise your baby dragon without my influence?"

"I did not barter the egg from you only to let you be its father figure, so yes, but also I am right. You have little time, and my magics are weak across water. I cannot easily influence the speed at which their fear travels."

"You would do that?"

"Not," I said, "if you do not go soon."

He nodded, then held his breath a moment, unusually human for a creature such as he. "I will see you again?"

"So long as I wear your rose you will never be fully free of me." The words were as much curse as promise to my way of hearing, but pleasure splashed over the vampire's countenance.

"And you will wear it always. Until later, then, Baba Yaga's daughter. Until later."

As ever, his words were left to linger on the air when he was already gone. I plucked them down and tucked them away in case I should need them someday. Then I knelt beside my sleeping daughter, collecting the pieces of shell from which she had emerged.

I was not Baba Yaga. I did not eat the baby dragon, only the remains of what had fed her within the shell. This, *this* was magic to sustain me, the very stuff that gave life to a dragon, but it was more as well. I ate slowly, each bite chewed thoroughly so it became a part of me, and when I was finished, I put a hand to my still-flat stomach, and whispered the word of what was coming to the world:

"Chimera."

Baba Yaga's Daughter

THIS IS THE NIGHTMARE: THAT I am lying beneath the still-warm bodies of my parents, my sisters, my younger brother. That I am bleeding, that the pain is unbearable, and that I cannot cry out for fear the heavy-booted Bolsheviks will hear me and finish what they began. I am not shot as my father and mother were, but stabbed, and that is danger enough: we bleed too easily, we Romanovs, and Maria who is next to me, breathing even still, will die before our murderers are gone. I cannot count the number of bullets and I must not flinch at any of their sounds, or I too am dead.

Maria rises up with a scream and is silenced, and I am alone, the last of the Romanovs. Our beloved friend Rasputin is gone, the empire is gone, my family is gone. This is the nightmare.

The dream is of a red-eyed white man who walks out of the bright summer night and does not shudder when the murderous traitors fire on him. The dream is of his strength as he casts men away as if they were dolls, and of exultance rising in me as I pray for their deaths. The dream is of his accent, strange, very strange, as he bows his head over mine. "I have no gift of healing. I can bring you to one who will save you, but the price may be high."

I am the daughter of tsars. There is no price too high for survival. For vengeance. I nod and the white man lifts me as if I have no weight. He puts me over his shoulder, and the dream itself becomes pain, red rolling pain, as my bloodied belly is pressed into bone and muscle. "Hold on," he says in his strange accent, and I gather what strength I have to wrap my arms around his ribs.

The world is knocked askew, and this *is* a dream, must be a dream, the way I am no longer grasping a man's torso, but instead lie sprawled and bleeding on the scaled back of a vast white monster. My ears ring with the force of—of something; I cannot quite convince myself that it is the force of the man's change from one thing to another. But there are wings pounding the air, and the ground falls away beneath me as if I fly in one of the Wright brothers' aeroplanes, and the air is crisp and cool and thin with summer stars.

Yes, this is a dream, with all the strange logic of such things, and so in the end it is hardly any surprise at all when the dragon lands at the edge of a forest, and Baba Yaga's hut comes to collect me.

"ANNA! *ANNA!*"

I was awakened by my mother's voice. By the sound of my name, which she used rarely. In the first moment I was confused, vestiges of my dreams clinging to me: *I am not Anna. You are not my mother, to use nicknames for me.* And my love, my white-winged savior, was gone. Gone as if he never was.

Then so too were the memories, and I was on my feet, bare feet, rough and calloused feet, one of them a twisted foot, but that made no difference as I ran to answer my mother's call. It was summer, a Russian white night turning to a long white day. Mosquitoes droned and wind rustled through silver birch trees. My mother was disturbed by neither as she hunched over the work that she did, grinding bones into dry brown blood. She must do this in the summer hours, so that the paint she makes is infused with sunlight. In the winter it will glow warm and bright on the skulls she dips it in, and we will have light through the darkest months.

The sun, which had never truly set, was low and white on the horizon. It blinded me as I looked that way, and in the eye-searing brilliance I saw a figure. A white man on a white horse, his trappings all in white. Something surged in me, an awakening of hope and fear, and for a moment I felt I was truly Baba Yaga's daughter, a witch in my own right. My hands felt bright and strong, not with the work that I did each day, but with the power that must be part of me. I had studied the grimoires and read the books of magic for as long as I could remember, but never before had I felt its fire in my veins. It was a sweetness, a transition, like the dawn itself, a change from dark to light. Like the white man in the sunrise, there for a moment and then when I blinked, gone as if he had never been.

Between us, between me and the sunrise, sat my mother, who looked at me and looked hard. She said, "Come," and I did, passing by her to collect a birch bark bucket. I filled it with water from a stream that lay beyond the fence of white bone that had built itself in the night, after the hut found its place to rest. I had never seen the hut stop so near to a stream that the bones could not stand between them, for my mother could not cross water. In her chicken-legged hut she could pass over any stream or creek small enough for it to leap, but even so, she preferred that I fetch and carry. Then again, what mother did not? I remembered doing this in my childhood, waking from rest on a hard cot to do the chores others would think below a princess.

I said "Hah" beneath my breath, because certainly no daughter of Baba Yaga's was also a princess, no matter how the old witch might hope it. She would grind *my* bones and drink *my* blood, if she thought I was Ana—

I stumbled, spilling water, and Baba Yaga leapt backward with a hiss. Leapt all the way into her mortar, and glowered at me from above. The soil darkened around her pestles and paints, water soaking in. I looked at them, then at the long-nosed hag who was my mother. I was fair, strawberry-haired, blue-eyed, and young. She was as brown as the earth, scraggly-haired, had eyes like black buttons, and was far too old to have birthed a girl my age.

"Forgive me, Mother. I stubbed my toe. Will I grind your paints for you this morning?" I knelt beside them, uncaring of the wet and mud, to continue the dirty work she had begun. My twisted foot, the one I claimed to have stubbed, was easy for her to see. I felt her eyes upon it for a moment or two.

"Clean the house and cook my dinner," she ordered, and I knew I was safe for another day. I dared not look up, though, not until I heard her mortar whistle through the air and the *whssht* of her birch broom whisking away her tracks.

Even then I kept my head down, my gaze fixed on the blood and mud that made up Baba Yaga's paints. Red blood, brown blood, drying blood, flaking and making a sick taste at the back of my throat. I knew that taste, and the scent that rose with it, too well. And yet I could not know it: never in my childhood had I been hurt, never had I slaughtered animals or been present when my mother ate up children or men to satisfy her hunger for fatty flesh, only seen the bones as they danced to their place in the fence around the hut. That she did these things, yes, I knew. Mothers threatened naughty children with Baba Yaga, as I had been threatened in my youth.

My mother, Baba Yaga, would not threaten me with herself. I dropped the pestle and clutched my skull instead. The red iron smell of blood clung to my fingers, and pain seared my belly. A hand went to my ribs, to the soft flesh beneath them. To the scars that lay there, white marks against white skin. Some round, others long and thin.

A child who had never been hurt could have no such scars.

I put my forehead to the ground and clenched my fingers in the dirt. Perhaps Baba Yaga had fed on me. Perhaps she had dug her long nails into my innards and sucked them out, the liver, the kidney, the spleen. Perhaps she had filled those spaces with magic, magic which I had felt stir in me for the first time this morning. Perhaps this was how one became a witch, first be born the daughter of one, then have all the insides eaten up so there is room for the magic.

Baba Yaga had done a poor job with me so far, if that was how it was. I could remember the number of summers I had seen: eighteen, and this was the nineteenth, and it seemed to me a witch should come into power with her woman's blood.

But the only blood I had now was in the paints I mixed, and those must be done before my mother returned. I lifted my face from the soil, feeling it stick and choosing not to brush it away. I would be dirty with the land of my mother, and perhaps draw more magic from that than she had given me of her own.

In summer the sun climbed the sky forever, shadows growing short but never disappearing underfoot. Nor did the sun ever reach an apex as it does in storybooks. It always offered an angle, a slant that made light softer here than I had read about it being in southern lands. But it reached its noon height with the same confidence in Russia's summer as it might anywhere else. I looked up, rubbing a mud-bloody hand across my face, and saw a flash of crimson on the sun.

A rider, like the white man this morning. A rider in red, all red, his horse a battlefield steed, and the man with a cloak that spread wide like flaming wings. He reeked of power, of the strength of a mid-day sun, and I drew that strength down into myself until it filled my chest and burned my lungs.

I knew the air, then. Knew the air and the wind and the breezes of Russia, knew them as they climbed the tall cold mountains and as they swept across the eastern steppes. Knew them as they carried cold from the far wintery north, and knew them from the distant sandy south. They carried to me all the knowledge of my country, all of its sorrows and joys, and that knowledge nestled within me, making a place for itself in the heart of the white strength that had come on me with sunrise.

I pressed a hand to my chest and gasped. When I could breathe easily again I lifted my eyes, but the red rider was gone. I had not expected him to be there, but I thought my mother would have expected it even less. I stood from the paints that I had mixed and went to the chicken-legged hut to clean, to cook, to mend, and to wonder at the power that contracted with every beat of my heart. Power that I felt was natural to me, though of course it would be: my mother was Baba Yaga, after all. But this was different from just the magic coming to life. This was confidence born and bred in my soul, trained under the loving and hard eyes of a Mama and Papa who believed that even—perhaps especially—those who ruled must also serve.

A papa. Baba Yaga would never suffer a father in her hut, and everyone knew that her children were the children of men she later ate. I stopped washing the dishes I was washing and turned away, eyes closed so my soul alone could guide me. One step, two steps, five, and that was as many as could be taken in Baba Yaga's chicken-legged hut without finding something to lay hands on.

A blanket. Ugly, worn, used and washed a thousand times, it had a name stitched into it: *Grigori*.

I spoke without thought, for I remembered the name, almost. "My dear friend. Our dear friend. Oh, we have missed you, dear Grigori!" Passionately said, though I barely remembered the wild-eyed man it belonged to. I could hardly recall why such sadness rose in me at the thought of his death. I did not know him, did not know why thinking of his dying made me fear my own. As if they were linked somehow, Baba Yaga's daughter and—

—and Baba Yaga's son. I gazed at the blanket in my hands, shocked by the knowledge. The scrap of cloth had not belonged to one I would call brother, but one I thought of in a very different way indeed. I had been a young woman when he died, no more than five years ago now, and I had wept as though my heart was broken. No, that had not been the death of a brother, that pain which I had felt.

Beyond the hut's windows the afternoon sun faded into twilight as I stood unmoving with Rasputin's blanket. I looked out a final time as grey shadows crept free of the trees, and this time was unsurprised to see a third rider leading the edge of those shadows.

A black rider this time, all in black, his steed a magnificent shade of night. He rode toward me swiftly, more swiftly than sense could say, and in the last moment his horse leapt the bone gate and the chicken-legged hut and he disappeared above me, but winter's darkness fell in his wake.

Its chill settled in my bones and crackled them from within, as the frozen lakes might crack, or as a tree invaded by frost could burst. That too was of my land, so much of it desolate and wild, and it belonged inside of me as much as the wind's whispers or the long days of summer did. It completed me, finished filling empty spaces I had not known were empty, and as those spaces swelled and cracked, so too did the thickness of thought which had hidden all my memories from me.

"Alexei." The name was a moan in my mouth. My brother Alexei, precious child, so dangerously ill. Shot in the head, as were my sisters, because the nightmares were no nightmares at all, only memory forcing its way through the spells Baba Yaga had cast.

There was no question of why, as I began to remember myself. Perhaps a white dragon came in the night to save me from the Bolsheviks, or perhaps that too was a story told to me by Russia's mother witch. Either way, it did not matter. I had nearly died, and I lived now because of her. She was a mother to me as much as Alexandra had been, and perhaps she had been wise to wash away my memories. They came on me hard now, a remembrance of things I had done and moments we had shared: the snowball I had thrown at Tatiana, after packing it around a stone. My cousin Nina, younger than me but also taller, for which I could not forgive her. How at the opera I had stained my white gloves with chocolates, too eager for them to remove the gloves.

And how my sisters and mother and I had wept over Grigori Rasputin's murder; how as a small child I knew I was loved and yet not the son my parents had prayed for; how Maria, two years my elder, and I had run together as The Little Pair; how we had put on plays during our captivity to make the family laugh and forget our troubles. How in defiance I stuck my tongue out at Yurovsky, our captor, when he turned his back and left our room.

How the next night we were murdered, all of us, and only I survived.

There was no dinner cooked when Baba Yaga returned home, only me, her daughter Anna, once known by another name, now standing alone in a small room and holding the baby blanket of a man I had loved. I had thought she would be angry, but she swept in and the door banged behind her. When I did not flinch she said, "Ah," and took the blanket away from me.

No. Did not take it away, but wrapped it about my shoulders like an embrace. Thus held, I found a seat and huddled in it, imagining the blanket to be Grigori's arms. He had been so kind to us, our dear friend. He had come to us when Alexei's bleeding would not stop, and he had saved our beloved little brother time and time again. He had extolled us to the virtues of prayer, of lady-like behavior, of, and only now did I think this strange, only now did I see it as the influence of his mother and not of Christ, of a passion for the earth and growing things and the connectedness of life in one thing and another.

I had been young when he died, only fifteen. Young, but not unaffected by his appeal. Not his beauty: he was wild-eyed and wild-bearded, but also wildly charismatic, attractive far beyond the physical attributes he had been granted. I would have stayed in his arms more happily than I hunched in his blanket, but the blanket was something: it was something. Baba Yaga left me be, making dinner herself, ground bone in dry bread, marrow and mutton to soften it. In time I ate what I was given, drank what there was to drink, and wondered at the dryness of my eyes. There should be tears, not hollowness, but perhaps time had muffled that as well.

"What did you see in the sunrise, daughter?"

"A rider." There was no sense to be had in not answering: Baba Yaga saw all, and I could not hide that I had seen something indeed. "A white rider, and at noon a red one and at night a black one. Who are they?"

Her black button eyes were wicked with interest. "They are my rising dawn, my love. My blazing sun and my darkest midnight, and they travel with me through all of my days."

"Why have I never seen them before?"

She clacked her iron teeth together and through them chattered, "You were a child." Then she pushed a book into my lap. A grimoire, bound by brass and locked with magic. She touched its lock and it snapped open, pages thickening and rustling as they were freed from compression. Power sparked within them, life and magic and secrets, all the things that I had known they contained, but had never felt in my bones. I had read this book and many others while I had lived in the chicken-legged hut, but they had been storybooks to me then. Now as I turned the pages they spoke to me, stirred me in my belly and beneath my skin. They told me how to draw power from the elements, from the wood and the metal and the sun and the stone, and with each turning page the emptiness inside me filled.

Filled with magic and with memory, clarity returning to me so that I knew the life I had led, so that I knew the faces and thoughts and touches of those who had shaped my childhood years. Again and again Grigori Rasputin, Baba Yaga's son, came to my mind, touching, guiding, caressing, so that I became a vessel for the power that he and his mother wielded. For the power that I too would wield, when my studies were done.

Baba Yaga left me again at dawn, but I did not care. I watched her go, saw the white rider in the sunrise again, then clutched Grigori's blanket around my shoulders and read further on. At noon I became hungry and set the book aside to find a meal.

And to see the red rider coming to me across the stream and over the fence of bones. He rode beautifully, as if he and his horse were one creature flowing sinuously toward me, until the horse was gone and the man was at the door, knocking thrice, and offering an insouciant grin when I opened it.

No. He was not a man on a horse at all, and I laughed that my eyes had ever seen him that way. There had been no horse, not ever, only the illusion of a creature too large to be a man for all that he walked in a man's shape. A man on a horse was all I had known to see him as at noon yesterday, but I saw more clearly now. He *was* red, though, red-haired with jade eyes, and a warm burnish to golden skin, and when I opened the door he said, "You are a jewel, the crown of the Russian empire, and I would like to woo you."

I could not help myself: I laughed. No man had ever said such a thing to me before, nor did I think one ever would again. "Would you, now?"

"I would," he said quite cheerfully, then looked back over his shoulder, returned his gaze to me, and still pleasantly, said, "but hastily, my dear, because Baba Yaga will eviscerate me if she finds me here."

I put my hand on his chest, keeping him from entering. I felt the heat in his blood, though his skin beneath his red red clothes was cool, and I said to him, "How does a witch, even such a witch as Baba Yaga, eviscerate a dragon?"

The sweetest pain I had ever seen crumpled the red dragon's face. Only for an instant, and then his jade eyes were merry again, and his sweet voice breathless: "The daughters of Baba Yaga will be my undoing. Let us say I don't care to risk it, my sweet. She's captured me once, and I'm still fool enough to cross the ocean and Russia's borders for the girl she calls her own. You are Ana—"

"Anna," I said firmly, because the other name belonged to a girl who had died and was not yet resurrected.

A beat of silence before he agreed: "Anna. You are not meant to have survived, Anna, so I couldn't resist returning when I learned Baba Yaga had another daughter."

"I am her only daughter."

Sorrow wrenched his face again. "Yes. Now you are."

Wariness crept up in me and I was glad I had not let him in. "What happened to the first?"

"I'm afraid I did. Myself and a friend of mine. But she happened to us first," and he spoke it not as an excuse, but as a matter of fact. "On the other hand, we sought her out, so we may have gotten what we deserved. Baba Yaga's daughters are not to be messed with."

I remained wary, but could not be afraid. "And still you came to me?"

He smiled, full of rue. "My heart demands it."

"You cannot possibly love me. We have never met."

"No," he said, so forthrightly it was impossible to be offended. "Love? No. But I can want you just for being what and who you are."

"A jewel in your hoard."

"A crowning jewel." He was a dragon: I knew that from my mother's grimoires, and from the new magic coming to life within me. He had no reason to apologize for that, nor, I found, did I have any reason to be affronted. I had no wish to be his jewel, but a certain delight pounded my heart and warmed my hands.

"Take me into the sky, then, my Blazing Sun. Fly me through the sun's arc and we shall see what you may have of me then."

A breath left him, quick and eager. He fell away from the door of Baba Yaga's hut, and the force of his transformation knocked the bone fence to the earth. He offered a great clawed hand, and I leapt from the door to his palm, then scrambled up to hold a red dragon between my legs.

He surged, flung himself skyward, and in a beat or two of mighty wings I saw the edges of mighty forests, the small villages nestled within them, the distant smudge of Moscow on the horizon. Higher, higher, he took us still, until all of Russia spread beneath me, and I thought *the other one did not fly so high*. That dream came back to me, the same powerful muscles beneath my body, the same rush of cool air tangling my hair. But he had been cautious, the white dragon who had taken me from the Bolsheviks and to Baba Yaga, whereas this red dragon flew as though he had no care in the world. He was power, raw and ready, where my white rider had been gentle and circumspect. I leaned forward, pressing my hands against and into flexing scales as though I could draw forth the heart of him, take the blazing sun's very heat into my hands and own it. Warmth flushed me, built inside me, and sizzled my skin. I raised my eyes to see that we flew so near the sun I could capture it in my hands. I reached, I stretched, I took it into me, a hot burst of pain and pleasure, and when we tumbled to the distant earth I lay tangled with a dragon, his cool flesh rich and gold against my milky white. He touched my breasts, my belly, kissed me and sought the pounding warmth between my thighs with eager fingers, but I caught his shoulders and held him away with the strength of a farm girl when he sought to put himself where his fingers had explored.

And then *he* was wary, though even in caution, humor lit jade eyes. "You do not," he enquired politely, "happen to have a red diamond necklace that you wish me to give me first, do you? No? That's something, at least." He rolled away when I pushed him, and lay beside me with an expression of curious interest. "I don't believe I've ever had a woman fly with me and then refuse me."

"Will you eat me now?"

A sly look came over his face, and though I had not lain with a man, an idea of what he was thinking came over me, and I laughed. Then he stood and offered his hands, and we flew together back to Baba Yaga's hut, where the burning sun faded toward the twilight hour. "I'll wait as long as I dare," he said to me as I climbed the chicken legs up to the hut. "I'll come again tomorrow at noon, and perhaps you'll have me then."

I said, "Perhaps," though I had no intention of falling to the red dragon's wiles, and then I went inside to make my mother's dinner.

But she was late in returning, which surprised me not at all. I watched for her at the door as the night grew darker, as dark as it ever did in a Russian summertime, and I was not surprised, again, when a rider came out of the dark.

Not a rider, again, no, nor a dragon to be mistaken for one. Blackness followed this one like an insect's wings, buzzing and beating the air. He moved quickly, far too quickly for the eye to follow, and that was what lent *him* the illusion of being a rider's size. He could be everywhere at once, so that the eye saw him as larger than he was. Not until he stood at the door did he stop his mad flickering motion and let me see him for what he was.

A plain man, not like the blazing sun-red dragon, but then a man of darkest midnight came in cover of darkness and had no need for beauty. "I suppose you wish for me to be a jewel in your crown as well," I said to him, and he chuckled.

"No. The blood in my veins, perhaps, but not a jewel in a crown. That's for dragons—" and then he breathed in deeply and murmured, "Dragons," again. "You know one, then."

"He has come to me," I agreed, and the small dark man pursed his lips.

"So high?" he asked, and lifted a hand to the height of the red dragon's human form. "With copper hair and jade eyes?" When I nodded, he muttered, "*Curse* him," and then with wry humor, "at least he's not at home trying to seduce Vanessa. Though if he knows I'm here he may betray me to her—" He ceased his ruminations and met my gaze again with a trace of amusement. "Forgive me. I shouldn't be worrying about the woman at home when I have one in front of me."

"You cannot think to seduce me," I half-asked in astonishment. "Not when you stand here and speak of the wife at home."

He winced. "Companion. But no, you're right. Will you walk with me, Baba Yaga's daughter?" He offered me his arm, a gentlemanly gesture.

I had known gestures like that in my past life, and now found it left me cold and alone. My answer came slowly, unconsidered enough to surprise me, but not so hasty as to offer insult in return for chivalry. "No. No, I think I will not. There is something you want of me, and I have no wish to play at games. For what you desire, I desire something in exchange."

"And what is that?"

I extended my wrist, bare and strong. "For my blood, your own. Two sips. One for health, one for life."

He went still, so very very still. Men did not go so still, could not be so motionless. Even if his fluid motion, his quickness that made him seem larger than he could be, had not betrayed him, the stillness would. It lasted only a moment, but I knew then that I was right, that the hunger for blood was born in him, and that mine was a potent cocktail indeed. So too was his, though, and when he spoke again it was on a breath: "You know a great deal, Baba Yaga's daughter."

"I would be no daughter of my mother if I did not."

He took my hand then, and drew my wrist to his mouth. Not to bite, as I might have thought, but to kiss, soft and sensual and in thanks. Then he moved closer to me, his breath warm on my neck, so much warmer than the dragon, whom I might have expected to be hot-blooded. "Close your eyes, Baba Yaga's daughter."

Perhaps I should not have, but I did. Mother's grimoires claimed no one looked on a vampire in its true, feeding form, and survived. Perhaps the books of magic were wrong, and my blood, exotic mix of royalty and witchery, might be enough to save me. But perhaps not, and in truth I had no wish to see the thing that drank my blood, for all that the pain above my pulse was sweet, and the warmth that flooded me was comforting. Warmth, when I should grow cold, but the vampire grew warmer with each swallow, and I could feel no chill while in his arms.

Only when I was dizzy did he release me, and bend his head to his own wrist. My blood, his own: it welled together and he pressed it to my mouth. *One sip for healing*: the wounds on my throat were gone before I drew a new breath. The vampire's blood was sweet, sugar-sweet, and thicker than mortal blood. I licked my lips and drank again: *two sips for life.* Rarest of gifts, immortality from an immortal. But I lifted my head and spat the last of his blood away, making certain not to swallow, for I remembered what my mother's books warned: *three sips to die.*

"A jewel in the crown I understand," I said then, "but blood is ephemeral, it is renewed and dies within the body. So why?"

He smiled. "Because blood is everything, witch's daughter, daughter of queens. Humans have never really understood that, but blood is everything. Blood is all. I thank you for the gift of yours."

He was gone before the words were: they lingered in his wake, and I stood in their portents a long while before I turned back to my duties, cleaning the house and making my mother's dinner. She looked me up and looked at me down when she returned, then sat and ate her meal before she spoke. "The blazing sun and darkest night have touched you, but I see no mark of the rising dawn."

Cleverness came into my tongue, and I remembered that I had been thought witty before I died. More than witty: sharp, and even cruel. "The blazing sun is all the power of life, and the darkest night all the depths of treachery. Who I am and who I was have no need for the encroaching light and hope that is the rising dawn."

My mother said, "Then you are ready," and slew me with an obsidian blade.

She slew me and yet I lived, my heart contracting around black glass. I lay naked, bound with leather straps across the hut's floor, my ankles and wrists spread wide as if to open me to the rising sun beyond the door.

A thing, a terrible thing, crawled toward me from beneath a blanket. From beneath the baby blanket that had *Grigori* embroidered on it, and I saw with horror that the hunched and wretched mess approaching me had once been my dear friend.

He bled from so many wounds: gunshot, knife stab, cut throat, unmanned. Poison foamed at his mouth, and drowning water gurgled in his throat. His skull was bashed in, and all of his body was blackened and shriveled with fire: no less would murder Baba Yaga's son, and now it seemed not even that had been enough. She capered around me, iron teeth clacking and long nails clicking as she encouraged the dreadful thing that was Rasputin to claw his way toward me. Onto me, a sticky cold bloody mass at my ankle and inching its way up my body.

Too late, too late, it took little imagination to understand why Baba Yaga might want a tsarina. Surely if anything might restore her son it might be the very blood of Russia herself, and now that blood had been filled with the magic that Baba Yaga lived by. She crooned, "Yes, and yes, and yes, my son. Crawl within her, have her as your own, seek her flesh with yours and become one, be reborn, my child!"

I should be afraid. Afraid of the coming violation, afraid of the magics worked by a mad witch, afraid of the shambling piece of flesh that had once been a friend. I should be afraid of the encroaching dawn which I so callously dismissed, and afraid of the moment of transition between night and day that will no doubt spell my doom.

Instead I am enraged.

It begins in the core of me, where the vampire's blood still lends me heat. It begins in the back of my eyes, a white fury that blinds me to all else. It begins in my hands, clenched against their leather bonds as if I might drag them from the floor. It begins in the very soul of me, and it whispers *Twice.*

Twice. Twice unwanted in favor of a son.

My wrath bursts forth, and a dragon destroys Baba Yaga's chicken-legged hut.

I WAS NOT CERTAIN I hadn't conjured the beast, though at the same time I knew him: my white knight, the rider of the rising dawn, no more a figment of imagination than the red rider or the black. Less so, for my life was his, a gift from a creature so vast it astonished me he had ever noticed me. Yes, even as a tsarina, I could be surprised that I had drawn a man's eye, much less this man, this beautiful white man with his red eyes and his fiery breath.

The hut's straw roof was aflame, the walls scattered and the bones that lay beyond all knocked askew. Rasputin mewled and sobbed, a pathetic lump of dying bones while the white dragon flew into the sky with Baba Yaga in his claws.

And I, I was free, with an ache in my arms and thighs that said I had snapped the leather that still dangled from wrist and ankle. I seized the mortar that was my mother's flying roost. I lifted it and drove it down once. Again. Again. Again. With each blow the Rasputin-thing became less than it was, a broken bloody smear of white and red. The mortar tugged in my hands, trying to escape, but I held it fast with will and magic, and smashed Rasputin again.

Baba Yaga crashed to the earth beside the ruined hut, splashing so deep into mud and muck that she made a crater of her own, and did not rise from it.

The white dragon flung himself from the sky, and snapped the broken bloody bits of Grigori Rasputin into his jaws. He met my eyes, and swallowed.

For an instant the world was silent. There was nothing in it but myself and my dragon lover, his eyes hot and hungry on mine. I went to him in solemnity, touched his broad white chest and reached for his long whiskered face. He transformed then, a tremendous inward rush of air that left me breathless. We were naked in each other's arms, eager in the face of death, and he no less claimed me than I claimed him. Raw and perfect passion, long since sparked and only now able to be consummated, for had I been anything less than I was now, he would have destroyed me, and had he been anything more, he would not have given that self up by feasting on Baba Yaga's son. Even now I felt Rasputin's power in him, burning hot and fierce but forever contained by a magic wholly different from human witchery. "Rumi," he whispered against my skin, a name to call him by. A name to possess him by, so that he might retain himself and still contain the warlock within.

"Rumi," I gave back, and did not say my own name. He knew it well enough, and there would be time enough later, when the rest was dealt with.

They were polite enough not to arrive until our need, the first flush of need, had been sated. It did not take long, which is as well: neither of them were patient, and my lover and I were still entangled when the vampire appeared bearing iron and wood and stone.

I paid him little mind: it was the red dragon falling from the sky who interested me more, because it was he who interested Rumi.

But the red dragon no longer cared for me at all: it was my mother, feeble in the pit of her own making, who held his attention. The vampire blurred, weighting her down with chains as he snarled, "Bound by iron, drowned by water, pierced by wood. Burned by fire—" and the red dragon drew breath for flame.

"*No!*" I flung my hand out, and the white power of a Russian night crashed forth. It caught the red dragon's throat, seized his fire, and the vampire sped toward me.

But I am immovable, intransigent, immutable. I am the last heir of Russia, and Baba Yaga is my mother. My bones are this country's earth, my blood its waters.

My breath is the wind that caresses its never-ending miles, my body the land upon which my people tread.

I am Russia, and not even a vampire can destroy me.

The black one bounced off me as though he had hit a wall, and even in his speed I saw the astonishment in his eyes.

The red dragon slammed into his mortal form, beautiful slim red-haired man, and spoke: "Have you lost your mind, girl? Do you know what she'll do to you? To us? We've killed her son!"

Baba Yaga's cackle rose from the mud-filled pit she was contained within. "A son, a son, what is a son when now I have a *daughter?* A son is nothing to a daughter, and I was old and blind to not see what I had been given in you, my child. Free me, daughter, my daughter, my Anna. Together we will teach these monsters the meaning of human magic."

Instead I said, "Go."

My mother screamed, but the dragon and the vampire wisely took one step away. Neither could resist, though. They looked at one another, then back to me, and voiced the question as one: "Why?"

"Because you have wakened in me the power to live, and because the witch belongs to Russia. Go," I said again, "and never return. I will know, and my amnesty will not last."

"What about *him,*" the red dragon said, and pointed petulantly at the other. At the white dragon, my dragon, my Rumi, gentle and ferocious, who had come to save me, treasure in his trove, from the revolutionaries. Who had come in the dawn to stop his enemy from slaughtering his love, and who now burned inside with the gobbled-up power of Grigori Rasputin, son of Russia, son of the Russian witch. He was greater now than he had been, an ancient dragon impregnated with human magic, and my body craved his touch.

I answered without thinking what it might mean to a dragon: "He is mine."

Shock, and perhaps envy, blanked the red dragon's face. Then he spoke another tongue, a deep growling language that had no business coming from a man's chest, and my white dragon sneered both fear and acquiescence. Not loss, though; not regret, and that was a great gift to me, for though I had not been meant to, I had understood what one dragon said to the other:

"Dragons are collectors, not the collected. Stay with her if you wish, but never imagine you are welcome among our people so long as you belong to a human."

But I am not human, I wished to say. *I have died twice and am daughter and mother to Russia. A dragon is my only worthy consort.* I did not say it, though, because the red dragon had told me something he did not mean to. *Our people.* They were not the only ones, these two dragons. My mother's grimoires had spoken of so many others, others she called *Old Races,* and had captured so many in their pages that I had thought they were nothing more than stories caught on paper. But no, there were two standing before me, and a third at my side, and many more in the world besides.

It was a sweet secret, rich with potential. They had lost much: so had I. Someday we might find a common ground.

"Go," I said one final time. I knew myself now. I had passed through death and rebirth. I had cast aside being Anna, but had become Baba Yaga's daughter, the daughter of Russia herself. "This is your order from the last Tsarina, from the mother and queen of all Russia. Go, and do not return."

And because I knew myself now, I reclaimed the name that had once been mine, and had no need to shout the last words, only whisper them with all the power of a witch: "So commands Anastasia."

Chicago Bang Bang

A MAN WITH A GUN BURST into the restaurant and shot Eliseo Daisani in the chest.

Dames everywhere screamed. Men bellowed. Daisani flew ass over teakettle, knocked halfway across the room as more bullets flew. Not just a gun, then: a Tommy gun, shining black and gleaming wood, fully automatic, tossing .45 calibre cartridges like they were shots of whiskey.

Even a guy like me thinks that's overkill, for just one man.

The broad with Daisani was the only one not screaming. She was a looker, if you like 'em hard around the edges. Wearing her hair long and soft couldn't hide that. But she had a body that wouldn't quit, and I can tell you that from personal experience. While everybody else was dodging bullets and hiding under furniture, she crawled toward her man, not giving a damn about what the gleaming hardwood floors might do to her grey satin gown. Grey: that was her name, Vanessa Grey, and that was the color she liked to wear. Dolls are funny that way.

Now this is the thing not a soul at that restaurant admits to seeing: Eliseo Daisani, mob boss and socialite lying there, his chest ripped to pieces, while the gun moll in the grey dress bit open her own wrist and fed him blood.

Maybe nobody saw it. With feathers from the upholstery flying and bullets still in the air, I'm not saying that's impossible. But if I'd seen it? I'd have forgotten quicker than you could say Jack Sprat. That kind of memory could shorten your lifespan considerably. Nobody heard her talking to him, either, using language a nice girl shouldn't, and giving a dangerous man what-for.

"Don't be stupid," is what they didn't hear. "Forty people just saw you take at least one bullet in the chest. You *cannot* just get up and kill the man, not if you want to stay in Chicago. Not if you ever want to come back to Chicago, and I will not be exiled from my home town, Eliseo. Heal most of it if you want, but you're going to the hospital and you're going to take weeks to recooperate, just like a normal person. I'll deal with this. Now lie down and play dead."

And if nobody heard that, well, by the time an ambulance got there, nobody was counting the bullet holes in Daisani's tuxedo, either. There was only one in *him*, and that was bad enough.

As for the tough with the gun, he was slick, but not slick enough. He backed out of the restaurant right into the cops' arms, and nobody thinks it was coincidence he got a bullet in the chest, too. The only thing dirtier than the cops in this town is the water.

I got all of this later, straight from the horse's mouth, not that a catch like Grey oughta be called a horse. But I'm the kind of fella a smart dame goes to when she's in trouble, and let me tell you, there couldn't have been a happier man in the world when she darkened my door.

The words *Private Investigator* were etched on the glass of that door. Used to be it'd said *Pinkerton Agency,* but they were too square for me. I'd had the glass replaced. I liked the way it looked, and I liked that there was no name on it. People who needed me didn't need a name. They needed a gumshoe, and most of 'em didn't want to know any more about me than that. To this day I figure Grey chose my door to walk through because a man without a name is easier than most to disappear, and once you've taken on Eliseo Daisani as a case, chances are you'll end up disappeared.

I knew what she saw when she stepped through my door. The lights were low, leeching color from the room. I was a shadow in the shadows, collar of my trench coat up and fedora pulled low over my eyes. A cigarette dangled from my lips, and hazy smoke in the room said a thousand like it had already been inhaled. Not even a glow lingered at its tip to highlight the lines of my face. It was better that way: even the clientele didn't need to have too clear an idea of what I looked like.

You hear her tell it now, she stopped in the door and said "You have *got* to be kidding." Me, I remember it better than that. I remember those dark eyes of hers, all anger and sadness. I remember the blood on her dress, smelling like a woman's chosen scent. I remember the way she crossed the room, looking like a drink of water in the desert. I remember the press of her body against mine as she whispered, "You're the only one who can help me now."

Doesn't matter who remembers it true. I remember it *better.*

It takes a stronger man than me to turn down a pretty woman when she says something like that, especially when he's been waiting a long time to hear it. I got the story from her, all the sordid details as she wrung her hands and paced the room. I had a healthy appreciation for that, too: satin shimmered and shone in all the right places. The look she gave me said that wasn't what she was here for, but maybe I read a promise or a hope in that desperate gaze. That was for later, though. Now we had business to discuss. "So what do you want me to do about it, doll?"

"Find out which of the bosses is gunning for Eliseo."

"And then what?"

She looked me up and down, fierce and bold as a broad can be, and said, "Eat him."

NOW THERE'S TWO PROBLEMS with a request like that. One is not even Daisani's doxy could pay me enough to eat a man. Long pig, nothing: humans are greasy and the bones stick in my teeth. At least, that's how I recalled it, and I wasn't in any hurry to see if I remembered right.

The other reason, and this was bigger news, was that Chicago was somebody else's territory. Even on the best day, eating someone on somebody else's grounds was rude, but as it happened, Chicago's dark mistress wasn't any too fond of me. I wasn't so much there on her sufferance as without her knowledge. And there's not a dragon in the world who can transform to his serpentine form without alerting the others in the area.

I should know. If anyone could do it, it'd be me. So I looked Grey up and down and said "No can do, doll. Got a second choice?"

She smiled, and I thought maybe this lady had been hanging out with a vampire too long. Something had happened to the smile I remembered from yesteryear. Something bad. I wish I was surprised when she said, "Then bring him to me."

I had a clear idea of what she might do in the name of love and revenge. Things we all did, maybe, except once upon a time, Vanessa Grey had been human. Sharp-witted and good at cards, but human. I wondered if this is what the Old Races did to humans they loved: made them more like themselves. There were proscriptions against dallying with mortals. We didn't have many laws, but that was a big one. I figured it was to protect them as much as us.

But introspection was for gargoyles, and I had a beautiful woman waiting on my answer. I turned my hand up, scraping fire from a fingertip to light the cigarette. "You ready to bring down the whole Chicago scene on your head, doll?"

"Chicago can't handle me."

I believed her, but no PI in his right mind would say that to a dame. "It's your funeral."

"No." She smiled again, that sharp smile born from living too long. It made her dangerous. Dangerous, and a little more provocative than a guy should find somebody else's doll to be. "It's theirs."

Nothing's ever that simple. Truth is, you can't throw a rock in this town without hitting somebody who wants somebody else dead. It only gets more complicated when you throw my kind into the mix. Technically, we ain't allowed to kill each other. For the most part, we don't. There was that dust-up with the vampires right here in Chicago back in the '70s, but even Daisani agreed they had it coming. I lost a lot that night. Some days I think it's why I'm here now, doing what I'm doing. Other days I don't kid myself. In a life as long as mine, playing the same role over and over gets boring. Sometimes it's fun to be the good guy.

Not that Grey would believe that.

Not that I'd want her to.

So just to be sure, I said, "How do you know it wasn't me, sweetheart?"

She took the cigarette from my lips. Broke it in half and smeared it under the sole of an expensive shoe. "Because you're not a power here. Not this time. Maybe not ever, with Serafina Drake still lurking in the sewers. You don't have any reason to force Eliseo out, and you know that's the most shooting him can do. You certainly wouldn't be trying to kill him with a gun, if you wanted him dead."

I had to hand it to her. She was smart. I was about to speak, but what she said next shut me up: "So it's not you, and it's probably not one of us at all."

It was the kind of silence you could hear a pin drop in. We stared at each other across the desk, me the dragon slinking around in human form, her the human who'd just elevated herself to equal with the Old Races. I said, "Us."

Vanessa Grey put both hands on the desk and let her head drop.

I'd known the woman more than two decades. Not once had she ever let her guard down that much around me. She didn't dare. We both understood the reasons. So did Eliseo. But for the first time, Daisani wasn't between us.

Dragons covet beauty, and things they can't have. I waited, heart in my throat, to see which way this coin would fall.

"Us," she said after a long time. "People who know about the Old Races. People like me. People like that bookseller."

"Chelsea." Chelsea Huo was a whole 'nother kettle of fish, but that wasn't something Grey needed to know. "That really what you meant?"

She lifted her gaze to mine. Cold, for all that eyes that dark should always seem warm. Maybe that was what Eliseo liked about her. But I was the cold-blooded one, and maybe like called to like. "Give it up. You'll never win this prize."

I smiled. Anybody else would have backed off. Anybody else wouldn't like the too-long canines. Grey didn't care. She'd seen it all before. That kept me smiling. "If I help you, you'll owe me a favor. I'll claim the prize I want."

"No." There was something about being refused by a woman. Something intriguing, even after all this time. Grey straightened, a vision in satin. "I'll pay cash, the going rate, or I walk out the door. A bum like you can't turn down that offer."

She was right. I couldn't. Not because of the cash.

Because Eliseo Daisani was *my* rival. Nobody else got to horn in on that.

She saw the decision in my eyes. I thought she might invite herself along while I sleuthed. I might have even wanted her to. But she took a step back, became a shimmer in the shadows, and reminded me: "I want him, when you find him."

I put a hand over my heart. "Whatever the lady wants."

For that, I earned a smile. With Grey, the smiles were everything. They were the admission I'd landed a hit. That the flirting and the teasing weren't completely unnoticed. When you're angling for somebody else's dame, it's the little things that count. "I'll call when I've got news."

She nodded, silhouetted as the door closed behind her. I listened to her footsteps fade away, and then I stood, a smile on my face. Hunting down killers and thieves was a job, but this: *this* would be fun.

GREY HAD ONE THING right: it probably wasn't one of us. That didn't stop me from padding into Chinatown in search of a certain bookseller. They knew me in that part of the city, and not just as a gumshoe. I'd never shown myself, but for some of 'em, I didn't have to. Humans weren't entirely stupid. Sometimes they recognized the impossible on a level they didn't even think about. It seemed to happen more in Chinatowns, like the Oriental knack for capturing our likenesses bled over into life. Or maybe that was just my fancy. Maybe I just felt more comfortable in my own skin in Chinatowns.

Truth is, you don't want a dragon feeling too comfortable. It's magic that lets us hold a human shape, but a shadow of all that mass follows us around. The more comfortable—or the angrier—we get, the more of that mass starts to throw itself around. Could be nobody had a hint of what I was at all. Could be I just had too much presence, and that would get me one of two things: respect, or dead. And dead was harder than it looked.

I swept into Chelsea's bookstore feeling full of myself and knocked over a stack of books taller than I was. Dust drifted up and I sneezed. Another tower toppled. I held still, trying to reel in some of that self-satisfaction. Anybody who knows me can tell you that's not an easy thing to do. But a third pile of books only wobbled, didn't collapse.

Chelsea Huo appeared from between floor-to-ceiling shelves, mouth pinched acerbically. "Don't you dare come in here again all puffed up like that, young man. Now pick up those books."

No one on earth could call me young and mean it. Not even an apple-wizened Asian lady who never answered a question straight. I picked up the books anyway. "You gotta get bigger premises."

"These are exactly the right size." Chelsea didn't help me clean up my mess. Instead she headed for the back, and after a minute I smelled tea brewing. That was as much invitation as I'd get. Books restored, I squeezed through the shelves and ducked under a low door into a peaceful back room.

I'd never known her to have anything other than a tiny bookstore and a tiny back room with a potted tea tree growing in one corner. The details of the back room changed, but Chelsea and the tea tree stayed the same. I sat down in a horsehair chair—Chelsea always had furniture you slid off—and she handed me a cup of tea I knew better than to refuse. A shot of whiskey couldn't disguise the flavor, even if she'd let me tip one in. "So who's in town I don't know about?"

Almond eyes gave me a stern look over the edge of her teacup. "I wouldn't stay in business long if I just handed that information out, dear boy. I take it you heard about Eliseo."

"Grey came to me."

The woman's feathery eyebrows shot toward a distant straight hairline. "Now that is a surprise. That might even be worth trading on itself."

I cursed myself a fool. Chelsea—helped. Helped the Old Races get by in a world peopled by men. Helped arrange meetings between factions who didn't speak in public. Helped by spreading one bit of information to somebody else. I wasn't sure anybody liked Chelsea Huo, but we needed her, and maybe, just maybe, we loved her. It was almost human of us.

And she was right. Vanessa Grey coming to me was a valuable piece of information. It meant maybe the woman who'd been in Daisani's camp for five decades could be bargained with now.

I knew better. She'd been looking for a PI, not a dragonlord. It was her bad luck and my good fortune that she'd walked through my door. But even if Chelsea knew that—and I would lay good odds she did—the important thing was, nobody else did. So I tried to look like I'd offered that tidbit up on purpose. I even took a sip of tea to be polite. I could play along. "So what's it worth to you?"

"You're looking for Mario Campanelli," Chelsea said, which meant it was worth enough. "Have you met him?"

I put my tea down. "No. The Campanelli syndicate wants Daisani dead? Why? He's a new face in town, not even a threat yet."

The woman had a dry look that parched a man just by glancing at him. "Do you wait for newcomers to become threats, yourself?"

"'Course not, but I don't do it so showy, not unless there's a statem..." A near-invisible smile twitched Chelsea's thin mouth, and a million pieces fell into place. None of us would go after Daisani with a gun, Grey had said. None of us, unless he was making a statement.

I knew a thing or two about statements. "...have *you* met Campanelli?"

"I have."

The last piece fell into place. "Son of a *bitch*."

I forgot to thank Chelsea for my tea on my way out the door. That was a mistake I'd pay for later.

Much later, as it turned out.

THERE'S A CERTAIN STILLNESS that marks the Old Races facing off. Part of it is we're inhuman. Nothing mortal can go quiet like we can. You'd think the gargoyles, who turn to stone, would be the best at it, but it's the vampires who are really eerie. Their gift is speed, so when they stop moving it's like the earth standing still. Normally it's so brief humans don't notice.

They noticed this time.

Some of that was me. The presence I mentioned before. The largeness that doesn't fit in a single man. I filled too much of the pool hall when I walked in. That disturbed even the least sensitive of Campanelli's thugs.

Lucky for them, I was there for Campanelli. I knew it and so did he. Our eyes met across the room. He went still. All other sound faded away. People cleared a path. It was the whole shabang. Coulda been romantic, if he hadn't been trying to kill my partner.

"You don't belong here, Dick." Emphasis on the last word, like being a PI was a bad thing. Italian-American accent, about as real as my own Chicago bang-bang slang. Good-looking fella. Small. Most vampires were.

I put on my best smile, the one that makes humans nervous even though they don't know why. It's the teeth, too long and too pointed, like vampire legends. But real vampires have flat teeth. Campanelli smiled back, proving it, and everybody backed up another couple paces. Me, I took a step forward, and let the weight of my attention land on Campanelli's men.

The women I've known have described it the same way every time. When a dragon transfers his attention, it's like he moves suddenly. Like force rippling down a cable. When I say *the weight of my attention,* I mean it. It knocked into Campanelli's boys like they were ninepins, and the smart ones scattered.

There were more smart ones than I expected. The dumb and ambitious held on a few seconds longer, until Campanelli flicked his fingers. Then they disappeared too, scents lingering: booze, smoke, perfume, blood. All familiar in one way or another. He spoke, same words as before, but this time they were thoughtful, not a threat: "You don't belong here."

I could see him trying to figure what that meant. I didn't want him to get too cozy with whatever he was thinking, so I interrupted with a mouthful of true:

"Getting Daisani off the board is one thing. Trying to kill his human persona in public, that's something else. That's making a bad enemy. Why do it?"

Mario Campanelli stood and sauntered to the bar. I knew a saunter when I saw one: it was my kind of walk. Vampires didn't usually dilly-dally around with that sort of thing. They got more effect by whooshing up, muttering something cryptic, and disappearing again before your heart even had a chance to jump. Then if they weren't gonna kill you, they'd stand back and listen to the way it jumped when they were gone. Daisani said it was a thrill that never got old. I believed him.

But Campanelli sauntered. Poured us each a drink—red wine for him, about as affected as you could get—and whiskey for me. Keeping us in the roles we'd assumed. I liked that. But I still wanted answers. I took the tumbler, raised it in thanks, and waited.

"When was the last time you saw a vampire?"

Whatever I'd expected, that wasn't it. Campanelli knew it, too: an ugly smile slid over his handsome mug, and now *he* waited while I thought it out. He didn't mean Daisani, and he didn't mean him. He meant any other vampire.

Now here's the thing about the Old Races. There were never millions of us. Not like humans. Even back when we were this world's dominant sentients, we lived too long and bred too slow to be that populous. Now what numbers we once boasted have been cut down by human expansion. It'd be a miracle if there are two thousand dragons left. I don't believe in miracles.

And there were more of us than there were of the vampires. Good thing, too: one vampire will wipe out a herd, a city—a whole species, sometimes. They don't do it for food. Mostly they're like human children: *it seemed like a good idea at the time* is reason enough. If there had ever been even tens of thousands of vampires, life wouldn't have evolved the way it did. That woulda been a shame: no pretty ladies like Vanessa Grey to while away the years with.

So you didn't see vampires often, just because there weren't many. I'd almost never seen more than a handful at once. Back in Rome, yeah: the decadence drew them like moths to fire. Here and there across the ages, they gathered where the pickings were lush and the people high-spirited. America in the twenties should have been big with the vampires, or London in the Gay Nineties.

Should have been, but now that Campanelli made me think about it, they hadn't turned out in force. They hadn't turned out at *all*.

"Chicago," I said, a long damned time after he'd asked. "Right here, sixty years ago. That's the last time I saw a vampire."

"We've all gone missing." Every word stood on its own. Campanelli had red wine at the corner of his mouth, like blood. "All but me. Daisani. Maybe a few others."

"Van Helsing. Dracula. Everybody knows the stories now. You're the stuff of talking pictures, Campanelli. Maybe they got smart and went underground."

Thing was, vampires didn't get smart. Daisani called himself the master of his kind. If he was, it was because he could control his impulses. Campanelli was running a mob syndicate, which meant he had to be the same sort. There's a few oddballs in every family, I guess. But as a whole? Not a chance. Vampires don't retreat.

Which meant something or someone had happened to them. "Van Helsing," I said again. "Almost the greatest vampire hunter mankind's ever had."

A nasty fluidity happened around Campanelli's jaw. The bones went soft, distending, before he got them back under control. "Almost?"

Blonde hair. Green eyes. An adventuresome demeanor almost crushed beneath convention. A hundred memories flashed through my mind, but I shook my head. "Nevermind. What's shooting Daisani got to do with this?"

"Self-preservation. Whatever's been hunting us, I want at least one more vampire between it and me."

"And you think a mook with a Tommy gun is the way to do that?"

Pain crept across Campanelli's face. Emotional pain, the kind of bone-deep wince you get from dealing with a moron. He took another sip of wine. "He was supposed to be using wooden slugs."

Everybody knew wooden stakes killed vampires in the pictures. *Nothing* I knew killed 'em in the real world. I almost said that. Almost, but I shut up just in time. This was information. More than I'd known before. Maybe more than Chelsea knew. If Campanelli was going after Daisani with wooden slugs, there was something to the myth.

It might seem strange a guy as old as I am doesn't know how to kill a vampire. On the other hand, they don't advertise it. I'd only learned recently you could imprison a dragon, and I *am* one. So vampires still having secrets wasn't such a surprise. What I did know was they're too fast to take down easily, and they don't *stay* down. That's the shapeshifting: it heals all of us to some degree, but vampires are masters at it. Subtle changes, not the big wallop of going from man to monster. It keeps them alive through injuries that would take out a gargoyle or even a dragon. If they get in a fight that bad, it takes buckets of blood to whip them back into shape after. Chances are their opponent will provide it, too.

"Still," I said, casual as I could. "Taking him out in a public place like that? Even if they'd been wooden slugs—"

Campanelli bared his teeth. He wanted to talk, and I was in no hurry to stop him. "I was there. I was *waiting.* I had the iron, and that would hold even Daisani until I could bury him."

Iron. Earth. Wood. A human's heart would've given him away by now. I was cold-blooded with a slow heartbeat to match. I'd never been so grateful for that. "And nobody woulda seen you snatch him. You're that fast."

He sneered an agreement. Truth was, all vampires were that fast. No harm in letting him think a little more of himself, though. Not when he was confessing the elements to bind a vampire. "But the idiot used normal bullets, and that *bitch* wouldn't leave his side. I'd just wanted Daisani, but now."

My ears were ringing. Somebody said "Don't be hasty," in a tone I recognized. Teasing. Compliant. Unctuous. It was me. Snake-oil salesman voice, the kind that so many marks fell for. "Dame that loyal can be good for more than just killing. With her at your side, you could walk right into Daisani's hospital room. Offer your condolences, straight-up and narrow. Put a wooden slug in his chest *then.* Let her see the mistake she's made before she dies."

Campanelli frowned. "They couldn't stop me getting in anyway. I'm too fast."

Vampires. I wanted to hold my head. Instead I lit a cigarette off one fingertip and waved the fag suggestively. "Sure, but what fun is that? Better yet, I can make you look official. Show up with a PI, everybody knows somebody's got dirt on Daisani. You and me are the only ones who gotta know he's going *in* the dirt. I'll make it up proper. Hire a hearse, put a coffin in the back for him."

"Yeah? You gonna bring the cistern of holy water, too?"

My gut clenched. Iron. Wood. Dirt. *Water*. Elements of earth, to bind a race that claimed they weren't from this world at all. I held my cool by the skin of my teeth. "Sure. Not like it'll burn me."

"Why would you do that?"

I leveled my best stare at him. "You got any idea how long Daisani and me have been going around, kid?"

Here's the answer: he took it when I called him *kid*. I nodded once and put a hand out. "Helping you out will rattle his cage. And you'll owe me one. I like that."

Campanelli considered that a minute, then walked over and took my hand.

I transformed.

IT WAS STUPID. CHICAGO was Fina's town. Now she'd know I was here. But there are things a man doesn't mess with, and a guy's arch-rival is one of them. So inside a breath I blew my cover, destroyed two floors of a downtown pool hall, and caught myself a vampire.

Poor bastard never stood a chance. Maybe the concussion of air coulda knocked him away, but I had a grip on him already. A grip that turned from a handshake to a flattening. Like I said, vampires are usually small. Campanelli fit under my palm, gold-tipped claws pinning him in place just in case. I reached out with the other hand—they were a hell of a lot more dexterous than paws—and took one of the splintered ceiling beams down with claw tips. Tilted my head to examine Campanelli, then did something a dragon's throat wasn't meant to do: spoke English.

"Grey? You want to do the honors?"

She was quiet long enough I almost thought I was wrong. Almost. But a nose like mine doesn't lie, and Daisani's blood was still on her dress. She came in, hair tumbled loose from its waves so she was no longer sleek and composed the way she'd been when she'd walked through my door. Her eyes were wide and she was quiet. Real quiet. After a minute I knew why.

She'd never seen a dragon before.

For twenty years I'd been trying to make the woman's heart race. Not with fear: that was easy. With desire. For twenty years she'd just barely humored me. Tonight, finally, I got what I was after. Shallow breath, pupil-eaten eyes, quick heart. She shed her shoes and climbed barefoot over my crimson coils while I watched her with one jade eye. Her weight was barely there, not even an itch. She walked along my spine to my shoulder, and slid down my forearm in a rush of satin whispers. Glanced at Campanelli, then met my gaze with a softness and a hunger I'd never thought she possessed. Then she put a hand beneath my nostrils, like I was a horse of immense proportion. I huffed. She laughed, bright trill of sound, and all of a sudden I knew Vanessa Grey better than I ever had. I knew what it was that kept her with Eliseo.

And I knew why I could never hold her attention, when he could.

She liked a little monster in her man. Eliseo Daisani could be both at once. Dragons, no matter what lay within, were one or the other in physical form. That would never be enough for her.

But just for a minute there, we were in love.

Then she reached for the splinter I'd pulled from the wreckage. It was nearly as tall as she was. She took it in both hands and stepped toward Campanelli. He was screaming. Probably had been all along. It didn't matter. Not to me, not then. I was too busy being crazy for this dame, this lady I would never have, as she lifted the stake and slammed it into Campanelli's chest.

Neither of us expected him to keep on screaming. His whole body shuddered, trying like mad to change shape. To prepare to feed, but the wood held him bound to human form. Vanessa looked at me with an arched eyebrow. I shrugged a massive shoulder. She copied it, small and delicate, then tipped her head toward an exposed iron girder. "Wrap him up in a couple of those. Then dig. I don't want to leave him here, but we're going to need a gargoyle to help move him. I'll call Biali."

Campanelli screamed until the dirt filled his mouth. I shoved a slab of concrete over his grave and became a man again. Grey's hair blew all around a second time from the force of air changing. Disarray looked good on her. Maybe that's why she never let herself look that way. "There are local gargoyles." It wasn't what I wanted to say. But she wouldn't want to hear what I wanted to say.

Her eyebrows went up again. "Can you trust them?"

Sometimes broads were smarter than me. "Call Biali."

"That's what I thought. Thank you for your help. I'll send you your money through Western Union. Just let me know where you go."

"Go?" The lady had brass balls, I'd give her that. "What makes you think I'm going anywhere, doll?"

"This is Serafina Drake's town," she reminded me, "and now she knows you're here. Considering what happened last time, I don't think she's going to be happy to see you."

"You weren't even *there* last time."

"Does that mean I'm wrong?"

She wasn't wrong and I knew it. I also knew the smart thing would be to walk out the door, climb a building, and take to the skies from there. But I couldn't help it. I transformed again, catching Grey in one huge clawed hand so she wouldn't fly across the room. Then I set her back on her bare feet and turned that hand palm up. An invitation.

Grey smiled. Then she shook her head and stepped back, arms folded across her chest. There was just a hint of sympathy in her eyes. A hint of regret. I nodded, and left her there with—just this once, just for tonight—the pieces of my broken heart.

But that's Chicago, kid.

The Age of Aquarius

THERE IS A MADNESS IN music. This, men have always known: that the beat of a drum, the shake of a rattle, the rise and fall of a voice, might waken something deep in the human heart and set it free. This is how a fiddle might bring a man to the edge of his seat, breath held against the last explosive moment of song; this is the reason for the instant of quietude when music ends, when the heart is overwhelmed and can show itself through no other means but silence. Such things are what have drawn the young, the beautiful, the faithful—faithful to music, not to a god above—here today.

There is, of course, also the promise of drugs and sex, to complete the triumvirate with rock and roll. All of these are why I am here, to spend three nights under a changeable sky and to gather strength and power from those who offer it.

My daughters are here for the same reasons precisely, and yet their reasons are far more base.

"Mother," says the eldest. Eldest, but not by much. Nine months, less than the space of a year. Little enough time even by mortal standards, and my daughters are close to seeing their first century end. "*Mother,*" Jana says again, and she is the less impatient of the two. The other, Emma, sways with the wind, her hands lifted to catch breezes in her fingertips. They say every parent has her favorite, but I cannot tell you which of my daughers is closer to my heart, the one I bore or the one I stole. It changes as easily as the light, and so to my mind, neither is favored.

Jana is her father's child in looks: tall, with red hidden in the depths of her black hair, and with challenging jade eyes. They're challenging only for their color: Jana is mild, thoughtful, steady, even shy, none of which her father is. She is also lovely and has no idea of it, which makes her shy charm all the more powerful. Men stumble to please her, and she hardly notices because her duty, to her mind, is to her sister and to me. She believes we need protection, and that she is the only one who can offer it. I think at times that we are her hoard: two objects of beauty, held precious. If that is so, I am content with it; certainly we are easier to carry than rooms of vast wealth.

"I am not keeping you here, child," I say gently enough. "Go and play as wild as you wish. If you waken things you would share with me, I'll be honored by your gift."

"But what about *Emma,*" she says in frustration, and we both look to the other girl, the one who still dances with the wind. *She* is my daughter in aspect: black-haired, blue-eyed, and far more beautiful than her father. And she is untethered, a drifting sweet spirit who acts on impulse and out of generosity, with little thought beyond the moment. Had I guessed the things my daughters might be, I would have been wrong beyond comprehension, as my mother has been about me.

"Emma," I tell Jana, "can take care of herself, just as you can. Just as we all can."

"But she's going to *miss* everything!" Jana all but stamps a foot, which is more dangerous than it might seem. She is young and small, but even at birth she was as long as I am tall, and with a hundred years of growth she is nearly twice that now. Not in mortal form, of course: she is only a tall girl, as a human. But her dragon mass lingers, and her foot stomped in anger can shake the earth.

Emma ceases caressing the wind and offers her sister a guilt-free smile. "I won't, Jana. Here, I'll come with you now." She offers Jana a hand, and peace is restored. I wave them away, and they melt down the hillside into a sea of gathering humanity. Hundreds of thousands of tickets have been sold, and hundreds of thousands more are coming. It is a pilgrimage, a thing that will never be repeated, though I know already that it will be tried. But there is a power in the first of anything, and the power of firsts is how witches are born. I respect that power, and choose to pursue it in my own way. I am not like most witches: they are born from first secrets, secrets so great they must be whispered once to release the burden, and that breach of trust is where my mother and her ilk rise from.

A few are born of white secrets: the hundredth name of God, perhaps. But most are born of the blackest secrets: the weight of man's first murder and of other bleak moments. A dozen or two, no more in all the world; that's the rarity of a secret strong enough to beget a witch.

My mother is one such, and I am not what she hoped for. We daughters never are: we are lesser creatures, myself only the child of a man my mother later ate. If I am born of a secret, it is that we daughters cannot thrive under our mothers' guidance. We must die to be free, and then our paths are our own to choose. But this is not a secret to bind me with, as there are a few others like me, and they too know the truth that engendered us all. We are something else, we daughters, and my daughters are different yet.

"You're alive," a man says behind me, his astonishment and pleasure clear in the words. An altogether more delightful response than the one his friend and rival gave me eighty years earlier upon discovering the same fact of my survival. My heart beats too fast just once, then hangs silent for the balance. Heat is rising in my cheeks, unheard of, but the man who has spoken is the one for whom I changed everything in my life, and I have not seen him since the day I died.

I look over my shoulder and laugh out loud. Not the kindest answer to his gladness, but I cannot help it. Fourteen decades ago ago he was beautiful, dressed in bright colors and expensive clothes. Today his beauty and brightness have not faded, but he wears the garb of the year, and it looks sillier on him than on most, perhaps because I knew him so long ago. His red hair falls nearly to his hips, held back from an angular face by a beaded headband, and he sports glasses like John Lennon wears, round and dark. Worse still, he has a goatee, golden-red and silky, and it is absurd. It goes with the costume, with the loose-sleeved and open-throated shirt, with the bell-bottomed brown pants and the moccasins, but it is absurd. I stand and offer him my hands. "You look ridiculous."

Mock offense flies across his face as he captures my hands and bows over them. "Dozens of young women assure me otherwise, my dear. You, despite your cruel words, are ravishing, and I say that without needing to take into account your improbable longevity. How on earth have you survived? Did Eliseo—?"

"Do you really believe my mother's daughter might need a vampire's blood to live forever, dragonlord?"

"I would not dare to presume, my dear. And how is your darling mother? Still in Russia with her chicken-legged hut?"

"Still furious and prepared to hunt you, yes. Be glad she is a witch, and cannot cross running water." A half-truth, that. Her hut can step over streams small enough for its legs to stretch across, and has been known to travel high and deep into the mountains to find the birthplace of rivers, circumventing them that way. But Russia, all of its great expanse, is Baba Yaga's. She stays within its wettest borders not just because of the difficulty of crossing rivers, but because there are other witches in other lands, and they do not lightly tread upon one another's territory. Not unless they know the secret that birthed their rival, in which case they tread and strike and rule.

"Really," Janx says with interest. "If I'm not mistaken, you're a witch and you're definitely not in Russia anymore. How is that, if a witch can't cross running water? There *is* an ocean between here and there, after all."

I have a head too full of thoughts of secrets, and a need, now, to keep secrets of my own. I am glad my daughters are gone, already a part of the breathless mass below us. I do not want them to meet this man, not today and perhaps not ever. Most particularly, I am not prepared to let him meet Jana, who is his daughter, and who was stolen from him before she ever hatched. I think he may never forgive me if he discovers she is mine, and that is a weight I am reluctant to bear. "I am not the same as Baba Yaga," is all I say, and Janx rolls his eyes to the heavens in exaggerated relief.

"She may be powerful, but she lacks beauty, my dear. My impeccable taste in women would be called into question had I been so misled as to bed her instead of you. You are most certainly not the same." He is willing, it seems, to take the answer because it gives him the chance to be flattering and outrageous, but curiosity piques in his jade eyes. I imagine he will make some effort to learn how it is I am not circumscribed by the same limitations as my mother. He will not, though, discover it today or tonight, or indeed during the entirety of this festival, and that is enough for me.

We speak at the same time, asking the same question: "What are you doing here?" and through mutual amusement I add, "And where is your yin?"

"Please," Janx says with a sniff. "I'm the yin, he's the yang. He's here somewhere. Attempting to monetize the greatest social event of the century. Why would you do that, when you have all of *this*?" He waves toward the flux of bodies, as alight with desire for them as he could be for any treasure. Jana is like that too: the things dragons covet are not necessarily as simple as gold and jewels.

"Perhaps it's dangerous for him," I say to the crest of people. "Perhaps the pursuit of profit helps dampen the desire for blood. He has learned some trick, after all, hasn't he? Something which lends him more control than his ilk are inclined to."

Janx's gaze sharpens in thought, softens with consideration, then sharpens again, suspicious now. "Do you know they've disappeared?"

Of course I know, but the circumstances under which I would confess to that are nearly unimaginable. "Who have? The vampires?"

Surprise turns Janx to an unmoveable object, just for a moment. It is not done, to speak the names of the Old Races in public. In daylight. In mortal presence. There are too many secrets to keep, too much danger, even for creatures as powerful as they are. But there are half a million people gathering here, and my voice, my insignificant words, are far too small to be picked out of the crowd. At the end of his moment of stillness, Janx understands that, and says "Yes."

I can see him trying to shape more words. Trying to say, "Yes. The vampires." But he can't: the weight of proscription is too heavy by far, and even the light and laughing dragonlord cannot throw it off. He will not acknowledge their names under the sunlight, no more, perhaps, than I would tell the secret that birthed my mother, if even I knew it. So we are silent together in that instant where he cannot make the words, and then I say "I've read my mother's grimoires, Janx. Once upon a time—"

"Oh no," Janx says. "That's a fairy tale, Baba Yaga's daughter. Start again, and make us true."

It is hard. Surprisingly hard. I start twice, and end with a smile on my lips before I say *"Once,"* very firmly. "Once, there were so many more of you than there are now. Perhaps they've died away, like so many others."

"No." There is conviction, if not certainty, in the single word, but Janx presses his jade eyes shut and makes a light gesture, throwing away the question's importance. "I hadn't thought of that," he says when he trusts his voice. "That his all-consuming fondness for building financial empires might be the bedrock upon which his bloodlust is sated. Here I've thought that it was me, all this time. How disappointing."

A part of him is serious, which is rare enough in this dragonlord. The only other of his species I have met is a cold and dour creature, but then, he has been my mother's slave in the frozen north for more years than I can tell. It was another of my mother's daughters, long dead, who provided the charm to capture him, and *she* never broke free of Baba Yaga's yoke. Poor Rumi is my mother's forever, unless there's another way to break the spell.

"Do yourself no disservice," I say to the part of him that is injured, and though I don't know it until I speak, when I do, I know I speak the truth: "You are vital to him. Your impulsiveness allows him to be reserved. The money," I add, and this is a guess, but a good one, "is only a prize because dragons hoard wealth."

"Beauty," Janx says absently. "We hoard beauty. It's hardly our fault beautiful things are precious and therefore worth money. *Who,*" he finishes in a breathless sweet tone, "is *that?*"

I know without looking that it can only be one of my daughters. Human women can and do turn Janx's head, as they do Daisani's, but there is something in the way he speaks which tells me he sees a member of the Old Races. Mortals are perhaps not quite so fascinating, and I am rushing through these thoughts to keep myself from flinching or turning too quickly. To keep myself from showing alarm, because I have no wish to explain my eldest daughter to the man who happens to be her father.

Janx does not, I think, see my sigh of relief when it is Emma tripping lightly up the hill. She moves more beautifully than Jana does, moves as though she's barely tethered to the earth, and the clothes of this era, silly as they are on Janx, are perfect for her. A spectrum of blues is dyed into her skirt and loose blouse, and her long hair is unbound save for a braided headband. I turn back to Janx, but he knows the answer now: sees it in the mirror of myself which Emma is. "Good lord," he murmurs. "Who is her father?"

I say "Not you," with a smile to take the edge away, and he gives me a complex look: surprise that I would say such a thing followed hard by a brush of regret and disappointment, though none of it loses his constant hint of amusement. "Emma," I say, perhaps too loudly, "this is Janx."

Her eyes widen and she glances over her shoulder. Looking for Jana, I know, but her sister is one of the thousands, no more distinguishable than any other. She looks back, blue gaze still rounded, and Janx is all but dancing with glee.

"You know me! You know who I am! Don't be silly," he says happily. "It's perfectly safe. All these people can have no idea what I am. You needn't look out for me." By the time he's said all that, he's managed to capture Emma's fine-boned fingers, and to bow deeply over them. She makes no more effort to extract herself than I would, and indeed, looks as delighted by his attention as any girl. She has lived longer than most humans, of course, but both my daughters still *look* like youthful teens, just as I have appeared to be perhaps twenty-two or -three for decades now. We are sisters to the eye, not mother and daughters, which suits us all. And if the girls are slow to mature, well, they have no cause for hurry. My own maturity came more quickly, but I was Baba Yaga's daughter.

Emma says, "But how?" to Janx, arresting his indrawn breath and the no-doubt forthcoming flow of flowery nonsense. "How?" she asks again. "*How* can they have no idea? Mother says you're—" She disengages herself from his hold so she can spread her arms, then spin on her toes, encompassing an impossible size with her dance. When she comes to a stop, she does so dizzily and with a smile that could break the strongest man's heart.

Janx is not the strongest man I have known, and is entirely besotted by the time Emma finishes asking, "Your true mass must be—well, massive! How do you not shake the earth and fill the room every time you walk?" It is an utterly practical question for a girl whose sister is a dragon, but Emma's delivery is breathlessly awe-struck, starry-eyed, and she has caught Janx's hands again to squeeze them and deepen the impact of her appeal. He has no idea he is being used, which, with this man, is an accomplishment all its own.

"I do," he says with perhaps the most honesty I have ever seen in him. "But my outrageous charm and devastating good looks distract people from noticing."

I can see the thought flicker across Emma's open face: that advice will do Jana no good. Jana has the beauty, but not the explosive personality to help hide her mass behind. Perhaps she could cultivate it, but neither of us would want her to. Her shyness is sweet, and it would be a shame to lose it in the name of safety. There have always been women who can arrest the attention of all when they step into a room. Reserved or not, Jana will be one such, and no one could possibly suspect the true reason for it.

But the thought is fleeting on Emma's face, and laughter follows, as it's meant to. Janx loves to amuse, and few women do not wish to find him amusing. "Tell me," Emma pleads. "Tell me about you. About all of you." *All of us,* she doesn't say, but she does not have to. There is a law among the Old Races, that they do not make children with mortals. Emma, by their law, would be proscribed, although my curious stance as a thing of human magic might confuse the issue. Might, but also might not, and so Janx understands that she is a secret, and that she will only know as much of her father's peoples as I can tell her.

He casts me a glance, half a question, which is more than I might expect from him. He seeks twofold permission: one, to talk with her as she wishes, and two, to be certain I have no questions of my own.

I nod. All I know of the Old Races I learned from my mother's grimoires, and while I have told my daughters everything I know, it is easy to understand that the knowledge I hold is not the same as experience. It is also easy to understand that what is enough for me may not satisfy daughters of the Old Races who are, after all, not witches themselves.

"Anything you want to know," Janx promises. A rash promise: my girls know much of a witch's power comes from knowledge, and so very often choose to share what they learn. But I will not press Emma on this topic, because even now I recall the squirming images on the pages of my mother's grimoires with discomfort, and do not ever wish to capture one of the ancient races with my knowledge. It is better, in this thing, to know too little, than too much.

Janx, given permission, has tucked Emma's hand at his elbow, and together they disappear into the crowd again, using numbers for anonymity. She will guide him into speaking of Daisani—no difficult trick, that—and will learn much of what she wishes to know about her father. I smile and kneel, re-establishing my space within the thousands. No one else has room to spread their arms or turn about, but the crush would disturb me. It's humanity's aspect I desire, not the touch of their bodies. For this is the rest of it: knowledge in one hand, essence in the other. Armed with those things, a witch might call a coal-shovel across the room to ride upon, or give life to a hut with chicken legs so it might carry her around the land. She might shape a life, or, with enough gathered power, even shape a world.

I believe a new world must be made, and have spent most of a century guiding two elements of that new world toward maturity. Tonight I begin the task of softening humanity with its own substance, softening it enough to let the changes I wish to see take place. My mother is ancient, eternal, but I am only the daughter of a man she once ate, so I do not know how long I might live. It is possible my work will take me all the rest of the long years of my life. I am content with that, because it is my choice, and because if I succeed, my daughters will live a life beyond their imaginings.

Jana enters the circle I've made, her presence announced by a sigh. "I've lost Emma again."

"She's found a curiosity, is all. She'll be back when she's done with him." It is not precisely a lie, though I think Jana wouldn't chase after them if she knew whom Emma walked with. She knows the story of how she came to me, and has never yet suggested she is prepared to meet her father. But she is satisfied with my explanation, and sits down, knees drawn up, within my circle. There are perhaps too many people here, though she was as eager as Emma to come and explore the masses. Still, dragons are large, and such a close press may be more uncomfortable for her than for her sister or myself. I am content to let her sit with me as long as she wishes, but almost before she is comfortable, an alertness strikes her spine and she radiates wariness. Astonished and concerned, I reach for her hand, but her attention is on the crowd below us.

After a moment, a small man steps out of the throng. Unlike Janx, he has not succumbed to the fashion of the era, though in this time and place a fastidious black suit makes him stand out. I climb to my feet with a more reserved smile than I feel, because Jana, her hand in mine, is trembling with rage.

I do not know what dragons learn while in the shell, but it was clear from before her birth that Jana recognized and loathed Eliseo Daisani, who took her away from the city she was meant to be born in. He did not steal her from her mother—that was another of his kind—but he failed to return her, and she harbors resentment a-plenty for that. I, too, of course, failed to return her, but I have earned forgiveness for that, or at least have been recognized as the one who took her from the hated vampires, and therefore am accepted. I tried to mitigate her fury against Daisani, but it is clear that I did not, and perhaps could not, fully succeed.

He joins us in our little clearing, small and lithe and very dangerous, though perhaps not to Jana and myself. His one concession to fashion is that his black hair is worn long, and drawn back in a tidy ponytail. I think him quite dapper, and dare a smile that begets a crushing squeeze from Jana's hand.

I wince. So does Daisani, which is unexpected. Jana draws breath to speak and I interject quickly before she can loose her tongue: "Eliseo, this is my daughter Jana. Jana—"

"I know who he is."

Fear is not a comfortable or usual cloak to settle on my shoulders, and it has never been laid upon me by one of my daughters. Now, though, its cold touch sinks through me, and whether I am afraid *for* Jana or *of* her, I cannot say. Magic flexes off her, her desire to take dragon form hardly under control. I hold her hand harder, but such restraint is like a flower trying to cup an iron chain. Nothing I am, nothing I can do, can stop her, not if she is determined to make this a fight.

Eliseo Daisani, my other daughter's father, smiles, and it is not a nice expression at all. His teeth are flat, like human teeth, but they look wrong somehow as his lips peel back from them. He says "Do not," and then again, "Do not, little girl. There is balance among the Old Races. The djinn can be contained by salt water, so the selkies were once their mortal enemies, and a dragon's size can be matched by a gargoyle's strength. But we vampires are not even born of this world, and no one, much less an infant dragon, might stand against me and win. Do not be a fool, child. It would do your mother a hurt to lose you, and I would prefer not to see that happen."

Poor Jana is flexing so hard I imagine I can see her scales bristling, for all that she shows only human skin. "Someday," she hisses. "Someday I'll be your match and this will come to an end, vampire."

Daisani smiles again, and this time he is actually amused. "No," he says, gently. "No, you won't."

Jana spits and hisses with impotent outrage, and to me, Eliseo says "Another time, perhaps," before walking away and leaving me with a gleam of regret under the darkening sky.

Smoke pours off my daughter, the sole dragonly indicator that breaks through her human form to reveal her. She strains to go after him, though his departure calms her enough that I can hold her in place. "The Old Races do not make war on one another, Jana."

Her green gaze flinches to me, and for the first time in her life I hear an undercurrent of accusation: "But I'm not *of* the Old Races, Mother."

It is easy for her to pull free of me then, and I watch her stomp away with an ache in my heart. I have not, I think, done badly by my daughters, but Jana is right. Unlike Emma, she is pureblooded, but nothing in her upbringing has taught her the ways and mores of her birth parents. I dislike feeling I have done her a disservice, but then, at the heart of me, I know I have been selfish. I took her for myself, after all, and kept her, and I do not think she knows that she and her sister have, all unawares, shaped the path I have chosen to walk along.

Perhaps I should tell them.

Perhaps I should, but not tonight. Tonight there is work to do in shaping the world to my path, and despite the men entering and exiting our lives, I must prepare. The girls are not like me: they are not witches, and do not harvest power from human interaction. There is no ritual for them, no need for a five-pointed star in a circle surrounding them, no need to sit in silence and strip away the thoughts of the world until they are receptive to its gifts. Nor, in truth, am I like *my* mother, who might cozy herself within the pentagram, but who seizes life forces rather than ask and take what she is offered. I tread more lightly than that, and have found the rewards beyond measure.

Tonight, in this place, among these throngs of people, it is entirely unremarkable to discard my clothing. It is more remarkable that no one notices, but I am not here to share the passion of bodies, and do not wish to explain that over and over again. Easier by far to twist a thread of power and make gazes slide off me, make myself unremarkable. A few, the especially astute, might still see me, but like me, they are waiting for the music, and there is little else in their worlds right now.

For my part, I want to feel the first beat of music against all my skin. It is the connection I am searching for, the moment where man and earth and sky are bound together, as rarely happens with tremendous gatherings. There is power in that when only one or two experience it; when hundreds of thousands do, then there is magic indeed.

A crone erupts from the earth and cuts me down just as the music explodes over us.

IT HAS BEEN TOO long since I was Baba Yaga's daughter. I am *astonished*, and humiliated, that I did not see this coming. That I was unprepared for it. There would be a witch in America's north-east; of course there would be. Were there not trials, after all? Were there not dozens done to death by those trials? Hysteria is rarely born of nothing, and a witch like my mother—which most of them are—would gain great power from such chaos and cruelty. All of this flies through my mind as abruptly as my blood flies through the air, the scarlet arc captured in a witch's palm.

Fear clenches my heart as she smears that blood on both hands, painting her fingers and nails with it. Now she is part of me, immersed in my blood, and my magic will think she is me. I have not been so vulnerable, not ever, for Baba Yaga wished me to live, not to die. I call on the oldest trick I know, the one my mother taught me first: that of whisking a coal-shovel to my hands that I might fly away on it. But that was a magic for another time: coal-shovels are not often found anymore, and there are none at this place beneath a starry sky at three o'clock in the morning.

The Salem witch pounces on me and sinks her claws into my skin, through my ribs, searching out the tastiest and most vital parts of me. I scream and dig at the earth, but no one sees me, hears me, comes to fight for me, because there is a spell laid to turn their gazes away. The Salem witch is canny: she has let me do all the work, and siphons every drop of power from me, from the music, from the masses. I buck beneath her, trying to throw her off, but magic is simple stuff, and only knows its own. My mind is wise to her trickery, but to the magic, blood is all.

I do not want to die.

Perhaps summoned by the thought, a tiny woman appears. I have seen her once before, as if in a dream, as the winter ice that birthed me thawed. I have no more than a glimpse of her this time, too, but I know her: as much as Baba Yaga, I think this woman gave me life. Wizened, wise, delicate, she rises behind the Salem witch and rips her head off and throws it away. It bounces across the shoulders of teeming humanity. Her limbs follow, flung terrible distances, and her eviscerated torso is left smeared across the grass.

My saviour is gone.

This will not kill the witch. I am numb, cold, staring at black blood on the flattened grass. This will not kill her, because it is not the revelation of the secret which gave her life, but she will, I think, have a very hard time recovering. Her arms will be easiest: they can crawl, inch by slow inch, back to her body, and fit themselves into ragged sockets.

Her head, which is small and being tossed like a balloon, moves farther away with each moment, and will take a long time indeed to find.

Emma, who is not human, and who therefore heard my screams, comes to me. She is fast, as fast as her father, but there is no room to run here, and so she could not be at my side in an instant. I cannot yet move: my limbs are still heavy, my heartbeat sluggish. I think perhaps the muscle there has been pierced, and am unsure how long it will take to heal. I am no easier to kill than any other witch, but no living thing can be pierced through and through and survive it comfortably. More, much of my magic has been stolen away, sucked up by the rival I should have anticipated. It, too, will recover, but it, too, needs time.

Now Jana is here, and although still human in form, she has strength her slighter sister lacks. Together they lift me to my feet, and in the darkness I can see Emma's pupils are huge, her nostrils flared at the scent of blood. I am safe: I am always safe with my daughters, but it is another reminder of the things they are.

Jana is puffing smoke with outrage, and the earth rattles with the weight of her footfalls. All my strength turns to reinforcing the charm to make mortals look away. Jana knows the feel of that bit of magic and wastes no time in transforming. Air pops outward, displaced by the change in her mass.

Although I cannot see him, I know that half a mile away, Janx stiffens, every inch of his skin alert. But he also cannot see us, and so his tension is no concern of mine. Jana extends a crimson and black leg. Emma leads me up, tucking me against Jana's ruff before snugging herself behind me, small and fierce and caring. Jana crouches and leaps upward, a powerful surge of muscle, and we're in the sky, climbing higher, higher, higher still. There is wind in my hair, Jana's ruff in my eyes, tears in my eyes as the air grows cooler. I have ridden on my daughter's back for decades, and each time it is a new wonder, a gift to break my heart. It is her strength which has taken me across oceans I could not otherwise cross, and that is a secret my mother would kill for: mortal means are not enough to let a witch cross oceans. It takes magic, and of the winged Old Races, only dragons have the range. Baba Yaga might leave her frozen homeland on Rumi's back, should she think of it, but in all the long cold centuries, she has not. Witches, too, are creatures of habit, and I would do nothing to put the idea in her mind even if I was still in her thrall.

I look back once, taking in the mass of people with a glance. I imagine that I can see him there, red hair falling long as he stares into the night sky, his gaze fixed on Jana's retreating form. His heart will be in his throat, his whole being wishing to fling himself into the air after us. But he will not. Long history and good sense will keep him on the ground, and so my daughter remains safe.

She remains safe, and I have survived, so I have only the smallest room to harbor regret in my heart. I would have said a farewell, had I any choice in the matter. But for the second time, I have not, and if it happens once more then I will know the red dragon and the witch's daughter are meant never to say goodbye.

There is a certain bittersweet relief in that. I am bleeding, drained, regretful, but comforted too, and so I look forward again, to the future—for that, after all, is where hope lies.

The Knight's Tale

Supersaturated sunlight made Rebecca shade her eyes as she exited the subway. Construction was going on, strong men in sleeveless shirts and hardhats climbing scaffolding with the confidence of monkeys. Long-haired women in bell bottoms and sandals slowed to admire them. Businessmen stepped swiftly to avoid running the women down. The colors would never fade in Rebecca's mind: brilliant blue sky punctured by glass-clad buildings, white and grey walls a backdrop for passers-by in orange and green and brown.

She wore brown herself, muted and tasteful, with a scarf tied at her throat. Businesswear, meant to oblige others to take her seriously. And across the street, half a block down, was Eliseo Daisani, one of the men she was meeting. Rumors flew through her office—an investment firm—about how he'd made his money. The favored story was that he had profited wildly at Woodstock, and was bankrolling that into an ever-increasing fortune. He didn't look like someone who would have even heard of a music festival, but then, Rebecca herself, in a business suit and her hair braided back, didn't either. Daisani saw her, mistook her raised hand for a wave, and waved in return. A shadow went wrong above her head, making her flinch internally, savannah response to danger from above.

The impact knocked her from her feet. She should have fallen, but didn't: a man was there, catching her, while a dozen steps away—in the very place she'd been standing a moment earlier—an iron girder smashed to the ground, shattering concrete and sending reverberations down the sidewalk. People screamed, scattered, all too late. Her heart hadn't yet had time to react, still thumping at its usual calm pace.

She was in Eliseo Daisani's arms, held in a bride's carry by a man who had been a hundred yards away when disaster began to unfold.

He put her back on her feet, carefully. He was a small man, shorter than Rebecca at the best of times, and at the moment she wore platforms that increased her height advantage by two inches.

Really, the speed at which he'd snatched her should have knocked her out of her shoes. She glanced at them, re-discovering the straps that kept them on her feet. Thick leather, as was the fashion; thick enough to withstand the collision. Mystery solved. She raised her eyes again, looking down at Eliseo Daisani, who could not possibly, not rationally, have saved her life. Not from the distance he'd been at. Not on the long side of a New York City block. Logically, she must have misjudged the distance. He must have been closer, perhaps only across the street, not half a block down. Even then he had been impossibly fast.

He had not been closer, and she knew it. He had crossed a hundred yards faster than humanly possible, and she was alive because of it.

Finally, finally, Rebecca's heartbeat accelerated. *Finally*, as if her feet didn't still itch with the sidewalk's vibrations, or as if screams weren't still filling the air. No time at all had passed, not really, while she internally debated possibility and rationality and rejected them both in the face of what had happened.

Daisani, brown eyes bright with rue, lifted a finger to his lips: *shh*.

As if there was anything that could be said. Rebecca's pulse thrummed at urgent speed beneath her jaw, but the ascot scarf hid that from prying eyes. She looked down the street once more, to where Daisani's driver still held the car door open. A woman was just getting out: Vanessa Grey, Mr. Daisani's assistant. Her face, even at the distance, was dangerous in its neutrality. She was not a woman Rebecca would like to cross, and there were very few people who brought that thought to Rebecca's mind.

Rebecca looked at Eliseo Daisani, smiled briefly, and in a smooth and steady voice said, "Good morning, Eliseo. I believe they're holding our table for us."

His own smile was a much fuller thing, peeling back to expose admiration and amusement. "Good morning, Rebecca. I believe you're right. May I be so bold?" He offered his arm, and Rebecca took it to be escorted beyond the shaken construction workers into the restaurant for lunch.

REBECCA KNIGHT WAS EASY to dislike. That was Vanessa's assessment, and she had had over a century to perfect those rapid assessments in. Rebecca had the austerity of genuine beauty, that cool and remote reserve that made her difficult to know. She should have been a ballet dancer, not a business woman; she had the long limbs and swan-like neck, the slim body and large eyes that would be vaunted on stage. She also seemed to have a ballerina's wiry strength, though that was conjecture on Vanessa's part, having not yet had cause to test the other woman's strength.

And she was, bluntly, looking for the excuse. Eliseo had been unbelievably foolish, darting through traffic to rescue a woman in broad daylight, when anyone might have noticed the inhuman speed at which he traveled. He never took chances like that, not in the hundred years Vanessa had known him. Not for any woman he'd ever met in that time, except Vanessa.

That, of course, was most of the reason she found Knight unlikable. Jealousy was ridiculous after so long, but she'd very rarely been tested on that front. Of course there were women. There were *always* women, when it came to Eliseo Daisani and the dragonlord Janx. But all of those women had been before Vanessa's time—or, if she had to admit it, when she was absent from Eliseo's side. He had been unusually thoughtful a few years ago after returning from the upstate music festival. Vanessa had not asked, but it ate at her and no doubt added to her dislike of Rebecca Knight.

If only the woman had screamed, or backed away in horror, or given some sign of disbelieving the rescue she'd just undergone. But she hadn't. Even half the block away, Vanessa had seen the swift resolution on Rebecca's face. She had seen and understood *perfectly*.

And she had ignored it.

No one was that unshakable. No one, which was precisely why Eliseo was now pouring Rebecca an unnecessarily expensive glass of wine and smiling avariciously at her. He was a moth to flame, when the flame was someone extraordinary.

Vanessa had never fully understood why he had chosen *her*. It had become clearer the night Janx told the story of the Chicago fire. Eliseo had seen her that night, looking through the smoke at dragons in the sky. No one else had seen them, but even so, it seemed a thin rope to bind himself to her with.

"No," Rebecca said, making it suddenly clear the expensive wine was going to waste. "The senior partners are eager to represent you, of course—"

"And you aren't?" Eliseo asked, amused. "Reeling me in would make your career, Ms. Knight. Both of your careers," he added with a nod toward Rebecca's partner. Russell something; Vanessa had the name written in her appointment book.

"Of course I am," Rebecca said coolly. "But the information you're proposing to offer is tantamount to insider trading, and neither of us will profit from even a hint of corruption."

Russell Lomax, that was it. His gaze slid sideways, sure indication of guilty interest. Unless Vanessa was mistaken, the young Mr. Lomax would shortly belong wholesale to Eliseo, and likely have an illustrious career because of it.

Rebecca Knight would likely have an illustrious career despite Eliseo Daisani, whose smile lit up again. "So certain of yourself, Ms. Knight. Perhaps we could discuss it further over dinner. Vanessa, will you arrange it?"

Vanessa smiled, took a note, and promised herself that if Rebecca gave one hint of telling anyone what she had seen, she would personally kill her.

THERE WERE WOMEN WHO would find Daisani's assumption that Rebecca would, of course, like to discuss it over dinner, and his impetuous request to Ms. Grey to arrange it, to be manly, decisive and flattering. Charming, even.

To her irritation, Rebecca found it at least amusing, and that was close enough to charming that she had agreed. And was glad she had: it was not actually possible that Ms. Grey had managed reservations at the Four Seasons, where it took months of advance notice to get a table, on a few hours' notice. Yet that was where Eliseo's driver delivered her, and she entered with a murmured, "Two impossible things before dinner."

"Four to go," Daisani said from behind her, "and I have all night before breakfast."

Rebecca startled, then turned with a laugh, her hand pressed to her chest. "I didn't think anyone would hear me. You look..."

He was never going to be handsome, was Eliseo Daisani. He was too sallow, not tall enough, and plainly, if evenly, featured. But in a sharp suit—not quite a tuxedo—and a sharper smile, he was charismatic, and that was perhaps more effective than handsomeness. His smile sharpened further, and he nodded. "Yes. So do you."

"You should have warned me," Rebecca said mildly. "I overdressed for anywhere in town but here."

"I thought you would, so you hardly needed to be warned. Our table is this way." He threaded his way to a window, one of the best seats in the house, and held her chair for her.

Rebecca stopped without sitting, taking in the view, then the restaurant, before looking at Eliseo. "You have a permanent table."

"It makes things easier." He waited for her to sit, then took his own seat, murmuring, "You said two impossible things," as he did so.

"A table at the Four Seasons doesn't qualify if you have a permanent one."

"And the other?" His gaze was unnervingly intent.

The memory of the morning's brightness lit Rebecca's mind, playing out the scene for the hundredth time. Playing, most vividly, the touch of his finger to his lips: *shh.*

"That you asked me to dinner without Ms. Grey eviscerating me," she said lightly. "I don't think she likes me very much."

Daisani tilted his head, bird-like, then was still for a few long moments before peculiar humor came into his smile. "Vanessa doesn't like anyone I like, as a matter of course. She's over-protective."

Rebecca's eyebrows shot up. "Of *you*?"

"Of us. Ah, here's the waiter. I saw your expression when I inveigled this dinner invitation, Ms. Knight. I think I'd better ask before making the same mistake twice: may I order for you?"

Of us. The brief phrase carried more weight than it should. Piqued more curiosity than it should, as well: it was none of Rebecca's business what kind of *us* Eliseo Daisani and Vanessa Grey might be. "Do you think you know me well enough to order my dinner?"

"Oh," Daisani said absently, "I can smell what you like. Chicken or pork rather than beef, but seafood is your first preference. Greens instead of starches, though you have a weakness for good soft bread and butter. And you like white wines more than reds regardless of what one is 'supposed' to drink with a particular meal."

Rebecca's jaw fell open and Eliseo Daisani laughed aloud. "I watched what you ate at lunch, Ms. Knight."

Which did not preclude the unpleasant idea that he *could* smell what she liked. He could cross a hundred yards inside a breath; the idea of another superpower was far from inconceivable. Rebecca closed her mouth with a soft *pop*, then touched her lips with a linen napkin. "I believe I can trust you to order my dinner."

SHE DIDN'T ASK. DIDN'T comment, all the way through dinner and into the idle walk through city streets after. Didn't ask, and it drove Eliseo mad. A wonderful kind of madness, one that set his heart racing and kept laughter on his lips. That was so much more Janx than himself, but the modern world was cruel. He and Janx were obliged by an increasingly media-driven world and the curious, idle masses to restrain themselves from too much communication, and so he, Eliseo Daisani, was also obliged to take on the role of curious flirt if he wanted that in his life.

Rebecca Knight, by all appearances, had no interest in such a flirt. He thought he amused her, which was not the usual reaction women had. Fear or fascination, but not amusement. Not careful disregard for the impossible thing she'd seen. That was not how women behaved.

He wanted to confess all so badly he could taste it. Could taste it like blood in his mouth, sweet and tempting. It had been centuries since the impulse to disclose all had been so strong, and the world had been a very different place then. More important, the woman in whom he'd then wished to confide had been drawn to him—and to Janx—in a way that Rebecca was not.

Either that, he thought, or she was the finest actress he'd ever met. "That information I offered this afternoon, Ms. Knight..."

Her heart jumped, which was something, at least. She wasn't entirely immune to curiosity. But her voice was as crisp and cool as it had been throughout the business day and into dinner. "I'm not interested, Mr. Daisani. Russell shouldn't be either. There would be consequences."

Daisani, lightly, murmured, "There's a double meaning to that," and Rebecca gave him a sharp look.

"Against my will, I bid thee come to dinner? No, Mr. Daisani, there's no double meaning. It's a very generous, very foolish, and borderline illegal offer. A federal circuit court has already ruled it *is* illegal, not just unethical. Russell may be foolish enough to trade on your potential upcoming partnership and investments with Global Brokerage Incorporated, but I'll have no part in it."

Eliseo's eyebrows shot up as she spoke. "You're extraordinary, Rebecca."

She looked exasperated, not pleased. "Am I."

"I can hardly choose where to begin. You recognize a not-oft-quoted line of Shakespeare. You lay out the situation as you see it with no sugar coating. Most people would have tip-toed around the details you just expounded on." She had not, though, quite been telling the truth. Her heartbeat, rushing too fast again, told him that much. There *was* a double meaning to it: there was the topic at hand, the question of whether she and Russell would succumb to the temptation he'd offered. But beneath that there was the matter of the rescue, and she laid that out too, with those same words. *I'm not interested. There would be consequences.*

Oh, she was right. So very right, but humans never believed that, not even when they were told from the start that they wouldn't walk away unscathed. But Rebecca Knight understood, and it made her delectable. Daisani's fingers curled toward his palms, aching with the desire to grasp her and hold on.

Rebecca gave him a level look. "Mr. Daisani, there are a vanishingly small number of women in stockbroking as it is. I may be the only black woman working in the industry in this city. Yes. You're right. I'm extraordinary. I am also scrutinized, and even if it was my nature to gamble on someone like you, I would refrain in order to keep my career. There is nothing with which you could tempt me."

"Not even immortality?" he asked rashly. She was enticing. Much too enticing. He needed Janx to make this scene a light and teasing one, instead of hearing an undercurrent of hopeful desperation in his own voice.

Rebecca's expression changed. Not piqued interest, but pity, and she shook her head. "Why would I want immortality, when my friends and family would die?"

He missed a step, and Rebecca took it as a stop. She paused, no more than that, and nodded to a nearby subway station. "This is me. Thank you for escorting me, Mr. Daisani. Dinner was lovely. I'm sure I'll see you at the office soon."

She left him there, gaping with astonishment and thwarted ambitions. He wanted to chase her, to discover where she would disembark and be there waiting, and the thought of doing so made his heart hurt. Not for himself, but for Vanessa. She had never understood fully that her seeing eyes, her quiet observation of the Old Races, her cleverness in manipulating them and her fearlessness had been the things that drew him to her. From the first night he'd seen her, little more than a child, she had been a shelter from the storm.

Rebecca Knight was the storm from which he needed shelter. Vanessa was extraordinary to him for having watched the skies over Chicago the night it burned, instead of watching the flames. For seeing dragons where others saw only destruction. For accepting that.

Rebecca was as extraordinary for her refusal.

He could not, in all conscience, abandon what he and Vanessa had. Not to pursue a fling with a woman whose calm stature denied such passion. Not in all conscience.

"The play's the thing," he whispered, and finally moved.

HE WAS *WAITING* FOR her at the other end of the line. Rebecca got off the train briskly enough, but slowed, then stopped, to see Eliseo Daisani lingering like an over-dressed panhandler at the subway stairs.

It should not make her laugh. It absolutely should not make her laugh. Rebecca stayed where she was, purse clutched against her stomach, until she was certain of her tone and expression. "You are incorrigible, Mr. Daisani."

"I like to think of myself as encouragable."

"I don't believe I've encouraged you."

He pursed his lips, considering, then made a gesture of agreement. "Perhaps that's encouragement in itself."

That, at least, took her humor away. She had no patience for men who refused to take her seriously; she wouldn't have gotten as far as she already had in her career if she did. There were women who molly-coddled and coaxed their way around difficult men, but it had never been Rebecca's way. Her voice crisped. "Not from me. You already have my answers on any topic we might need to discuss. Anything else can and will be addressed in the workplace."

He paused a moment, then smiled, sharp and dangerous. "I'll be informing your partner Russell this evening, but I thought you should be the first to know."

Rebecca's stomach tightened, anger already burning to replace dismay. Women were far too often expected—even subtly instructed—to go to bed with a big client in order to land him. She would not play by those rules, and if it cost GBI the Daisani accounts, it would probably also cost her her job. Jaw lifted, she waited on his next words, and wondered if she might ever work again.

"I'll be coming by your offices tomorrow to sign the paperwork for my accounts to be handled by GBI," Daisani said so smoothly she almost didn't understand. "Would one o'clock suit, or do you prefer earlier?"

He had not come this far to tell her that. Not this far, nor this fast. He hadn't, she was certain, been on the train with her, and even late in the evening road traffic would be too intense for him to have already come the distance. But he was fast; she knew that already. Impossibly fast. Still, he wouldn't have come so far to tell her about the accounts in person. He could have called, and could have waited till morning, for that matter.

"One o'clock would be fine." Her voice had gone hoarse. "Thank you. Thank you for informing me, Mr. Daisani."

"Yes." His eyes were very dark, almost black, in the poor subway lighting. He didn't appear to be breathing, only waiting, and she knew all too well what he waited for. Rather than give it to him, she nodded once and walked by. Walked away, for the second time that day. And was not surprised to hear him say, "Rebecca."

It would be easy. Despite her protestations, it would be too easy to turn back and ask. How had he gotten to her Queens neighborhood so quickly? How had he rescued her only that afternoon? How could it have been only that afternoon, when the world seemed to have bent and reshaped itself so much? She turned her head and heard his breath catch. Somehow she gathered willpower from that sound. Enough, at least, to murmur only, "Goodnight, Mr. Daisani," and to hurry up the steps without another word.

It was not coincidence that he signed the paperwork twenty-four hours to the minute after he had idiomatically swept her from her feet and saved her from certain death. Rebecca was certain of that: Daisani paused a moment, looked at the clock on the wall, and didn't sign until the minute hand ticked over to mark the precise moment. Vanessa Grey noticed, too, and her mouth grew ever-more pinched, though she said nothing as the senior partners broke into spontaneous applause.

Russell held Daisani's handshake a moment too long; spoke with a shade too much enthusiasm as he said "Thank you" to the business mogul. No one else would hear it, or care if they did, but Rebecca was watching and listening for it, and sighed. He—Russell, Daisani, perhaps none of the men in the boardroom—would never quite understand her distaste. More than distaste. If Russell were anyone else's partner she would find it distasteful but say nothing to him. But her own career, her own future, depended on an impeccable record; that was one of the predicaments of her position. It would change as more women became involved in high-end business deals, but for here, for now, she had to be flawless. A partner who profited off closed-door deals would eventually tarnish her reputation, and it wouldn't matter if it was accident or malice when it happened. When Russell made his exit, she followed, feeling weariness more than anything else.

"You haven't shaken my hand yet, Ms. Knight." Daisani insinuated himself between her and the door, one hand extended and a glass of champagne in the other. "You wouldn't want my new associates to think you dislike me, would you?"

She took his hand, if not the champagne he offered next. "That would be unfortunate, yes. Of course, having tested us with landing your business, I expect Russell and I will never see you again. You're much too important to leave to junior partners."

"Then why send you at all?" He sounded genuinely curious, and Rebecca's gaze strayed to Vanessa. Daisani followed it, then said, "Ah. I have a weakness for women, do I?"

"I believe that's their interpretation, yes."

"And yours?"

"Your weakness is for the extraordinary. I imagine it's most appealing when wrapped in a feminine package. Excuse me, Mr. Daisani," she said to his shout of surprised, pleased laughter, "but I have other business to attend to. Good afternoon."

She left with a smile, as if they parted good friends, and heard the approving rumbles of the senior partners rise behind her as the door closed.

"RUSSELL?"

He startled guiltily as Rebecca tapped on his door and slapped his account book closed when she came into his office. He would spend the rest of his life assuaging guilt, but her conscience would be clean.

Clean, at least, if this one thing went her way. She closed the office door and sat across from him. A man would stay on his feet, imposing, but she didn't want to threaten. Just to be...understood. "I've just listened to the stock reports. Quite a bump there."

Russell wet his lips and looked away. "We did a good job for GBI. The senior partners are pleased with us. We've all made a lot of money today."

"Some of us more than others."

He looked back, gaze blank before understanding and dismay hollowed it. "You, um. You didn't..."

"You've done so extraordinarily well in such a short time, Russell," Rebecca said. "So very well that I imagine you're thinking of taking an early retirement. You have a family, don't you? Young children at home?"

His eyebrows crinkled. "No..."

Rebecca smiled. "Perhaps you should look into that. Sooner rather than later. No one will think twice about a decision to focus on a family now that you're set up for life. You'll go out on a good note. The senior partners are, after all, very impressed with you."

"Are they?" His voice was hoarse.

"Of course they are. We landed Daisani's corporations as a client and there hasn't even been a whiff of scandal."

His jaw relaxed, though the skin around his eyes remained tense. "Oh." And then again, more quietly, "Oh."

Rebecca stood, smiling once more. "I'll miss you very much, Russell. It's been good working with you." She left with her hands icy and her stomach in knots, the adrenaline of making the deal always hitting her after the fact. He had understood clearly enough. A youthful retirement in exchange for her never saying a word about how he'd come into so much money so early. In exchange, more importantly, for her untarnished reputation, but that was never going to be enough to convince him to walk away from profiteering.

Rebecca returned to her desk and spent the afternoon in a pantomime of activity, knowing all that would be seen if someone should glance in was industrious attention to work, and not a woman who desperately,

desperately wished for even just one other female at the firm in whom she could confide.

A CAR WAS WAITING for her after work. The same one as the day before; the same driver, with the same look of polite expectation. Wisdom dictated she not get in, but she wasn't, in the end, that strong. She was driven to the Empire State Building as rain began to fall, tires hissing on the streets, and she was offered an escort to the observation deck.

A table was laid out there, protected by an enormous umbrella, and a meal had been placed on the table, still hot enough that steam rose against the humid air. There was only one setting, and no one else—no one!—on the deck. "Extravagance," she said aloud. "Two impossible things before breakfast. Very well, Mr. Daisani. I haven't eaten, so if you insist."

Delicate shrimp in a garlic sauce, halibut in filo dough and filled with seafood stuffing, a white wine so subtle she couldn't imagine its expense, and a prosaic but splendid cheesecake for dessert. A bribe, all of it, though why she might be bribed by food when she wasn't swayed by millions, Rebecca didn't know. Perhaps not a bribe, then, but an offering. A suggestion of the lifestyle she could enjoy if she would simply *ask*. Private meals in public settings, private drivers—her every wish catered to, no doubt. She rose from the table, wine glass still in hand, and stepped out to the uncovered deck. The rain had stopped and sunset glowed on the horizon, pink and blue stormclouds satisfied with the job they'd done. Somehow she wasn't surprised that he didn't come to her until after the sun had set. That, after all, was properly dramatic, and if nothing else, Eliseo Daisani had a flair for the dramatic.

Nor did she hear him approach. There was no bell on the elevator, no sound of footsteps, just his voice and then a moment later, him standing at her side.

"You haven't asked."

"No." The view was magnificent, city sky clear of smog after the evening's rain. Streetlight reflections shone in the gutters, and even from the height of the observation deck she could still hear tires on wet roads and impatient horns echoing down steel canyons. "Russell works for you now, I suppose."

Daisani's silence held a long moment, hearing in her change of topic the promise she had no intention of making aloud. *You haven't asked,* he'd said. *No. And I never will.*

She could live without his secrets. Preferred to live without them. *Of us,* Daisani had also said, and Rebecca had thought he meant Vanessa and himself. To a degree, no doubt, he had. But the *us* of whom Vanessa was protective was a larger collective. There were others like Eliseo Daisani.

It was enough—perhaps more than enough—to know that. To know that the extraordinary lived side by side with the ordinary on New York's busy streets. It was something to tuck away, to let tease the edges of her dreams, but not something to explore. That was for someone else, in some other time, some other place.

"Don't be silly," Eliseo finally said. "I spoke to him this afternoon. I understand he's going to work for Legal Aid. I like that in a man. A willingness to give back to his community."

Rebecca nearly laughed. "It's easy to give back when you have a few million dollars in the bank."

"An amount I expect you'll have in time. You're very brave, Rebecca Knight. Almost no one can resist the easy path."

"There's no such thing. There's always a price. It's usually much more expensive than the harder path."

"Oh, Rebecca." Daisani's voice carried a note of genuine sorrow, enough to make her look away from the view. He looked much older than he should, ancient regret in dark eyes. "Oh, you are too wise for me. What ill luck to meet you, when you have no use for me."

"For both of us." There: there was the concession she had never intended to make. The admission that Eliseo Daisani and his secrets were, after all, tempting. Rebecca turned back to the city, to the hurrying headlights below. "I've already chosen the road less traveled by, Mr. Daisani. I can't afford its branches."

"And you choose to be adamant in this."

"I do." Those were weighty words, small as they were. Spoken to seal relationships in the eyes of God and of the Union. She used them now with great deliberation, and Daisani took a small breath that acknowledged them.

"If you ever need anything," he said after a moment.

"I won't." Rebecca stepped back from the wall and he turned with her, making one last small gesture. An offer. An invitation. Open fingers, not so much as beckoning. Simply extended. In hope, Rebecca thought, and though she hadn't intended to, she smiled. "Goodbye, Mr. Daisani."

Rue shot through his own smile and he closed his fingers as though the invitation had been an unintentional one, and now noticed, an embarrassment. "Goodbye, Rebecca Knight."

HE DIDN'T FOLLOW HER. Didn't come to stand beside her at the elevator, didn't appear ahead of her as he had done before. She was unsure if he would until she reached her own doorstep; reached the warmth and comfort of her own home. She even stood there a moment outside the house, a hand on the doorknob as she waited, heart hammering, to see if he was waiting.

It was relief, not regret, that burst in her chest at the count of thirty. If he was waiting, if he was going to come to her, he would have in those thirty seconds, and curiosity would have had her at last. *That* would have been regrettable, not the other.

The doorknob turned under her hand and she startled, then smiled as her husband's broad frame filled the doorway. "I thought I heard you. Couldn't find your keys?"

She stepped into his arms, still smiling. "There you are. I missed you last night."

"Surgery ran late. It went well, but I wanted to keep an eye on the patient, so I stayed at the hospital. I didn't want to call and wake you." Thomas kissed her hair, then rolled her away from their embrace in a luxurious ballroom dance spin before drawing her close again. He didn't look like a dancer, her husband. Too big, too broad-shouldered, too imposing, aspects that were belied by gentle surgeon's hands. She had fallen in love watching him on the dance floor. Watching him with someone else, in fact, which still amused her when she thought of it.

He threaded his fingers through hers, tugging her toward the kitchen. "I made dinner. I'm sure you've eaten, but come tell me about work. How's it been?"

"Successful. And complicated. Russell and I landed the Daisani account. Now Russell's rich and retiring."

"Really. And you're not?"

"I'm not." Rebecca sat at the kitchen table, watching Thomas turn the heat off beneath a pot of pasta. "It was a choice, in the end, that's all."

"A difficult one?"

She loved that about him, too: that he would ask, even as he opened the refrigerator to take out a bottle of white wine, a square of parmesan cheese, an already-prepared salad. Chin in her hands, smiling as he puttered around the kitchen with his beautiful, human, grace, she murmured, "No. Not at all."

Last Hand

THE ELEVATOR DINGED QUIETLY AND a girl—a young woman, really, but then, everyone was young now—exited, her posture brash with confidence that lasted no more than two steps into Eliseo Daisani's reception room. Then she took in the sumptuous rugs, velveted chairs, gleaming hardwood floors, and slowed. It was nothing against her: everyone did. The entire purpose of fitting a business office so luxuriously was to upset expectations.

After more than thirteen decades with Eliseo, Vanessa had come to truly appreciate how badly most people could be disconcerted by such things. This girl, though, recovered well, managing not to trail her fingers over a velvet chair as she passed it. She was in her late twenties, African-American, and very pretty, with a few dark brown corkscrew curls escaping their bindings. Her cafe au latte skin contrasted well with her cream business suit, and she had enough vanity to wear a short skirt instead of tailored pants. A good presentation, Vanessa thought, though she knew the appraisal wouldn't be readable on her face. Nothing was: that was the point of the sharp expression she adopted.

Nothing, including the fact that Vanessa recognized the girl. Her name was Margrit Knight, and she was a rising star in the city's Legal Aid department. She'd won a case just a day or two earlier, achieving a clemency grant from the governor for a woman whose attempt to save herself from domestic abuse had turned to homicide. Eliseo would want to see her, of course, but it would hardly do to simply usher the girl in.

"Do you have an appointment?"

Margrit startled, then blurted, "You have a beautiful voice," clearly not her rehearsed response. A twist of satisfaction went through Vanessa. Her voice was completely unlike her physical demeanor, yet another thing meant to upset expectations, and she was always pleased when it succeeded. More pleased when her opponent recognized and admitted to her own surprise.

Opponent. If it wouldn't break character, Vanessa would roll her eyes at herself. Eliseo and Janx had filtered too much of their ways of thinking into her mind, if a young woman appearing on the doorstep was automatically classified as an opponent. "Thank you. Do you have an appointment?" They both knew she didn't: a leather appointment book lay in front of Vanessa, still closed, but inside, its thick pages were unmarked.

Margrit gave a self-deprecating smile. "I don't. I was hoping—"

"Mr. Daisani," Vanessa said crisply, "is a very busy man."

"I understand." Margrit gestured to the lobby chairs. "I'd be glad to wait. I only need a few minutes of his time."

They looked at one another a moment, cat and mouse, before Margrit's attention slipped above Vanessa's head and she asked, cautiously, "Your grandmother?"

Unable to resist, Vanessa turned to look at the painting she knew was there. It looked very like her, indeed, save for the clothes and hair were Roaring Twenties instead of modern-day. She had just won the speakeasy and Eliseo had commissioned the painting in amused celebration. Everything had changed since then; even the speakeasy was no longer hers alone, thanks to the streetwise 'pirate' Grace O'Malley. She resented the loss, but life was change.

That became more difficult to remember, the older she got. It should be easier, she thought, not harder, but bitterness tended to well where an ease of acceptance had once sat. She'd foreseen that once, the very day she won the speakeasy, but when the change had begun was a question that Eliseo or Janx would have to answer. Janx, probably: Eliseo would no doubt be kind and lie, if he had even noticed the severity that had crept into her.

"Vanessa Grey," she said, to distract herself. "And Dominic Daisani, Mr. Daisani's father." Grandfather, by all rights, given the turning of the years. She would have to remember that next time someone asked about the painting. "I was named for her. My family has worked for the Daisanis for a long time."

"She was lovely. You look like her." Margrit Knight offered Vanessa a genuine smile, then stepped back. "I really don't mind waiting. Just a few minutes of his time, maybe?"

Vanessa nodded very slightly toward the chairs, and let pleasure dance across her features in the moment Margrit's back was turned. She let the girl wait nearly half an hour, then gestured her in to see Mr. Daisani. Let Margrit think it was flattery which had gotten her through the door. There was no need to admit Eliseo would have insisted, had he been asked, that Margrit be allowed in. Even if she wasn't making a name for herself in the papers, everyone knew already that first Alban Korund, then a selkie woman, had gone to her for help.

Selkies, for pity's sake. The selkies had been extinct, or close to it, since before Vanessa's time. She had never met one, not in a hundred and thirty years, but Margrit Knight seemed to draw the Old Races to her like moths to a flame.

She had no idea, of course, what world she was rubbing up against, and probably never would. They were too cautious now, so cautious that Janx and Daisani hadn't so much as seen each other in years. Too many people had cameras now, and were too eager to spread gossip. The business mogul and the crimelord couldn't afford to be seen together, nor could they stay in any one place too long with their unchanging faces. They worked alone now, ancient rivals pursuing parallel empires without ever risking their paths crossing.

Eliseo hadn't said as much, but he missed his partner. The emptiness where Janx was meant to stand was a void Vanessa could never fill.

Margrit left Eliseo's office, closing the doors with such care that it clearly disguised outrage, and murmured her thanks to Vanessa again as she went to the elevator. Her shoulders were drawn back, pinched, and her posture rigid. Vanessa waited until the elevator had enveloped her before turning an expectant, amused gaze toward Eliseo's doors.

He exited the moment the elevator doors closed, black eyes bright with merriment. "That's Rebecca Knight's daughter, Vanessa. Can you believe it?"

Vanessa glanced after the girl, eyebrows elevated. Margrit was much lusher than she remembered Rebecca Knight being, but there was something in the cheekbones, perhaps, now that Eliseo had mentioned it. "What on earth did you say to get her back up?"

"Oh." Eliseo sat on the corner of her desk, looking pleased with himself. "I offered her a job. It offended her to no end. No wonder Korund likes her. She's forthright, stalwart and true. Like her mother, but less devious. He's going to tell her, you know. He has to. She'll never help him unless she knows what he is."

Vanessa arched a skeptical eyebrow. "Gargoyles never tell anyone."

"Alban isn't like most gargoyles."

"And if she's like her mother, she won't help him even if she knows."

Eliseo shook his head, eyes on the elevator and the memory of the girl who'd just left. "No. Rebecca would never have risked jogging in Central Park. Margrit needs to fight the system. She'll help." Satisfied with his conclusion, he looked her way with apology suddenly strong in his gaze. "I'm sorry about the speakeasy, Vanessa."

A pang went through her and she breathed deeply to send it away. "It's all right. Everything changes."

"One of that woman's hideaways is beneath the derelict building I own uptown. I'm having it taken down. It won't expose her, but it'll inconvenience her. A fair trade, I think."

She took another breath, this time to object, and let the protest go unspoken on an exhalation. Eliseo was rarely swayed once his mind was made up, and a part of her—small, petty, oh-so-human—wanted the revenge. The speakeasy had been hers for almost a century, and to lose it, even to a grateful city, would always sting. "Thank you."

He smiled and stood. "Anything for you, Vanessa. Now, I'm about to be late for my next meeting, unless I go by myself. Is there anything I should remember about the gentlemen I'm seeing?"

"The one with the bad toupee always thumps the table when he's got a bad hand. Don't sign anything until the lawyers look it over if he's not getting physical."

"I never do anyway." Eliseo tipped her chin up and stole a kiss, rare treasure in the workplace, then was gone between one blink and the next. The fire stairs doorway brushed shut long seconds later, but by that time he would be at his meeting. Vanessa smiled at the sound, then arched her eyebrows in expectant curiosity as the elevator chimed a second time. These were nominally Eliseo's public offices, but almost no one visited them unannounced: one did not simply waltz into Eliseo Daisani's presence and expect to be seen.

Three women exited the lift. They were of an age at a glance, but one walked a step in front of the other two, somehow denoting her as the elder. She was stunning, black hair framing an ageless face, and she carried an unfamiliar chill of power.

The girls behind her were nearly as lovely, both with hair as black as their mother's. Vanessa twitched an eyebrow again, wondering what made her think they could be mother and daughters when they appeared so close in age, then nearly laughed at herself: certainly over a century of living with Eliseo had inured her to superficial age appearances meaning anything. Curious, interested, she said, "May I help you?"

"Vanessa Grey," the older woman said, traces of a Russian accent marking her voice. "A pleasure to finally meet you. Do you still play poker?"

VANESSA DIDN'T REMEMBER THE last time a blush had colored her cheeks, but surprise brought one now. Not just surprise: excitement. Whether it was long exposure to Eliseo and Janx, or her grandfather's cardsharp skills still lying deep within her, the thrill of an unexpected game could still delight her. She nodded once, then waited.

"The stakes," the Russian said, "are very high. My daughter wishes to meet her father."

"Eliseo," Vanessa said after a moment. The Old Races had rules against breeding with humans, but it had always seemed to her inevitable that somewhere in his long life Eliseo might have fathered a child or two. She had never particularly wanted children herself.

The low thump of jealousy in her chest startled her. All rational discourse aside, it was unpleasant to have her idle suspicion confirmed. One's lover, she thought, should not have fathered someone else's child, regardless of when that may have happened.

"No," one of the girls said. The more delicate of the two: she was small and blue-eyed and wore diaphanous layers even in the winter chill. She spread her fingers, indicating the other girl. "Janx."

Vanessa laughed this time, astonishment deep enough to run to delight. Janx's daughter had emerald eyes and no more than red highlights in her black hair, but she could see him in the length of the girl's jaw and in her slender height. "You look like him," she said, and uncertain pleasure crossed the girl's face.

Agreement filtered through the mother's expression as Vanessa looked back at her. "What does this hand have to do with me?"

"Eliseo Daisani took Jana away from Janx and her mother the night he first saw you." Simple words, with no more explanation offered.

Vanessa held herself still, not so still as the Old Races might, then let a slow sigh escape. "He should not have done that."

"No," Jana said, loathing in the single word. The other girl took her hand, sorrow etched in her features. Complicated sorrow, and complicated anger, from both the girls and the mother too. They were a family, full of love for one another, but torn apart by a kidnapping decades in the past.

But Eliseo should have raised the girl, not this Russian beauty with a daughter of her own. "How did you come to be her mother?"

"I took her from Eliseo," the woman said. "Will you play the hand?"

She could say no. It was clear in all their eyes; clear most particularly in the anger and hope and fear in Jana's. She *should* say no, because to lose was to lose all.

It was simple, really. What went around came around, for want of a better phrase, and this circle had, all unbeknownst to her, spent fourteen decades coming to its close. A daughter lost the same night a lover was found; there was only one way, in truth, that it could end.

Vanessa, clearly and quietly, said, "Of course I will." Then, with humor, because there was no use in anything else in this moment, she added, "And I won't even cheat."

FIVE CARD DRAW HAD won her the speakeasy. There was no other game she would play, not with stakes this high. Winner take all, of course: a single hand was as much as they needed. This was not a game for wits and canny intuition. It was luck and nothing more, and after all the lifetimes Vanessa had lived, that was more than enough.

The deck of cards, still sealed, came out of her desk drawer; the one she played solitaire with was on the other side, but one never knew when the opportunity for a hand of poker might arise. The other daughter, the diaphanous one, shuffled and dealt just two hands: one to Vanessa and one to the Russian woman, who sat on the desk corner just as Eliseo had a little while earlier. Jana stood aside, fingers made into fists and held rigid in front of her stomach.

The Russian glanced at her cards, discarded two, and took up the new ones her second daughter dealt. Vanessa lifted her own, studied them, and did the same. A moment later both hands were on the desk: two pair of sixes and tens and a queen besides, from the Russian. A single pair of aces and a scattering of number cards from Vanessa: a losing hand.

Jana gasped, both hands covering her mouth, and the other daughter gave Vanessa a look of regret as she stood.

Vanessa shook her head and murmured, "It's all right. Good luck, Jana. He's…remarkable."

The girl nodded behind her hands, and their mother edged them toward the elevator. "Go. I will follow." Obedient, nervous, they scurried away, and not until the doors had closed did the Russian reach out and overturn the two cards Vanessa had discarded.

Aces both. High cards. Winning cards. There was no surprise on the mother's beautiful face, and her accented voice was soft when she spoke. "I will tell him you did this."

"If you wish."

"It may save your life."

A tell: a miniscule shake of her head, almost too small to be seen, but unstoppable. "Do you think so?"

Cool power filled the woman, more by far than what she had come into the room with. She wasn't one of the Old Races: Vanessa knew them too well to think that. She was human, but not wholly, and it was with a tone of prophecy that she said, "No. I fear not."

Vanessa nodded once. "Who are you?"

"I am Baba Yaga's daughter."

She knew the name from folklore: the Russian witch who lived in a hut with chicken legs, and who scoured the countryside looking for men to make meals of. She'd thought that was all it was, folklore and fairy tales, but she should have known better. Eliseo, after all, was a fairy tale, too.

"No," she said after a moment. "Not if the stories of Baba Yaga are true. Baba Yaga wouldn't have given me the chance to choose, and she wouldn't have offered to tell Janx what I'd done. She may be your mother, and you may be a witch, but I think you're not Baba Yaga's daughter."

Genuine pleasure flashed through the Russian woman's eyes. "I will tell him," she promised, then, like her daughters, went to the elevator.

"Wait," Vanessa said. The woman turned back as the doors opened, one hand holding them from closing again. "The other girl…?"

Now sympathy shone in the Russian's gaze. "Yes. Before he knew you, if it matters at all." She nodded a farewell and stepped away, leaving Vanessa alone with a scattering of cards on her desk and an ache that had little to do with her own fate, and entirely to do with what Eliseo would do in the next few days.

She would not say goodbye. That was a given: he couldn't be warned. He would try to rescue her, and that would cause unnecessary strife. Besides, she wasn't certain she wanted to be rescued. Not after thirteen decades, and wasn't thirteen an unlucky number anyway? Smiling, cool, calm, aching, she gathered her belongings and left Eliseo's office as she did every day at lunch. It felt odd, knowing she wouldn't return.

What would you do if you had only one day to live? An eternal question, asked curiously, seriously, playfully, by millions.

Go home was her answer, but home was a riverboat on the Chicago River, and had disintegrated decades earlier. There were other things to do, though: a walk through the park, and dinner with Eliseo. She ordered filet, a rarity for her, and Eliseo teased her for it. They spoke of inconsequentialities, for she could say nothing else without warning him, and the lightness of regret within her promised everything had been said already, anyway.

She did stop as they parted—her position as his secretary dictated they keep separate homes—she did stop to say, as she did not often do, "You know I love you, Eliseo."

He turned back, pleasure and concern in his answer: "I do. Is everything all right, Vanessa?"

"Entirely," she said, and it came easily enough to not even seem a lie. "I just couldn't remember if I'd mentioned it this decade."

"You did." His smile was lightning quick, just as he could be. "The day the towers came down."

"Oh yes. Well, all right, I shan't beleaguer the point, then." Vanessa smiled back and Eliseo laughed, pulling her close for a kiss that he clearly didn't care who saw. Vanessa hit his shoulder with her purse, scolding. "Stop that. We'll have to start all over somewhere if someone catches us."

"It's nearly time to do that anyway. Perhaps Paris next, my love? Or should we go to the Orient and be exotic?"

"I think we're seventy years too late for that. Paris would be lovely."

"Not," Eliseo said, in an excellent approximation of his rival, "as lovely as you. I love you too, Vanessa. Will you come home with me tonight?"

"Maybe later. I'm going to go look at my speakeasy one more time. I'd like to be alone."

He softened, as he did so easily with her, and kissed her knuckles. "Later, then. Give it my farewells, as well."

"I will." She left him then, sometime long after sunset. The gargoyle would be gaining Margrit's help by now, and Baba Yaga's daughter would have introduced Jana to her father. It had been enough time for all the cards to be played, all save the last hand.

There were motion sensors installed in the speakeasy now, and cameras, as well as the guards outside. Hundred dollar bills laid on the table until the security chief broke a sweat was enough to have the guards removed and ensure cameras and sensors suffered a catastrophic failure. Assured of privacy, Vanessa slipped through familiar tunnels, and into the darkness of the speakeasy that had for so long been her refuge.

"My dear Vanessa."

"Oh." Her heartbeat soared, bringing color to her cheeks a second time that day. "It's you. I'm glad."

"You've earned that much, at least." Janx came out of the shadows, a candle sparking to life in his hand. Unnecessary, of course: there were electric lights, but even now Vanessa preferred the flames.

Appropriate, then, that it was Janx. She smiled a little and took the candle as she stepped past him, bringing it to the first of the stained glass windows. Color reflected the light, illuminating her face: not such a different face, save for the drawn angles of it, than the one that had first looked at these windows more than half a century earlier. Janx was a fainter reflection in the windows, his changeable expression holding solemn. She traced not his face, but the lines that made up a hint of dragon, then those that were the vampire in the stained glass, moving to each of the other two windows to complete the images before coming back to the center of the room.

The chess board was laid out as it ever was, part way through the last game played. She moved a piece, then another, until the black queen was threatened by the white king. Janx came to touch a finger to the queen, but she caught his hand before the figure toppled, and he let himself be stayed.

"I've hired a man," he said ever so softly. "A man who will do terrible things to your body, Vanessa. It must be made to look like the other murders, you know. The ones Alban's accused of."

She exhaled, tiny cold rush of sound. "I suppose I won't mind anymore, when it comes to it. Did you meet her, Janx? Jana? Your daughter?"

"I did." Pride and anger warred in the dragonlord's voice. "And then I sent her away, after promising her her revenge on Eliseo."

"It's fitting," Vanessa said. "A full circle. When did I become bitter, Janx? When did I become angry?"

"Chicago. Campanelli. Before then, but after the speakeasy. That was where I noticed it, though. You got cold, Vanessa. You became too much like us."

"Is that what happens to us? The women you choose?"

"Most of you don't last long enough." He finally touched her, a caress of her jaw, and his jade eyes were utterly serious as he murmured, "I am sorry, Vanessa Grey. I am sorry."

"Yes," she said. "I know."

The queen fell.

Chimera

I WAS A BARMAID, NOT FOR the money, which was poor, but for the ear to the ground; for the hearing of secrets told and of visitors arriving. A hundred years and more I had listened for certain tales, hoping, shaping, shifting the world around me to make them possible. They are fairy tales, perhaps; dreams of hope and magic, and this is the secret I have learned today: that they were coming true. A child was coming, and she would be the shape of our future.

Her mother knew neither me nor my daughters, but I knew her, thanks to the keeping of my ear to the ground. She had been given a title by the Old Races themselves, and that is a rare thing indeed. They named her *Negotiator,* and they went to war and changed tradition because of her. Nothing was proof of that more than the girl she was set to bear, and this was why I had invited myself and my own daughters to a party for those who know who and what the Negotiator was.

I knew only one of the many who were there, though another is unexpectedly familiar: a tiny woman, wizened and wise, whom I have seen twice in my life, both times as if in a dream. She was, I thought, my saviour, and it was both my wish and my fear to speak with her. But before I could, the one I *did* know was at my side, his jade eyes bright with pleasure as he bowed over my hand. "How long has it been, my dearest white witch?"

"Have you a less-dear witch?" I wondered, and laughter sparked in him.

"Your mother, to be sure. Do you know, it's been two hundred years since I've visited Russia?"

"And will be two hundred more, at least. My mother does not forgive easily, and you cost her not only a dragon, but a daughter."

"Only one dragon, though," Janx said thoughtfully. "Poor Rumi is still there, freezing his assets off. I may be obliged to do something about that someday. Perhaps you would help me."

Caution rose in my breast. I had helped the Old Races before, and would again, but obligations ran deep, particularly with this man and the one with whom he was an eternal rival. "At what cost?"

The endless humor in his eyes went cold, green fire turned to green ice. "At a cost I have already paid, witch's daughter. You owe me."

We both looked to a black-haired girl across the room, a tall and rangy beauty, before I cast my gaze down. He was right; oh, so bitterly right. I had stolen the girl, not from him, but from Eliseo Daisani, who had in turn taken her from the fool who dared pilfer a dragon's hoard. We might both of us have returned her to Janx, but we had not, and so it was true, true, true: I owed the dragonlord, and could perhaps never repay that debt. "I will aid you, of course."

"And how will I find you, when I have seen you thrice in a century?"

I shrugged and nodded toward the daughter we shared. "She visits you, I know. She will call me to you, when you have need."

Impishness lit his face again, jade eyes gone wide with assumed innocence. "I will *always* have a desperate need for you, my dear."

I cannot help but laugh. Janx is irrepressible, and I have desired him for it since the day we first met. "Will you introduce me to your Negotiator?"

His eyebrows rose. "You don't know her? What are you doing here? How did you even know to come?"

I nodded again toward Jana, and then to the woman she spoke with: a redhead, not so fiery as Janx himself, but fierce and green-eyed too. His other daughter, half a dragon and half mortal, and half sister to my oldest. "Her name is Kate, yes? Girls, no matter their ages, love to share news, and so I knew to come. They are chimeras, Janx. All of them, these mixed children of the Old Races. They are our future. They are our hope."

We counted them silently, he and I: Emma, my other daughter, who is the child of a vampire and a witch. Like Margrit's babe, Emma was the shape of a future I had worked decades to create. As the world stands now, they are strangers in the strange land, unable to show themselves for who they truly are. Kate and her sister Ursula, who was Eliseo's daughter as much as Kate was Janx's, had lived centuries on the borders, neither human nor

Old, and that was the fate I hoped to spare my own girls. Chimeras all: Jana was the only trueblood child of the Old Races here, and she, having been raised by a witch, was not what her birth mother might have imagined. With each new chimera born, the hold humanity had on this world lessened a little, and the possibility of magic grew stronger.

"And our Negotiator," Janx said in the silence that had come up between us as we studied our children, "is she our hope as well?"

"Would she have survived this long if she was not?"

Janx inclined his head, then offered his arm, and together we made our way through the gathering so he could say, "Margrit, my dear, may I introduce you to an old friend of mine? I'm afraid she has no name, but that's very nearly the least of her peculiarities, so I'm sure you won't hold it against her. And this, of course, is Margrit Knight. Her husband," he added dismissively, "is around here somewhere. Looming, no doubt. You're not missing anything with him. I'm much more charming."

Margrit is smaller, even large with child, and younger-seeming, than I might have thought. The years, after all, had spun by, more and fewer than I might imagine. Age showed on human faces: the Negotiator's girlhood friends had lines on their faces and white in their hair. She, of course, did not; no one who has sipped twice of a vampire's blood is marked by the years in that way, not until far more of them have passed, and Margrit Knight had done more than that. She had a dragon's blood in her veins as well, and her coming child was the daughter of a gargoyle. Her hands, though, were strong as she shook mine, and her smile was genuine. My girls were chimeras, but Margrit's would be a wonder indeed. "It's nice to meet you. You're Emma's mother, aren't you? She looks like you."

I wondered how my youngest had met Margrit already when I had not, but nodded and offered my congratulations. Her smile brightened and she smoothed a hand over her belly, delight running through and through her. But her attention was for Janx, not me, which could hardly seem remarkable, given the way he drew the gaze. Her words, though, were not what I expected: "Have you seen him, Janx? Is he well?"

The dragonlord's countenance darkened, his presence weighting the room. Others moved away unconsciously, but the Negotiator stepped forward, crossness on her face. "Stop that. Be normal, and answer my question."

Janx's presence lessened again, though a sulk stayed in place. "No, I haven't, nor do I wish to," he said petulantly, and I felt ill-advised amusement splash over my face. Margrit saw it and shared a smile with me, which undid Janx's threatening demeanor entirely. Laughter rose up in me, and I understood suddenly why she had gained her title, and how pleased I might be to be friends with this woman. I had not known it in coming here to meet her, but a certainty clicked within me, the gift of being my mother's daughter after all: she and I could change the world.

And our daughters, ah, our daughters.

Our daughters will be everything we could hope them to be.